GUARDING AUTUMN

CRIMSON POINT SECURITY SERIES

NEW YORK TIMES AND *USA TODAY* BESTSELLING AUTHOR

KAYLEA CROSS

GUARDING AUTUMN
Copyright © 2024 Kaylea Cross

∼

Cover Art: Sweet 'N Spicy Designs
Developmental edits: Kelli Collins
Line Edits: Joan Nichols
Digital Formatting: LK Campbell

∼

This book is a work of fiction. The names, characters, places, and incidents are products of the writer's imagination or have been used fictitiously and are not to be construed as real. Any resemblance to persons, living or dead, actual events, locales or organizations is entirely coincidental.

All rights reserved. With the exception of quotes used in reviews, this book may not be reproduced or used in whole or in part by any means existing without written permission from the author.

ISBN: 979-8-308029-73-1

She's guarding a big secret…

Long ago, single mom Autumn buried her feelings for the man she's loved in secret for most of her life, knowing he'll only ever see her as a friend. Then unexpected news blows up her entire world, leaving her in an impossible situation. If she tells him the truth, it could ruin everything between them. But she won't be able to live with herself if she doesn't.

And it could destroy everything.

Autumn has always been a central pillar of Gavin's life, but their friendship isn't enough for him anymore. He's in love with her and wants to make a life with her. An upcoming security job finally gives him the chance he's been waiting for, but then everything goes wrong. From the moment she arrives, she's distant, putting up walls he's desperate to tear down. When a planned protest spins out of control and her daughter goes missing in the fray, he finally learns her secret. As they fight against the mounting danger, a hard truth hangs between them, threatening to rip them apart forever.

AUTHOR'S NOTE

Get ready for more mayhem with the Crimson Point Security crew! When I first started plotting this one, I really wasn't sure about the premise I came up with. It contains a trope I usually dislike, but in this case it fit the storyline and the characters so well that I decided to give it a tweak and wound up falling in love with it. I hope you enjoy it!

Kaylea

PROLOGUE

Twelve years ago

Maybe it was the Jack Daniels. Or maybe it was because this was his last night in his hometown. Whatever it was, as he stood beneath the thick branches of the old sycamore and looked up at the two-story white colonial bathed in moonlight, Gavin was overcome by a wave of nostalgia. Almost homesickness.

It made sense. In a lot of ways, this house had been more of a home to him than his own throughout the years.

Autumn's window on the second floor was dark, but he knew she had to be in there. She hadn't shown up to the party, so he'd left early because celebrating grad just wasn't the same without her. And there was no way he would leave town without saying goodbye in person.

Her family had given him a key to the house when he was nine, but he never used it at this hour because he didn't want her parents to hear him sneaking in and out so late. He jumped up and caught the thick, lowest limb of the sycamore and swung himself up on top of it. From there it was a short climb to the sturdy branch that ran close to her window. He'd done it so many times over the years that the bark was worn away in places.

Crouched on the thickest part of the gnarled branch, he stood, wobbling once before steadying himself, and peered through the window. A shaft of moonlight arrowing into the room revealed Autumn curled up on her bed, awake and facing the window, a pillow hugged to her chest. She looked so sad and alone, his heart squeezed.

He tapped on the window quietly. Her head came up.

She pushed up into a sitting position when she saw him, shoved her long sandy blond hair back and switched on the bedside lamp to its lowest setting. Gavin lifted the sash with a slight squeak and climbed over the windowsill into her room as she pulled the folds of her silken robe around her more securely, covering bare legs that he refused to let himself stare at.

His mischievous smile faded when she watched him with a sad expression that twisted his insides. "Hey." He paused there just inside the window. "You didn't come to the river, so I stopped by to check on you." Pretty much their whole graduating class had gone down there to celebrate—and as a sendoff for him and his twin, Tristan.

"I'm not in a party mood." Her voice was dull. Flat as her expression.

Unsure what to do or say, he came over to sit on the edge of her bed. Only a foot or so separated them, but it felt like a mile, and worry flickered in his gut. The antique grandfather clock on the upstairs landing struck one. The house was still and quiet, her parents sound asleep in their room down at the opposite end of the hall.

Gavin reached for her hand and held it gently, unsure

what to say. They'd been friends for so long, he hated to see her hurting. "Bad night, huh."

She nodded, swallowed, and blinked a couple of times.

"Wanna talk about it?" Her dad had cancer. She was upset and scared about the battle he faced, the treatment that was often worse than the disease, and what the outcome would be. But he knew it was more than that. And that it was partly his fault, because he was leaving town tomorrow.

"Not really." She pulled her hand free, leaned past him to switch off the lamp before lying back down and curling up on her side to face him.

He studied her for a long moment, willing the lingering haze of alcohol to clear from his brain so he could figure out what to do or say to make her feel better. "Scootch over."

She shifted to make room so he could lie down next to her. He stretched out on his back, hands resting on his stomach, their shoulders touching. The little glow-in-the-dark stars all over her ceiling spun for a second. Man, the Jack had hit him harder than he'd realized. He'd helped her stick them up there last summer in the shape of the dippers and a couple of her favorite constellations. "Did your dad hear back about his treatments yet?"

"He has his first chemo appointment Tuesday."

"That's good. I mean, that he gets started so soon," he added quickly. "But I'm sorry you guys are going through this. It sucks."

She closed her eyes, drew in a breath, and let it out in a sad sigh that made him wince inside. "I'm just…worried."

"Yeah." He knew what that was like. His stepdad had died of a heart attack when Gavin and Tris were seven. Then they'd watched their mom work and drink herself to death.

He reached for her hand again, needing the connection. It was hitting home real hard now that he was down to his last few hours here. Their lives were about to change forever. After tonight he wouldn't be climbing through her window again for a long time.

Maybe ever. "That's rough. But he's got good doctors, and they caught it early. He's going to fight this and win."

"How was the party?" she asked in that same dull tone.

"It was all right." He turned his head on the pillow to look at her. Would give anything to see her smile right now. "Not the same without you there." Not even close. He'd ditched everyone to come here, not understanding why she hadn't at least wanted to see him before he left.

She sniffed, frowned at him as if she had just smelled the alcohol coming from his pores. "Are you drunk?"

"A little, yeah."

"You didn't drive here, right?"

"Course not," he said, insulted. "I walked."

"You walked all the way here from the river to see me? That's…miles."

A little over five and a half. "Yeah." Why wouldn't he? Had she really thought he'd just leave without seeing her? They'd been friends for thirteen years. Close friends. A few times he'd wondered if they could be more, but she'd never given any sign that she was interested, so he'd shoved all that down and pretended he didn't feel anything else for her. He was going to miss her like hell.

"What time is your bus tomorrow?"

"Eight. I'm all packed, but I gotta be home by seven to spend a bit of time with Marley before we go." He and Tristan were both close to their sister. "I can stay until then." His house was only two blocks away down a well-worn path through the woods. He could walk it blindfolded.

The silvery moonlight washed across her face, making her pale green eyes glow as they stared at each other in silence.

An overwhelming rush of sadness hit him, along with a surge of protectiveness he'd been feeling a lot lately where she was concerned.

Who was going to look out for her when he left? Who would be here for her if things didn't go well for her dad? She and her parents were such a big part of his life, had treated him as one of their own since kindergarten, always made him feel welcome and safe, and Tris too. They were family to him as much as his brothers and Marley were.

Autumn hitched in a breath and reached for him.

Startled, he rolled to face her, drew her to him and wrapped his arms around her, not knowing how else to make it better. He wasn't the silent type, but he didn't say anything as he held her there in the moonlight, giving her the only comfort he could…while trying not to notice how incredibly good her soft curves felt pressed against him.

The heartbroken sound she made hurt his heart. He kissed the top of her head, already missing her. He'd wanted out of this town for years, and he and Tris had always dreamed of following Decker's example and becoming US Marines. Now that the moment was at hand, the thought of leaving was harder than he'd imagined. Because it meant leaving her behind too. They would always stay in touch, but everything was going to change starting tomorrow.

Autumn wriggled closer, and he tried to ignore the sudden spike of arousal at the way they were pressed flush together. The way his pulse kicked when her lips brushed the base of his throat. He'd held her like this before a few times, the most recent when her dad was first diagnosed a few weeks back. But tonight…it felt completely different.

This was goodbye. They both knew it. And right now with only that thin, silky robe covering her sweet curves, he was struggling like hell to repress every non-brotherly thought and feeling he'd ever had for her.

She felt so small up against him like this, and the way she burrowed into him stirred all sorts of confusing feelings. Along with certain parts of his anatomy that he had no control over.

Thankfully she didn't seem to notice. She pressed her face into the crook of his neck, the fresh scent of her shampoo filling his nose. He tensed when she moved closer still, because there was no way she could miss what was happening in the crotch of his jeans.

But she didn't pull away. And just as he started to ease his hips away from her, she nuzzled a sensitive spot at the side of his neck.

He froze, all his muscles bunching, even as tingles spread out from where her lips caressed his skin and more blood rushed to his dick. Was she…?

He eased his head back to peer down into her eyes, convinced that either he or the alcohol was misreading the situation. But Autumn stared back at him with complete clarity and cupped the side of his face in her hand while his pulse tripped and went into double time.

Because the look on her face told him he definitely wasn't imagining this, or the intent in her pale green eyes. More heat streaked through him, leaving him hard and aching.

He hadn't planned this. Hadn't dared even to let himself dream this would happen when he'd climbed into her room minutes ago, or that she would ever want him this way. He'd only meant to comfort her. But if she truly wanted him, there was no way he was stopping this.

They both leaned in at the same time. Their lips touched. A tender grazing that shot sparks right through him before he settled his mouth over hers and brought one hand up to hold the back of her head.

Autumn slid her hand into his hair and pulled him closer to deepen the kiss. He moved slow at first, his brain still trying to process that they were kissing. Then her hands started moving over him, and he stopped thinking entirely as they slid up under his T-shirt to glide over bare skin. Tracing every ridge and dip of muscle she found before trailing down to cup the aching bulge between his legs.

Shit. He sucked in a breath, broke the kiss to stare at her. The feel of her hand blocked from his naked skin by only a few layers of fabric was the sweetest torture. His breathing turned unsteady, the urge to rip open his jeans so she could stroke his naked flesh overwhelming.

Say something. He felt like he had whiplash. Had to be sure she truly wanted this and find out exactly *what* she wanted before they did anything else. "What—"

Her lips cut off whatever he was about to ask, her tongue delving in to play with his. The question he'd been about to ask withered and died under another rush of heat, the feel of her hand stroking him through his jeans taking over everything else.

Autumn sat up suddenly, got to her knees, and undid the sash of her robe. He stared up at her in shock, barely able to breathe as it fell from her shoulders to puddle around her legs. The moonlight made her pale skin glow, the shape of her round, firm breasts and tight pink nipples making it impossible to speak, let alone think.

Oh, damn, she was stunning.

Before he could move or find his voice, she was undoing his jeans. He didn't stop her. Was praying she *wouldn't* stop.

The moment he was naked, she straddled his thighs and bent over to the side to look for something. He grasped the indent of her waist in his hands, still unable to believe this was happening, and was about to cup her breasts when she sat back up and ripped open the condom he'd been carrying in his wallet since last summer. His reputation as a stud depended on it.

He swallowed. He hadn't had sex before. Not full on. Had she? He didn't think so. If she had, she'd never told him, and he hadn't heard any rumors about her.

She fumbled to get it on him. By the time she got it rolled down to the base, he was struggling to breathe, every tiny touch and caress of her hands sending pleasure shooting up his spine. He shifted his hands to her hips as she straddled him, steadying her, using his last few functioning brain cells to give her a chance to change her mind before they crossed the point of no return.

"You sure?" he managed, even though he was dying for her to continue. The thought of her being his first was his deepest fantasy come to life. He was so hard for her.

"Don't talk," she whispered.

Yes, ma'am.

They stared at each other wordlessly for a long moment, the sound of his uneven breathing harsh in his ears, then she shimmied up to ease him into place between her legs and slowly sank down on him.

His fingers dug into her hips as warm, wet heat enveloped him, unlike anything he'd ever known. His eyes slid closed, and his head moved back on the pillow, his whole body arching. Ecstasy rocketed through him, the intense pleasure knocking the air from his lungs.

"Autumn," he managed to choke out, holding her tight. He wasn't sure if he was trying to give her one last chance to stop or begging her not to. Chances were high this was her first time too. Was she okay? Was he hurting her?

She placed her palms flat on his chest and began to ride him. Slow at first, a little hesitant and unsure, and his heart practically exploded with tenderness. But the friction and view were incredible.

He sucked in a sharp breath when she sank down fully on him, groaned low in his throat, and fought to hold back as she picked up her pace. Ordered his brain to hold on, not to let himself come yet, make sure she was enjoying it too.

But he couldn't even force his eyes open. The pleasure was too much, rendering him helpless, and suddenly he couldn't take it anymore. He thrust up into her, his breathing coming faster, face contorting and jaw locked to hold back a shout of ecstasy an instant before he started to come.

Autumn muffled his strangled groans with another kiss. It felt like his whole body was melting into hers. He sank into the kiss and moaned into her mouth, the intense pulses slowly, gradually fading into soft ripples until they left him boneless and panting against the bedding.

His head spun. The whole room did, a deep lethargy stealing through him.

Autumn eased off him and lay down on his chest, tucking her face into the crook of his neck. He wrapped his arms around her, struggling to get his bearings and find his voice. He'd been so caught up in the moment he hadn't even noticed if she'd enjoyed it. Hadn't even made an effort to try and make it good for her.

He stroked his fingers through her hair, in awe but still unsure why she'd done it. Why him? Why now? Because he was leaving?

"Are you okay?" he whispered, worried it had hurt and that she thought he was a selfish asshole for not taking better care of her. She'd taken him so off guard.

She nodded and made a soft affirmative sound, her soft hair caressing his cheek.

He was still stunned. "Autumn, what—"

She put her fingers over his mouth to stop him. "Don't." Then she cuddled closer, telling him without words how much she craved the comfort of being held. "Just stay like this with me. Don't leave yet."

His heart turned over. He held her tighter. Closer. "I won't."

He drew the covers over her, savoring her warm weight, the silken softness of her skin as he held her to him. He didn't know why this had happened, but he was grateful it had and wasn't going to spoil this amazing moment by asking for explanations she obviously wasn't ready to give.

They only had a few hours left together before he had to climb back out her window and follow the path through the woods down to his house. Before he left her and this town behind and began the next chapter of his life away from everything and everyone he knew and loved.

Autumn needed him right now. He would get answers from her later. Tonight, he was going to hold onto her and this moment for as long as he could.

ONE

Present Day

"Mom, where's my pink unicorn hoodie?" Autumn's twelve-year old daughter Carly called from upstairs.

"Either folded in your closet where I put it, or dumped somewhere *you* left it," Autumn replied from the little work nook in the kitchen where she was quickly going through the morning's emails. Her dad was due to arrive any minute now to take them to the airport. She'd packed a suitcase for Carly last night, leaving her daughter to gather her own personal items for the trip.

"I can't find it!" There was a definite note of panic in Carly's voice.

"Keep looking." There was always a mound of clothes hanging off Carly's desk chair, and more piles all over her bedroom floor.

One of the joys of parenting a tween.

In the lull that followed, she read and responded to a few more emails, mostly from work. The conference coming up next weekend was a big deal for her. Originally slated for Seattle, the organizers had opted for Portland instead at the last minute, which suited her perfectly since it was only a couple hours' drive from Crimson Point where all the Abrams siblings now lived.

The owner of the advertising company she worked for had chosen her to head up the team presenting their most important pitch ever. This was the biggest career opportunity she'd had since joining the firm, and she intended to kill it.

"Find it?" she called up when a few more minutes passed without anything from Carly.

"Yeah, it was on my chair."

"Amazing," Autumn murmured to herself and kept typing. No wonder it had taken ten minutes for Carly to find it.

A new email popped up. "Ah! Great." She'd been waiting for this response from the company for weeks. Excitement and curiosity sparked inside her as she clicked it open, read the message, then accessed the site.

Several interesting things jumped out at her right away as she studied the information on the screen, capturing her interest completely. Wow. This was so cool. Carly was going to be ecstatic.

She clicked on another tab.

Her hand froze on the mouse. She stared in incomprehension at what was written there on the screen in black and white.

Her heart lurched.

No. Impossible. "What the *hell*?" she whispered as shock morphed into a sharp stab of panic.

She read it again. Checked everything a third time against the previous information she'd been given that had begun this whole process in the first place. Because they couldn't be farther apart.

She clicked on more tabs to verify.

No, no, no...

But no one was listening to her silent, desperate prayer, because everything pointed to the same unbelievable conclusion.

She sat back, staring blankly at the screen as her stomach plummeted and the blood drained from her face. My God. This couldn't be happening.

How? Her mind raced, trying to make sense of it. There had to be a mistake, but...the scientific proof staring her right in the face said this was all too real.

Carly's hurried footsteps sounded on the stairs. Autumn quickly shut the laptop, heart thudding. She felt sick. Like she was having a bad dream.

"Okay, I'm ready," Carly announced as she came around the corner carrying a loaded backpack and wearing her pink unicorn hoodie. She stopped, frowned at her. "What?"

Her daughter looked the same as always, slender and gangly, long strawberry blond hair pulled back in a ponytail, eyes the same pale green as Autumn's. Yet now it felt like she was looking at Carly for the first time and seeing a stranger. And no matter how hard she wanted to, she couldn't deny the truth of the evidence she saw with her own eyes.

Oh, God. Oh, my God...

"Nothing." She put on a smile and hoped it looked convincing, her insides churning like a washing machine. Shit. Just...*shit*. "Ready to rock?"

"Yep. Are Gavvy and Trissy picking us up at the airport when we get to Oregon?"

The coffee she'd finished ten minutes earlier turned to battery acid in her stomach. "Yes."

"Good, I can't wait to see them. Oh, I hear Papa's truck!" Carly turned and raced from the kitchen toward the front door, oblivious that their world had just been shifted permanently on its axis.

Autumn closed her eyes a moment, pushed out a deep breath, and then opened her laptop again. She hid the email in another folder for later, shut everything down, and then packed the device and the power cord away in her bag, still in a haze but out of time to dig into it more. She was just zipping up the case when her dad's voice called out from the front door.

"I'm here, and I've got Carly outside. We'll load the suitcases into the back and wait for you in the truck."

"Okay." Her legs felt a bit weak as she stood and hurried up the stairs to do one last sweep of the upper floor, still reeling from what she'd just learned. A sort of mental fog and numbness was starting to creep in.

She couldn't unsee what she'd read on that screen, didn't know how to process it, let alone what the hell she was supposed to do about it.

After setting the alarm and locking up, she climbed in the back of her dad's truck cab, letting Carly sit up front with him. It gave Autumn a bit of privacy, and the constant stream of chatter Carly kept up with her grandpa saved Autumn from having to talk.

The ride to the airport passed in a blur. Then it was the usual rushed chaos of quick goodbyes, getting their luggage checked in, the frantic unpacking and repacking of carry-ons to get through security, and finding their way to their gate. Still on autopilot, she bought Carly a snack, and they sat together in the waiting area with a few minutes to spare before the boarding announcement started.

Autumn stared out the terminal windows at the planes

coming and going, not really seeing anything. Her mind was in complete turmoil, circling around and around without finding a solution.

Except one. The only one.

And that solitary choice could destroy the stable, carefully constructed life she'd built for herself and her daughter from day one.

"You've been staring at that same spot for like, twenty minutes. Is something wrong?" Carly asked her.

Autumn surfaced as though waking from a dream. "No." Yes. Yes, there was very much something wrong. Although buried underneath everything, there was also the tiniest flicker of relief. Which was nuts. "You excited?"

"Yep." Carly adjusted one of her earbuds and went back to the current drawing in her sketchbook. Another character for her portfolio. She was getting better and better every month it seemed.

The boarding announcement came over the PA. Autumn reached for her bag. "That's us." But now she was dreading this trip. Dreading it with every fiber of her being.

She spent the short flight to Atlanta trying to work on final prep for the conference. Failed miserably because she couldn't concentrate for shit with the recent bombshell clanging around in her brain.

Later, as their connecting flight to Portland roared down the runway for takeoff, it felt like there was a hot coal lodged in the pit of her stomach.

The final countdown to her unexpected moment of reckoning had begun.

TWO

Gavin leaned back against the pillar in the baggage terminal and eagerly scanned the arriving passengers for two of his favorite faces in the world. "See 'em yet?" he asked his twin. Autumn and Carly's flight had arrived a few minutes early. They should be here any minute.

"Not yet." Tristan eyed him in amusement. "And not sure if you know this, but checking your watch every five seconds isn't gonna make them show up any faster."

Gavin shoved his hand in his jeans pocket and adjusted his stance. He'd been counting down the days since Autumn had told him about her upcoming work conference here on the West Coast months ago. That was the last time he'd seen her in person, and the weeks had dragged for him since.

Now it was finally happening, and he was impatient to maximize his time with her and Carly before he and Tris had to report for their security detail in two days' time with the rest of their Crimson Point Security team. The upcoming weekend summit in Portland was going to be a huge security operation for them, meaning all hands on deck, so even the owners would be on assignment.

Before then, he desperately needed as much time alone with Autumn as he could get to figure out whether she was open to the idea of moving them out of the friend zone. Permanently. Because he finally knew what he wanted, and he was playing for keeps.

"What's up with you? You're as wound up as a long-tailed cat in a rockin' chair factory," Tris muttered.

Gavin cracked a grin and stopped fidgeting. His twin had no clue about the recent, major shift his feelings had taken with Autumn, and though Gavin trusted him more than anyone else in the world, there were a few things he just didn't want to share with him. This being the most important of them.

"Haven't heard that expression in a while. And that made you sound like a total hick, by the way." Their mom used to say that one when they were kids. Back before everything had gone to hell for all of them pretty much overnight.

"Well, I gotta keep rotating 'em, don't I? Keep it fresh."

Through the stream of passengers heading their way, he caught a glimpse of strawberry blond hair and zeroed in on it. Carly appeared through the crowd carrying a backpack. Autumn was right behind her, and something in the middle of his chest squeezed hard at the sight of her.

A sense of rightness, like a missing puzzle piece clicking into place. Suddenly everything in his world was right again.

Shelving that startling thought for the moment, he straightened and lifted a hand. Carly saw him first, broke into a wide smile and rushed toward him.

Gavin stepped past his brother to greet her. "Hey, squirt." He picked her up off the ground in a big bear hug that made her giggle and melted his heart. She was so tall now. A few inches shy of his shoulder already, and she was only twelve.

"Damn, you've grown since the last time I saw you. Didn't I tell you to stop that?"

"Hi, Gavvy," she said, her thin arms hugging him tight.

"I'm so glad you're here." He set her down and passed her off to Tristan, shifting his attention to Autumn. And shit, all his insides tightened when she got close.

He couldn't pinpoint exactly when his feelings for her had taken a sharp U-turn, but he'd known the moment he'd seen her after coming home following his honorable discharge from the Corps several months ago. Having her right in front of him now, the way his pulse skipped confirmed what he'd been wrestling with all this time—that and the way he couldn't take his eyes off her.

He was in love with his lifelong friend. And she had no damned idea.

Smiling, she moved toward them at a more sedate pace, wheeling her carry-on beside her. Her sandy-blond hair was tied back in a ponytail that swished along the tops of her shoulders with each step, and the black leggings she wore hugged every sexy line and curve of her legs and hips.

"Hi." She stopped a few feet away rather than greeting him with a hug.

He frowned slightly, closed the distance and wrapped her up in one anyway. His entire body sighed in contentment at the feel of her. The top of her head came up to his chin, the familiar vanilla scent of her shampoo filling his nose. She'd always made his world feel right, but now that feeling was more powerful than ever.

"Good to see you," he murmured. God, he'd missed her these past few months he'd been settling in out here on the West Coast.

She returned the hug for a moment, but it was almost over

before it started. When she started to pull away he held on for another second, until the stiffness in her body registered.

He let her go, unsure what was going on. "How was the flight?" he asked, searching her eyes and trying to read her.

"Fine." She stepped back and tucked a lock of hair behind her ear, the gesture almost nervous, then quickly moved past him to hug Tristan. "Thanks for picking us up." Her Kentucky drawl was sweet music to his ears. His and Tris's had faded a little over the years since leaving home.

"Yeah, of course. How've you been?" Tristan asked as he embraced her.

Gavin might be overthinking it, but it seemed like Tristan's hug was ten times longer than his own. He'd never been jealous of his twin before, but he definitely was now, and he didn't enjoy the feeling.

"Good," she answered. "Busy getting ready for the conference." She stepped back from Tristan, not as far as she'd stepped away from Gavin, did that hair thing again that confirmed she was nervous, and avoided looking at him.

What was up with that? He couldn't think of anything he'd done. "You guys ready to roll?" he asked, letting it go for now. He was all tied in knots over her and overthinking shit. Probably making something out of nothing, as Tris liked to tell him.

"Yes," Carly said, coming up to wind an arm around his waist. At least she seemed genuinely glad to see him.

"We're parked out front. You guys hungry?"

"*Starving*," Carly said in that dramatic way pre-teen girls had. "All we got on the plane was a package of nuts, and it wasn't very big."

Sounded about right. "I know just the place, and it's on the way to the coast," he said, taking her suitcase and guiding her toward the exit with a hand on her shoulder. Autumn hung back with Tristan, who had taken her bag. What was going on with her? Her stiff, slightly remote reception to him was weird. "Can you hang in there another twenty, thirty minutes?" he asked Carly.

"Sure."

"Perfect. It's an Italian place."

"I love Italian."

"I know." He'd known her all her life, which meant he also knew all her favorite things. Autumn's too, and he planned to use that insider knowledge to his advantage over this week.

Autumn got in the back of his SUV with Carly. Tristan took shotgun. Gavin kept glancing at Autumn in the rearview mirror as she told them about her conference on the way to the restaurant.

At dinner, she took the seat across from Tristan rather than him, did the hair tuck thing twice when she made eye contact with him, and yeah, it wasn't his imagination—she was definitely doing her best to avoid looking at him whenever possible. Like she was uncomfortable. What the hell?

Throughout dinner he was increasingly conscious of the distance coming from her, but the food was as good as always, and Carly was happy. The drive down to Crimson Point afterward took just under two hours. By the time they got there, the subtle, lingering tension coming from Autumn had his nerves on edge. Maybe she had somehow picked up on his more-than-friends vibe and felt awkward?

No, that was impossible. He'd been careful not to give away that things had changed drastically for him.

He and Tris carried the luggage up to their condo. The entire place was spotless and sparkling because they had both cleaned it from top to bottom this morning in anticipation of Autumn and Carly's arrival.

"Wow, this place is all yours?" Carly asked from the living room, looking around the large, modern space with wide eyes.

Gavin grinned. This unit was a big step up from the one they had bought together back home. "Yep. And wait until morning. There's an unobstructed view of the water from this whole side of the unit."

"Which room's mine?"

"You're in Tristan's."

"Come on, I'll take you," Tris said, and led her down the hall.

Gavin turned to face Autumn. "You're in my room." He'd wanted her in his bed. In his sheets. In his shower. It was completely territorial and caveman, but having her in his most intimate space did it for him on a lot of levels. Though given her current standoffishness, his whole plan may have just gone to shit.

Her hand tightened on the handle of her suitcase briefly, her expression giving nothing away. "Okay. Down there?" She nodded in the opposite direction Tris and Carly had gone.

"Yep." He took the handle from her and wheeled the case down the hall to his room.

His king-size bed dominated one side of it, the tufted charcoal leather headboard positioned against the wall and facing the huge window overlooking the bay. "I washed the sheets this morning, and all the towels in the ensuite are fresh."

He wanted his scent all over her from being skin to skin with him, not from his sheets and towels.

"Thank you," she murmured behind him.

He put her suitcase on the foot of the bed and turned around to face her. She was still hovering near the door. As if she didn't want to get too close to him.

He couldn't take any more. "Autumn. What's going on?"

She blinked at him, those gorgeous green eyes a few shades lighter than his. "Nothing. Why?"

"You're acting like you don't want to be alone in the same room as me." It cut deep.

"What? No, it's—I'm just tired. Long day traveling, didn't sleep much last night, and I'm preoccupied with the conference."

He didn't buy it, her actions and body language told him otherwise, but he knew her well enough not to push the issue now. So when Carly called for her and clear relief flashed across her face as she fled the room, he didn't try to stop her.

Tris was waiting for him by the front door. "You ready to head out?"

They were bunking at Marley and Warwick's place. "Yeah." Carly and Autumn were both standing in the kitchen doorway, waiting to say goodbye. "Fridge and pantry are fully stocked, but if you need anything just message or call one of us," he told them, fighting a deep disappointment that Autumn would probably reach out to Tris instead of him. He'd envisioned this all going so differently, and he didn't know what was going on with her. It was making him nuts. "We'll talk to you in the morning. Sleep well."

Autumn nodded, put on a smile that was a tiny bit strained at the edges. "Thanks."

He walked out to his vehicle with Tris, unable to figure out what was wrong. "Autumn seem off to you?" he asked as he started the engine.

"No. Why? She seem off to you?"

"Yeah." He pulled away from the curb, glancing up at his lit bedroom window on the way by. Autumn was up there right now. Would be climbing into his bed soon. And, shit, what he wouldn't give to be climbing into it with her and doing all the things he'd fantasized about for too damn long.

He'd planned to feel things out over the next few days before she left for the conference and he and Tristan started the security gig in Portland, see how things went before he told her about his true feelings for her. But given her reaction to him tonight…

Hell, he didn't know what to do now, didn't know what was bothering her. Unless… Wait.

There *was* something between them that had never been dealt with. Something huge they'd both just ignored and never talked about again.

No, he thought with a mental shake of his head, that made no sense. Why would that suddenly be an issue now?

Neither of them had ever brought up what had happened the night before he'd left for boot camp. Not once, for a variety of reasons. But something told him they had to now. It was long past time they talked about it like adults and got it out of the way so they could both move forward.

Hopefully together.

For more than two decades, she'd seen him as her best friend, the sarcastic, fun-loving, sometimes reckless guy she'd grown up hanging out with. He needed to make her see him in a whole new light.

And step one meant laying everything on the line and telling her how he felt.

THREE

Autumn set one last curl in her hair and unplugged the hot curling wand on its stand on the bathroom counter, conscious of the anxious energy humming through her. Gavin might not be here physically, but it felt like he was with evidence of his presence all around her. The scent of his body wash she'd just used hung in the air, clinging to her freshly washed hair and skin.

She'd now had twenty-four hours to absorb the news, but she was still in shock, still had no clue on how to best handle the situation. Other than to accept the one option—the morally correct option—that would blow her life apart.

It was so damned ironic. For years, she'd let herself dream about being with him, fantasize about having a family together someday. That it was happening this way was more painful than bittersweet.

And how was she going to tell Carly? How many times had Carly told her she wished she had a dad? Two Christmases in a row she'd written to Santa asking for one. For her to find out it had been Gavin all along was either going to be the best news Carly could ever get, or—

"Mom, you ready yet?" Carly called from out in Gavin's bedroom. Sleeping in that giant bed had made it tough to keep her mind from wandering to forbidden places Autumn really couldn't afford it to go now. "I'm *starving*."

"There's a fully stocked fridge in a gorgeous kitchen just down the hall."

A distinctly pre-teen sound of frustration answered her. "You promised we could get something to eat in town and then go shopping to get Gavvy and Trissy a birthday present before I start my genealogy project."

Her stomach grabbed at the reminder. It was their birthday. The big three-oh, and Marley was having them all over to celebrate tonight.

She couldn't not go. Wasn't so much of a coward that she would no-show on his birthday just to avoid feeling awkward. He'd always been good to her. He deserved better than that. "Yes, I know. Gimme five minutes."

"You said that five minutes ago."

"Patience, please."

"Ugh, *fiii-nuh*." Carly gave a long-suffering sigh, and her footsteps retreated.

Autumn took another deep breath and confronted her reflection in the huge mirror above the sink, forcing down the tension in her belly at the thought of seeing Gavin later. She only had a few days until the conference started, and then she would be swamped for that whole weekend. She'd been so excited about the start of this trip, the chance to make the most of her time here with Carly and exploring the area with the twins and Marley.

Crazy how life could suddenly turn on a dime.

She found Carly sitting at the kitchen island waiting for her with an annoyed expression and smothered a grin. "Ready?"

"Been ready for half an hour," her daughter muttered, hopping off the stool and heading for the door.

Ah, to go back to that time in life when being mildly annoyed at your mother was the worst thing that happened in your day. "It'll be cool down by the water. Bring your hoodie."

Carly dutifully tugged on the pink unicorn hoodie on the way out the door. The morning was overcast, but already Autumn could see signs of clearing in the cloud deck when they stepped outside onto the path. Lush, shiny dark green rhododendrons lined both sides of it, covered in brilliant blooms of red, pink and yellow. In between, purple foxgloves and multicolored poppies popped through.

"It's so pretty," Carly said, taking a picture on her phone.

They headed down the hill together toward the waterfront, the salty breeze whipping off the water making it feel more like fall than almost summer. The vibe of the town was immediately welcoming, a relaxed, charming place that soothed the jagged edges of Autumn's anxiety.

It would all be okay. It would.

Down beyond the curving edge of the bay, long lines of rolling waves washed onto the strip of sandy beach that stretched north as far as the eye could see, the dull roar of the ocean growing louder as she and Carly approached the base of the hill. People were out walking their dogs, young families strolling along the beach and the sidewalks past the brightly painted shops, restaurants, and other businesses on Front Street.

"I love it," Carly announced. "No wonder they all moved here."

"I think it's hideous," Autumn joked.

Carly shot her a look over her shoulder, then her gaze

caught on something around the corner. "Whoa, that place sure looks popular."

As Autumn rounded the edge of the building onto Front Street, she saw the lineup of people extending down the sidewalk and into the bright blue open front door of a little café. A hand-painted wooden sign of what looked like a humpback tail hung from the edge of the building, announcing that it was called Whale's Tale.

"Clever. Love a good pun." The smell of freshly baked goodies carried on the air. Autumn breathed it in appreciatively. "Must be good. Should we wait it out and see?"

"Oh, there's a bookshop inside it too!" Carly turned to her. "Can I go look for a present in there while you wait in line?"

"Sure." Autumn joined the back of the line and watched her daughter disappear through the open bright blue door of the bookshop, feeling a sharp pang. Carly was all the best parts of her. Her daughter was the most precious present she could ever give Gavin, but it wasn't the kind of news she was going to drop on him on his birthday.

She *was* going to tell him. But she had to pick the right moment, and despite their lifelong friendship, part of her was afraid of his reaction. Afraid that he might initially accuse her of hiding it from him all this time or reject Carly outright, saying he didn't want the responsibility.

No. That wasn't just unfair, it was ridiculous. She and Gavin had known each other almost all their lives. And while he wasn't one to shy away from conflict, he was also quick to forgive, at least with people he cared about. When she explained that she had only just found out herself, he would believe her. She couldn't believe he would reject Carly; he adored her. Maybe once the initial shock wore off, there was a chance he might even be happy about the news.

Yeah, keep dreaming the best-case scenario if it makes you feel better.

It did, thanks.

But she also intended to make it clear she didn't expect anything from him, other than his relationship with Carly. Autumn didn't want money from him or for their connection to change. He meant too much to her to lose that.

Seeing him at the airport yesterday, the way his face had lit up when he'd seen them… The shock of the news must have rattled her more than even she'd realized because her emotions were all over the place, and the old feelings she'd worked so hard to bury all those years ago had come rushing back the moment she'd seen him.

And that hug. The feel of those familiar, powerful arms locking around her. The overwhelming urge to melt into him, hide there in the safety of his embrace. For some reason it had seemed like he'd held onto her longer than normal. Like he didn't want to let her go.

She shook her head at herself in annoyance. *Wake up, Autumn.* She needed to lock those old feelings down hard, shove them back into the box she'd buried them in when she was eighteen. She couldn't afford for him to see that truth. Not now.

The lineup outside the café had moved enough that she had a clear view into the bookshop. The smells of cinnamon, caramel, and freshly brewed coffee wafting out the door made her stomach growl. Carly was in plain view through the large windows at the front, holding a couple of books while chatting away to a young, pretty blond woman wearing an apron.

Carly turned to look at Autumn and rushed toward the door, a wide smile on her face. And in that moment it hit Autumn like a gut punch. The red hair that she had always thought belonged to another man. The shape of Carly's mouth and chin. All Gavin. She'd just never noticed it before.

"Look what I found," Carly announced, holding up the books. "What do you think?"

Autumn grinned at her daughter's excitement, stifling the nervous flutter in her belly. *Oh, God, please don't hate me.* "I think they're perfect." She handed over her credit card. "Ring 'em up, then go have a look at the pastry case and see what they have so I can decide while I'm in line."

Carly took it. "Okay. That's Poppy, by the way. She owns this place, and told me everything here is made from scratch. That's why it's so busy." She hurried away to pay for her purchases.

Autumn looked over at Poppy, who smiled and gave a friendly wave. Autumn returned it, mentally gearing up for seeing Gavin later on. Tonight she would set all this drama aside and let him enjoy his time with family. Tomorrow…

He would find out that family was one person larger.

FOUR

Hands aching as they gripped the iron bar above him, Gavin clenched his jaw and powered through the last few pull-ups, the muscles in his arms and chest screaming. He'd been so keyed up about Autumn all day through the endless meetings for the upcoming summit, he'd needed the punishing workout to burn off the restless energy.

"You about done there yet, tiger?"

Arms quivering, Gavin gritted his teeth and forced his exhausted muscles to propel himself up the final few inches until his chin cleared the bar. Immediately, he swung down and dropped to the mat, could barely get his hand up in time to catch the towel Tris chucked at his face. "Thanks."

"Sure." His twin perched on the edge of a weight bench and took a long swig of water, eyeing him. "You good?"

"Yeah, why?"

Tristan didn't answer. Just kept looking at him with that measured, X-ray stare that silently called bullshit.

Technically, they were identical, but they were different enough to be told apart if people paid attention, especially where their personalities were concerned. Tris was quiet and contained. Wound a little too tight, truth be told. Gavin leaned more in the opposite direction. And that was partly why people had tended not to take him seriously in the past.

It had always rubbed him the wrong way, so over the last few months he'd begun working hard to change that. He needed Autumn to notice.

"You don't know what's going on with you?" Tris finally asked. "Or you don't wanna talk about it."

"Nothing going on, so nothing to talk about." This was one of the rare times he didn't want his other half to know something.

"'kay." Tris got up and walked away. "I'm hittin' the shower. Better get your ass in gear. You know how Marls is with being on time."

Maybe it was their military background, but in their family, if you weren't ten minutes early, you were late. And then you got chewed out. Their sister had always been strict, though to be fair, she'd had to be, considering she was only two years older than them and had been forced to take on the role of their mother as a teen. Although compared to their big brother, she was a softie.

Decker was a total hardass, didn't like anyone knowing he was actually human. It was a damned miracle that any woman would fall in love with him, but somehow he'd managed to snag Teagan. Though she was a badass in her own right, and Gavin had never seen Deck so settled or, dare he say it, happy.

He hustled to the fancy shower room, sighed as he stepped under the warm spray in the spacious luxury cubicle. The showers here in the company gym at Crimson Point Security had awesome water pressure. He quickly scrubbed himself down, then let his mind wander as he washed his hair. Inevitably, it wandered to a vision of Autumn, standing in here with him, water sluicing over her naked curves while he traced every single one with his tongue.

He went rock hard instantly.

The one and only time he'd seen her naked, they'd been eighteen. He'd been drunk as shit, not expecting her to suddenly flip the script on him, and more than happy to lie back and enjoy the ride once she had.

He regretted that now. Wasn't proud about how it had gone. If he could go back and do it again, he would handle it so differently. Take charge, make sure he took care of her needs. Make her come at least twice before he'd climbed back out that window as rays of dawn light lit the eastern sky.

If he got another chance now... He would give her everything.

Ignoring his raging erection because there wasn't time to deal with it, he roughly dried off and took out the dress shirt and pants he'd hung up in his locker. Tris's eyebrows shot up when Gavin walked out rolling up his cuffs. "What's happening?"

"With what?"

"I thought this was just a family dinner. Who you tryin' to impress?"

A certain someone he'd taken for granted for way too damned long. He wanted her to see him differently. Dressing sharply would help. "No one. Just felt like classing things up a bit."

"Well, now I look like a bum compared to you," Tris complained.

He shrugged. "Then swing home to grab some different threads if you think you can still make it to Marley's on time. Easier for Warwick to tell us apart this way though." Their Brit brother-in-law was former MI6. Retired now, but volunteered his time helping Ivy, another badass female in the

Crimson Point circle, run a charity with one of her sisters to protect vulnerable orphans from trafficking. In his free time, he did occasional consulting work for Crimson Point Security. Helluva good guy to have join their newly reunited, albeit somewhat dysfunctional family.

But what family didn't have some level of dysfunction? His was better than most, and Gavin loved all his siblings despite their unconventional familial roles. Decker forced to be the reluctant father figure way before his time, Marley the willing mother-slash-big-sister figure, and then Tris, Gavin's self-appointed keeper. Much good that had ever done him.

His twin grunted and headed for the door. "Loser."

"I'm telling Warwick you said that."

Tris threw him a dark look over his shoulder. "Not him. You."

Gavin stopped and put a hand to his heart. "Ouch. Dude, it's my birthday."

"It was my birthday first."

He snorted. "Because you're a whole seventeen minutes older?"

"Damn right."

"'kay. Hope you're in a better mood by the time we get there. Nobody likes a party pooper."

Tris held up a middle finger as he hit the bar on the steel security door. "See ya there."

They'd driven here separately because Gavin wanted to drive Autumn and Carly back to his place later—alone. "Not if I see you first."

Tris stopped in the open door to look at him, challenge stamped all over his face. They both bolted at the same time and ran for their vehicles, but Tris had a second's lead time.

Gavin reached his SUV just as Tris's truck peeled out

onto the street. Gavin raced to the lot entrance and turned the opposite way.

He sped up the hill away from the water, took an alternate route across town and—would you look at that—Tris's headlights turned onto Marley's street a few seconds after him.

Grinning smugly, he took his sweet time parallel parking in the single remaining spot out front of the sweet little cottage. Tris pulled up beside him on the street, rolled down his window and gave him a long glare. "*How*?"

"Magic. See you inside, but I guess you'll be a while, huh? Prolly have to park a block or two over at least."

Tris stared at him another moment, then pulled up slightly so that his truck was exactly aligned with Gavin's in the right-hand lane and turned off the engine.

Gavin couldn't even open his door now. "You can't park there."

"Watch me."

"Okay, well, enjoy getting towed out of spite."

"I will."

Chuckling, Gavin did up his window and climbed across the front seat to get out the other side. Tris's pounding footsteps came behind him. Gavin put on a burst of speed. He beat Tris to the door by a few steps, was the first to walk inside.

"Happy birthday!" a chorus of voices shouted.

Carly rushed toward him, arms held out expectantly. "Happy birthday, Gavvy."

Aww. Grinning, he picked her up in a bear hug. "Hey, squirt. Thanks."

"Welcome." When he set her down she reached for Tris, who was still standing behind him because he'd made a point of blocking the doorway. "Happy birthday, Trissy."

"Thanks, cutie." Tris shoved him aside to hug her, and Gavin moved to greet their sister.

"Look at you, all shined up and looking so handsome," Marley said as she embraced him.

"What? I'm always handsome."

"Happy birthday, mate," Warwick said beside her, extending his hand.

"Cheers." Gavin shook with him, his gaze moving to the others hanging back by the kitchen doorway. Decker, Teagan…and Autumn. He received a shake and a back slap from his eldest brother, a hug from Teagan, then turned his full attention on Autumn, who still hadn't made a move his way. "Hi."

She smiled up at him. A real one that set his heart thudding. God, she was beautiful with her sandy blond hair curling around her shoulders, pale green eyes sparkling, a purple wrap dress emphasizing her sweet curves. "Hi. You look nice."

"Thanks. You look beautiful." Good enough to eat, and he wanted to do just that. Desperately.

Finally, she stepped forward to hug him. The moment her arms came around him, everyone else in the room seemed to disappear.

Gavin pulled her close and squeezed her, burying his nose in her hair to fill his lungs with her clean, feminine scent. Christ, she smelled good, and the feel of her all soft and curvy nestled against him like this had a low growl forming in the back of his throat. How the hell had he taken her for granted all these years? She was everything he'd ever wanted. Kind, constant, loving, smart, hardworking. Down to earth. Independent. Always put Carly first, making countless sacrifices as a single mother. He was in awe of her.

"Quit hogging her. I already gave you the prime parking

spot." Tris gave him a push. Gavin reluctantly released her, a startling possessiveness streaking through him.

He'd never wanted anyone the way he wanted her. Needed her. He had to make her his. Because she'd always been his, he'd just been too fucking blind to realize it.

He stepped back but kept his attention on her. Drinking in the sight of her, the sound of her laugh at whatever his twin was saying, then glanced around. Marley had his and Tris's favorite meal waiting on the carefully set table.

She was an incredible cook. Growing up, she'd sometimes seemed to conjure meals out of thin air when money she and Decker earned ran out. She'd done her best with whatever they had on hand, which often hadn't been much, and that was why cooking was such a core part of her personality now that she could afford whatever ingredients she wanted. Now food was one of the ways she nurtured the people she loved.

He eyed the presents and cake sitting on the kitchen counter. "Oh, yeah, you made the cake." The amazing chocolate cake she'd made for them every year without fail. That included the times she'd had to go door to door up the street or to Autumn's mom to ask for the eggs, cocoa powder, and mayonnaise to make it. Making them that cake had been more important to her than her pride.

"Of course, I made the cake," she said with a laugh. "There'd be a revolt if I didn't."

"Damned right." He looped an arm across her shoulders and kissed the top of her head, contentment and pride filling him. Everyone he cared about most was in this one room. Autumn and Carly fit in so seamlessly with the others, had always been accepted as part of the family.

And if birthday wishes came true, he would be making that official in the very near future.

FIVE

"Oh my God, I'd forgotten about that! In fourth grade they tricked their teachers and swapped classes for two weeks before they got caught," Marley said to the others with a laugh and shook her head, gazing fondly at the twins. "You guys sure liked keeping me on my toes."

"Well, we didn't want to let you get bored. Right, Tris?" Gavin said, helping himself to a second slice of the cherished triple-layer devil's food cake Marley had made them. It was her signature dessert and an Abrams family tradition, the decadent chocolate cake made with mayonnaise and topped with shiny, dark chocolate ganache.

Autumn loved chocolate as much as anyone, but it was so rich she could only handle a small slice.

For her, the evening had been bittersweet so far. In a lot of ways, it felt like the old days, like going back in time when she had been welcomed into the Abrams' house growing up. Before their stepdad had died, and then Marley and the twins' mother—Decker's stepmother—not long afterward.

That double tragedy had affected Gavin and the others deeply, in ways she hadn't understood when she was young.

Unless he had practice or a game after school or on the weekends, Gavin had preferred to hang out at her place rather than be at home, sometimes even sleeping over.

Autumn had still been to his house plenty of times over the years, but usually just for special occasions when Marley would somehow find the time and energy on top of all her other responsibilities to make a homecooked meal and dessert for someone's birthday or to celebrate one of the twins' sporting achievements.

Tonight, Marley looked happier than Autumn had ever seen her. Probably because her whole family was back together again. Her husband Warwick was a little intimidating at first sight with that big scar running down the right side of his cheek and throat. But he and his Geordie accent were completely charming—even if she didn't always catch everything he said.

Decker, the eldest, she hardly recognized, since he seemed to have undergone a complete personality transformation compared to the last time she'd seen him. She couldn't remember him ever being this relaxed and at ease before, the grim set of his features gone. He'd even laughed a few times tonight, which was wonderful to witness. His girlfriend Teagan was harder to get a read on, however. She was all mysterious sitting beside him and taking everything in, radiating a quiet kind of confidence that Autumn found intriguing.

As for the twins, some things never changed. Like always, Gavin was the life of the party, with quieter Tristan delivering sarcastic zingers every now and again to keep things lively. Carly was clearly having the time of her life being in the center of it all, getting endless attention from her favorite people.

If it wasn't for the heavy weight sitting in the middle of

her chest, Autumn would have felt the same way and been sorry to see the evening end.

But when Carly stifled her third yawn in five minutes, Autumn took the opportunity to call it a night and make her escape. "Well, this has been amazing, but I need to get this young lady home to bed to sleep off this jetlag so she can get up bright and early and get to work on her final school project."

Carly's expression was mortified. "Mo-o-o-m. I'm almost a teenager, and I'm not tired."

"Yes, you are, because you're still on Kentucky time." She stood, grabbed her sweater and purse.

Gavin rose from his chair. "I'll take you back."

Autumn waved him off. She wasn't ready to be alone with him yet. "No, it's fine. Stay. We'll just get an Uber."

He shot her a you-gotta-be-kidding-me look and shook his head. "Not happening." He reached over to ruffle the top of Carly's hair, earning him narrowed eyes but no snarky comment. Carly worshipped him too much to dole out the snark Autumn received on a far too common basis these days. "Come on, squirt. Let's get you home. Mom's orders."

Carly huffed but dutifully got up and said her goodbyes to everyone.

Autumn followed suit, doling out hugs and wondering how these people she loved, who had always made her and Carly feel so welcome, would react once they found out the news.

Don't borrow trouble, she scolded herself.

Marley wrapped her up tight in her arms and gave her a hard squeeze. "It's been so good to spend time with you guys. Call me in the morning once you know your plans? I can take an extended lunch break from work and come meet you." She managed a care home in town.

"Will do." As a single parent, Autumn had so much respect for Marley. Barely in her teens when she'd been left to look after the twins, she'd raised them and run the household while going to school and working part time, living off the little money their parents' life insurance had left them, and whatever Decker had been able to send home to them.

Autumn had always had a lot of support from her parents. Marley had had no one once Decker left right after his graduation, and she'd basically been a kid herself.

The evening air had a damp, cool edge to it when she and Gavin stepped outside and walked the short distance to his SUV. Marley paused partway down the walkway when she saw it. "Um, how are you gonna get out?" There was another truck parked beside his—literally parked in the middle of the street.

"Because we're taking Tris's," Gavin replied, pointing a fob at the double-parked truck to unlock its doors.

Autumn shot him an incredulous look. Tristan was the mature, level-headed one. "What the…"

"Ooh, what did you do to make him mad?" Carly asked eagerly.

"Beat him here when he was sure he'd win—and took the last parking spot on the street," Gavin said, opening the right rear passenger door for her.

Carly smirked. "Nice." She climbed inside.

Autumn reached for the front passenger door, but Gavin's hand shot out and grasped it first. "I got it," he said quietly from right behind her.

Autumn stilled at his nearness, his scent wrapping around her. Clean and dark and masculine, and he was standing so close she could feel the heat of him along her back. His arm brushed hers, sending tingles right up to her shoulder.

Seriously, how was she going to sit him down and tell

him the truth when she was ready to crawl out of her skin just being this close to him?

"Thanks," she murmured when he opened the door and quickly climbed in, unsettled by this strange new effect he had on her. She had to figure out a way to stop these feelings.

"So, what's this project you're working on?" Gavin asked Carly as he put the truck in gear and started driving up the quiet, leafy street.

"My family tree. I signed up with a genealogy site to try and find stuff about my dad's side of the family."

Gavin slanted Autumn a questioning look and it was a miracle she didn't choke. "Yeah? Find anything?"

"I haven't had time to check yet, but Mom said we got an email from them before we left. I'll look at it in the morning."

Oh, God. Autumn stayed silent, lost in her turbulent thoughts while he and Carly chattered about the project on the way to his building. The ten-minute drive felt more like an hour, and by the time they arrived, she couldn't wait to get out of the truck and run inside.

She opened her door as soon as he stopped at the curb out front. "Okay, thanks for the lift."

"I'll walk you up."

"No, that's—"

"There a problem?"

Oh, hell yes. "No."

"C'mon, squirt." He hooked an arm around Carly's shoulders and escorted them into the building, up the elevator to the top floor. "Just need to grab a couple things from my closet quick," he said to her as he unlocked the front door.

"Sure." She stayed in the kitchen, anxiously counting down the minutes until he left.

Carly disappeared down the hall into Tristan's room to get ready for bed while

Autumn wiped down the already gleaming countertops to give herself something to do. The view from up here through the kitchen windows was spectacular, the ocean breeze pushing fast-moving clouds across the face of the half-moon shining over the water.

Gavin appeared a couple minutes later and paused in the kitchen entryway, one finger holding the hooks of the garment bag draped over his broad shoulder. She couldn't help but notice that the position of his arm made the bulge of his biceps stand out even more.

His phone beeped in his pocket, but he ignored it, his expression uncharacteristically serious as he watched her. "So. You gonna tell me what's bothering you?"

Hell. "Nothing's bothering me," she said a little too quickly, moving to the island. It was already spotless too, but cleaning it again was better than having to look at him right now. And it put some distance between them.

He came over to the island, draped the garment bag over one end of it and planted himself on a stool, facing her. Taking up way too much space in the large kitchen even though there were several feet of gleaming granite between them. "You gonna make me drag it out of you?"

She stopped, gathered herself, and met his gaze. The instant she did, a sharp pain stabbed her chest.

Her fingers tightened on the damp cloth in her fist. Why did this have to happen? Why did he have to be so damned gorgeous and irresistible, and everything so complicated all of a sudden? It was late, and she was tired, not to mention overwhelmed. This definitely wasn't the right time to tell him, and Carly was just down the hall.

His phone beeped again. "You gonna check that?" she asked, hoping for a reprieve.

"No."

It was clear he wasn't about to let this drop. She chose her words carefully. "I just... We need to talk about something important. Alone."

"We're alone now."

She shook her head. "Carly's here." No way.

He frowned in concern. "What's wrong?"

She shook her head again, darted a quick look past him to the hallway as her ears strained for any sign that her daughter might come out of her room. "I can't with her here," she said in a lower voice. In case Carly came out of her room for some reason and overheard. Or worse, in case telling him didn't go well. She didn't want Carly to witness them arguing.

He crossed his arms. His incredibly big, sculpted arms that had felt like heaven around her. "Is it about the night before I left for boot camp?"

She almost gave herself whiplash snapping her head around to stare at him in shock. Nearly tripped over the corner millwork on the base of the island as she took a step back.

His gaze was level. Unwavering. "Because we never did talk about it. Ever. I think it's time we did."

Oh, Jesus. Her heart was galloping, a thousand bittersweet memories from that night invading her mind. And he was way closer to the truth than he realized. "I...it's not..."

Another beep from his phone, loud in the sudden, brittle silence. He kept staring at her, unrelenting. "For the record, I regret that."

As the silence stretched out, her face grew so hot she was sure she was only a second away from spontaneous combustion. "You...regret it?"

He nodded once. "The way it went. And that we just left it like that."

With effort she swallowed the golf ball-size lump stuck in

her throat. He regretted the way it went. What did that mean? She was afraid to ask. Because she was pretty sure she wouldn't like the answer, and that would make what she had to tell him even harder.

His phone chirped again. Then again, several times in a row. She gestured toward it. "You should—"

Mouth compressed into a hard line, he reached back and impatiently pulled it from his pocket. Scanning the screen, he rose, still reading. "Damn, I gotta go."

The rush of relief almost weakened her knees. "Everything okay?"

"Work-related. About the security detail this weekend." He shoved his phone into his back pocket and looked up at her again, annoyance burning in his green eyes. "But we're not done here."

Her insides grabbed. *Crap*.

But rather than head for the door, he rounded the island and came toward her. Somehow, Autumn stood her ground to keep from retreating.

He stopped right in front of her and settled his big hands on her hips. His expression was determined, and she could feel the imprint of his long fingers through the thin fabric of her dress, their intimate position making her heart thud painfully against her ribs.

"Just tell me you're not sick or in trouble," he said quietly.

Oh, she was in trouble all right. More trouble than she could handle. She forced a weak smile, shook her head. "No, I'm okay." Sort of. But not really.

Seeming satisfied, he relaxed. But his hands stayed put on her hips, his fingers tightening on them in a way that felt weirdly possessive. They were inches apart, staring at each other. This close to him, she was reminded again of just how big he was. He towered over her, the physical power of him stealing what little oxygen she was still able to suck into her lungs.

And the intent way he stared at her. Almost as if he… No, she had to be reading that wrong. It was…confusing.

And arousing.

Before she could quiet the chaos in her brain, he leaned in and pressed a kiss to the middle of her forehead. The tender gesture made her insides clench painfully. "Whatever it is, we'll figure it out," he murmured against her skin. "Okay?"

Not trusting her voice, she nodded, her eyes stinging.

He squeezed her hips gently and released her, stepping back to grab the garment bag and swing it back over his shoulder. "We'll talk tomorrow after I'm done with work, all right? Just you and me in private."

She dreaded it as much as she wanted to have it over with. "Okay."

He stopped in the entry to the kitchen, that penetrating gaze making her pulse skip. "Sleep well."

"You too."

When the front door clicked shut behind him moments later, she could still feel the imprint of his lips on her skin… and on her heart.

SIX

TJ tugged the brim of his ballcap down lower on his forehead as he stepped out onto the sidewalk. As always, the men's shelter was full. He'd been lucky to get a bed here again last night and didn't hold much hope for one tonight based on the looks of things.

In either direction outside the front entrance and across the street, long lines of homeless men lined the sidewalks, the ones unable to get a bed huddled in doorways or sleeping out in the open next to their small piles of worldly possessions.

He would worry about tonight's sleeping situation after his shift. And if he wound up having to bunk on the street again, well, there were worse things. These past few months, it seemed like he'd spent as many nights on the street as in a bed anyway.

Shoving his hands in his coat pockets, he kept his head lowered and walked north for two blocks before turning west and heading for one of Portland's busiest waterfronts. The morning sky was blue overhead, but a cool mist had rolled in off the river overnight, covering the edge of the waterfront in a pale haze so thick that only the tops of the cranes were visible above it.

This construction job wasn't steady work, but it was the best he'd had in almost a year and paid decently for a day's labor. He'd been out here on Portland's streets for more than six months now, but it felt like years. Every day, he passed by countless other homeless people, a disproportionate amount of whom were military vets like him. Every single one of them had a story and a reason why they'd ended up here. Abuse. PTSD. Mental illness. Depression. Getting hooked on prescription meds. Booze. Hard drugs.

They were the forgotten. Living ghosts. It was an eerie feeling to be invisible, for people to walk by without even seeing him. Like he didn't exist. That had been the hardest thing to adjust to.

Life on the streets was hard. He'd learned early on to keep to himself and whom to avoid. Knew who most of the dealers and gangsters were and where they hung out. But even though he kept a low profile, there had been times he'd had to fight for his life out here while the cops looked the other way because they considered him and the rest to be unworthy of protection. And every day, more of them died out here, unnoticed.

Right on cue as he turned the next corner, he saw a fire crew and ambulance blocking the street. A group of first responders was trying to revive a guy sprawled out on the sidewalk while other homeless looked on without emotion and people in business suits crossed the street to avoid the scene, shaking their heads in disgust.

TJ moved closer. He stopped, recognizing the man lying there on his back. A local addict he knew. Not former military, but a decent guy who had wound up here after losing his job, home, and wife, and getting hooked on progressively harder and harder drugs to escape his misery.

Today he must have taken a hit laced with fentanyl. These days, there was no telling what was in the shit the dealers sold their desperate clientele.

One of the paramedics working on him stopped, shook his head and stood, stripping off his gloves. TJ edged closer as the other responders drifted away and paused to look down into the man's face. He'd seen so many men die out here. Way more than in combat overseas.

Staring into his acquaintance's face, he felt…numb.

"Can I help you?" a cop asked him brusquely.

TJ met his gaze. Saw the judgement and disdain in those hard brown eyes. Telling TJ he thought he was just another piece of shit, to wind up out here. Fuck him.

The cop jerked his chin at the dead man. "You know him?"

Not well. "His name's Ritchie."

"Ritchie what?"

"Holmes."

"He got any family or next of kin?"

TJ shook his head. "Not that I know of." He didn't want to get involved. Ritchie's troubles were over now.

Not for the first time, he wondered if one day he would wind up like this too. God knew he'd been tempted to exit this life many times over the past few years because death was the only real escape from the burden he carried every day. Instead, he was out here just going through the motions of living from one day to the next.

He told himself there was still a point to his existence, that he still had value as a human being, but at this point he wasn't so sure anymore. Despite all the efforts to stop it, the drug scene up and down the West Coast was the worst it had ever been.

The whole country was infected now, the drug and housing crisis leaving a tide of homeless addicts left to suffer and die on the streets of American cities and towns while the dealers, runners, and cartels got richer by the day, along with the politicians and billionaires.

It made him sick and angry. Somehow he'd wound up here after serving his country with honor for the best years of his adult life. And for what? What was the fucking point anymore when guys like Ritchie kept dying day after day after day without any sign of it stopping?

He walked on, clearing his mind on the way to the river. Dan was waiting for him at the entrance to the jobsite, nodded at him. "Hey, man." He looked rougher than usual, flannel shirt and jeans dirty and torn in places, a bruise under one eye and his beard in serious need of a trim. "Got anything extra to eat?"

"Sorry." Dan had served in the Army before landing on hard times and had been on and off the streets for a few months now. He wasn't a drug addict as far as TJ knew, but he'd been hitting the bottle pretty hard lately. Based on what TJ had witnessed during his time out here, it probably wouldn't be long before Dan went for something harder to numb himself. And then only a matter of more time before he became another Ritchie. "You good?"

Dan touched the bruise under his eye and grunted. "Yeah, some stupid motherfucker thought he'd try and mug me last night. He got my phone and a couple twenties I had."

They walked into the site together, collected hard hats, vests, and work gloves from the foreman's trailer before punching in for the day. They both had ten hours of manual labor ahead of them before clocking out.

TJ didn't mind. Most days he looked forward to the mindless work and the physical exertion that let him drop into a dreamless sleep later.

"Hey, you're comin' to the protests this weekend, right?" Dan asked.

TJ shook his head and tugged his gloves on. He'd seen all the security barricades going up around the big conference center downtown. Some elitist global political movers and shakers were coming to town to sit around and congratulate themselves for being better and richer than everyone else while deciding how the world should be run, and people here were pissed as hell about it. "Gonna pick up an extra shift or two if I can."

Dan shot him an accusing look. "Come on, man. Those fucking rich hypocrites are all gonna be here. Liars and criminals who cover each other's asses, every last fucking one of 'em. These out-of-touch assholes run the country, send people like us off to fight in shitholes around the world while they live the high life on the backs of the taxpayers they send overseas to die, then forget we exist when we come home, and leave us on the streets like trash. You seriously gonna sit back and let 'em get away with what they've done to us?"

He shrugged. Protesting wouldn't do jack shit to change anything. The rich would just keep getting richer, and the poor would just keep getting poorer, flooding these streets with human misery. "Not my fight." His fight was different and more specific. Although lately, it was getting harder and harder to remember exactly what he was fighting for anymore.

Dan shook his head in disgust. "The fuck it's not. We need all hands on deck." Seeing TJ wasn't going to budge, he sighed. "Whatever, just think about it. If you change your mind, you know where to find me."

TJ didn't answer as he headed for his workstation for the day. No way he was getting involved in that shitshow. A blind man could see it was a powder keg waiting to go off.

He didn't want to be anywhere near the city center when the spark was lit.

SEVEN

Gavin couldn't tear his eyes off Autumn when she came into view up the street with Carly. Snug, dark jeans hugged her hips and thighs, and the thin athletic jacket conformed to every curve of her breasts and waist. Her hair was pulled up into a clip, the ocean breeze blowing little tendrils around her face and neck.

He'd learned how to hide his feelings at a young age, but the longer he tried to suppress what he felt for Autumn, the harder it was to keep it under wraps.

"Mornin', pretty ladies," he said when they got close.

"Morning. Tris joining us?" Autumn asked. He was worried about her. Wished the hell he could figure out what was wrong.

"Yeah, he and Marley are gonna meet us in a bit." He managed to pull his attention from her long enough to smile at Carly. "Get a good start on your project this morning?"

"Yep, but Mom said she couldn't find anything about my dad's side, so I guess I'm just gonna write my report on hers." She looked as disappointed as she sounded.

"Ah." He glanced at Autumn. Carly's father had never been in the picture. He and Autumn hadn't been in an actual relationship when she'd wound up pregnant, and she had never pursued child support. Gavin didn't even know the asshole's name, but he hated him on principle. Fuck that loser.

Autumn avoided looking at him as she steered Carly toward the café. "Let's get in line before we end up halfway down the block like yesterday."

He was impatient to have their private conversation as soon as possible. Had been up half the night wondering what was so major that she wouldn't just tell him and refused to talk about it with Carly around.

Poppy greeted them at the counter with a warm smile. "Are you guys regular customers now?" she asked the girls.

"Absolutely," Autumn said, and gestured to Carly. "We've both got our hearts set on trying the strawberries and cream croissant."

"Excellent choice. They're my husband Noah's favorite, and we only make them when the local berries are in season." She switched her attention to him. "What'll it be for you today, Gav?"

"Caramel pecan sticky bun."

"Ooh, lucky for you there are two left. Because the other one's already held for Boyd."

Boyd Masterson was former Delta and lived up in the hills outside of town with his wife, Ember, who did occasional freelance work for Crimson Point Security's IT department. "Haven't seen him around lately."

Poppy smiled. "You know how he is. He prefers to come in right at opening and avoid having to socialize too much."

"Ah, yeah, that tracks." Good guy, but a hermit.

He ordered his own breakfast, paid for their order over Autumn's protests and took everything to go. "Ever flown a kite?" he asked Carly on the way out the door.

"No."

"Want to?"

She grinned up at him. "Yeah."

"Okay. Right this way." He led them down the street, pausing to greet a familiar figure coming toward them pushing a stroller. "Morning, Danae."

"Morning." She stopped just in front of them, and Gavin introduced them.

"Danae's married to my boss, Ryder. She works at the local vet clinic," he explained.

"I'm just giving Walter his walk in between patients while Sierra finishes the first surgery of the day." Seeing Carly's curiosity, she pulled the canopy back and a furry face appeared over the edge with a grayed, spotted muzzle and long ears that drooped along with his eyes. "Walter, say hi."

Carly's delighted smile was priceless. "Oh, he's so cute!"

"He's a rescue and extremely spoiled, as you can see," Danae said. "He's too old and stiff to walk much these days, so he gets paraded around in this. He's a total celeb around town, everyone knows him. You can pet him if you want."

Carly reached in and stroked the dog's head. Walter's mouth opened in a smile, his pink tongue lolling. Carly wrinkled her nose. "Ew, Walter, you have really bad breath."

Danae laughed. "He's an old man. But don't let that fool you, you should see this guy when he's out dune buggying. He's an adrenaline junkie at heart."

Carly's eyes widened. "Dune buggying?"

"He *loves* it, has his own doggles and helmet and everything. Where are you guys off to?"

"Gonna get us a kite and take it for a test run before I have to get to the meetings," Gavin said.

She nodded. "Ryder's been so busy with this upcoming job he hasn't been home in two days. Tell him I said hi?"

He chuckled. "Will do. See you later."

"Bye. Nice to meet you both," she said to Carly and Autumn, and carried on toward the clinic, where Walter liked to lie just inside the front door like a furry floor mat for everyone to walk around, watching the comings and goings along Front Street through the glass.

"The people here are so cool," Carly said.

He smiled at her enthusiasm. "It's a small-town thing. You get to know the locals pretty quick in a place this size. Here's the kite shop." The front of it was all decked out in a rainbow of various kites in all shapes and sizes fluttering in the breeze.

Inside, Carly quickly zeroed in on a unicorn kite. "This is the one?" he asked her.

"Yes." Her eyes shone with excitement as she took it to the counter.

The elderly woman behind it smiled at her. "This is such a lovely kite. Your dad can have it ready to go in just a few minutes."

Carly's cheeks flushed. "He's not my dad."

The woman blinked. "Oh, I'm sorry." She glanced anxiously between them.

"Don't be," Gavin said. "It's the red hair, right?"

The woman hesitated a moment. "Um, yes."

He glanced at Autumn to see her reaction and was surprised to see her face was pale as she stared back at him, then she almost immediately turned away. "I'll wait outside," she said, already heading for the door.

What the hell was wrong? He paid for the kite, then he

and Carly quickly put it together inside and exited the shop. Autumn was waiting for them, sunglasses hiding her eyes but her color back to normal. "Ready to rock?"

"Yep," Carly answered, a bounce in her step as she carried her kite. "Are Tris and Marley still coming?"

"They just texted me saying they're already at the beach." He hung back a bit and stopped Autumn with a hand on her waist. "You okay?"

"Fine," she answered, pulling free to follow her daughter. "What time do your meetings start?"

"About ninety minutes from now. Not sure when we'll finish up, and Tris and I may have to work late after that. What time are you guys checking into your hotel tomorrow?"

"Around three, but we'll head into Portland before that to shop and get something to eat first."

"There'll be extra security downtown all weekend, but just keep an eye out while you're walking around the city."

She glanced over at him. "Why? Are they expecting trouble from the protests?"

They always had to expect trouble. That was part of the job. "They're anticipating more protesters will arrive starting tonight, and with that comes the risk of trouble. You don't need to worry though. The security at your hotel has been beefed up, too, and you're a few blocks away from where the protests will be staged."

"I'm not worried. I'll be so busy I won't have time to leave the hotel, and Carly will be working on her project."

"Didn't find out anything about her other side of the family tree, huh?" Yeah, he was fishing. He knew next to nothing about the guy who'd gotten her pregnant except that it was a short fling that had gone nowhere. And that it had happened less than a week after Gavin had left for bootcamp. That still stung.

Her shoulders tensed slightly, but she kept walking. "No."

When she didn't say anything more he let it drop, because he knew full well she didn't like talking about Carly's sperm donor.

At the far south end of the row of buildings on Front Street, they came to the Sea Hag bar and the mile of sandy beach beyond it. The breeze picked up as soon as they passed the protection of the bar, whipping off the rolling waves and across the wide stretch of sand, their steps leaving a trail of indistinct footprints in their wake.

"There they are," he said. Tris and Marley waved and started their way from the opposite direction.

They met in the middle of the crescent-shaped beach that hugged the bay. He and Tris immediately taught Carly how to get her kite in the air, then stood by to coach her while Marley and Autumn took video and pictures. Once Carly had the hang of things, he walked over and sat down next to Autumn to eat their breakfast, tamping down his impatience to get her alone.

She seemed more relaxed as she chatted with Marley and called out encouragement to Carly, but he couldn't help shake the feeling that she was still ignoring him a little. He didn't like it.

After the better part of an hour, Carly and Tris reeled the kite back in and came over to join them. Marley handed out food she'd brought along as a young family passed by, two parents with a little boy who looked around two or so.

He heard the mother say no, and the toddler suddenly launched into an epic tantrum, lying face down on the sand while screaming bloody murder and flailing his fists and feet. Gavin and the others all stared while the father tried to pick the kid up, getting clocked in the nose for his efforts. He cursed and a wrestling match ensued, both parents struggling to subdue their demon child.

"And that's just one reason why I'm never having kids," Gavin said, feeling sorry for them and glad Carly was way past all that.

Autumn's head snapped toward him, eyes still hidden by the sunglasses. "You don't want kids?"

He made a face. Given his background, he didn't think he would be good dad material for a little one. He hadn't exactly had good parental role models, and wasn't sure he could give a kid what it needed and deserved. "Can you see me dealing with that?" He nodded toward the continuing meltdown.

"Nope," Tristan answered.

Exactly, so Gavin let the dig go without argument. "What about you?" he asked his twin. "You want kids?"

"Dunno. Maybe. Never really thought about it, to be honest. Been kinda busy putting up with you." But Tris was also watching the meltdown as if it was a trainwreck in motion he couldn't look away from.

"Whatever. You'd both be great dads," Marley said with complete confidence. "A lot of guys don't have any experience with babies or kids before they become parents. You'd figure it out fast."

He grunted, wishing they'd change the subject. He didn't see himself parenting a little one. Ever. Didn't want to risk screwing up a kid for the rest of its life.

"Why not?" Autumn kept staring at him, unwilling to let it go.

Her insistence surprised him. She was well aware of his bleak childhood. "You know why."

"It doesn't mean you wouldn't be a good parent. You're fantastic with Carly."

He appreciated the praise, but Carly was half grown up

already, and his relationship with her was good because he was like an honorary uncle. Autumn had already put in all the hard work to this point by herself, and Carly had thrived because of it. "Yeah, because I'm the funcle. Besides, she's practically already an adult. Aren't you, squirt?"

She'd been a few weeks old the first time he'd met her while home on leave. He'd been terrified of dropping or hurting her somehow, and for the handful of hours he'd spent with her in total as an infant, he'd handed her back the instant she fussed or needed a diaper change. Babies freaked him out.

Carly nodded. "Pretty much."

The agitated parents were now struggling to get the toddler strapped into the stroller. The kid was having none of it, arched taut like a bow, fighting like hell against confinement and screaming like a banshee. He suppressed a shudder. "You never had meltdowns like that, did you, squirt?"

"Never," Carly answered. "I've always been mature for my age."

"You certainly did have meltdowns like that," Autumn told her dryly.

"I don't believe it," Gavin said. "Carly would never."

"Well, she did," Autumn insisted, and there was a definite edge to her tone that made him pause and drop the teasing.

Whatever was bugging her today, he knew it was connected with whatever she wanted to talk to him about later. But he was done with her attitude, and later was too fucking far away, so he reached over, grabbed her, and put her over his shoulder.

"What are you doing?" she cried as he pushed to his feet, trying to scramble off him. "Put me down!"

"Nope." Enough was enough. He turned and started jogging down the beach, arms locked across the backs of her thighs to hold her in place while she braced her hands on his lower back to keep from bouncing against him.

Her protests died within moments, and her grudging laughter was music to his ears. "Gavin, you idiot, I just lost my sunglasses. Where the hell are you taking me?"

"We'll get 'em later. And not far." He ducked into a little alcove up ahead formed by a low cliff that blocked them from view of the others and set her on her feet. Slowly, so that she slid down the front of him inch by inch until the soles of her shoes finally touched the sand.

She steadied herself on his shoulders a moment, her cheeks flushed pink as she pushed her wind-blown hair away from her face. When she went to step back, he stopped her by catching her hips in his hands. Those pretty, pale green eyes flew up to stare at him, startled.

He released her hips and framed her face between his hands instead, desperate to fix whatever was happening between them. "We're alone. Now talk to me, Autie."

She stared back at him a second, the look in her eyes softening slightly at the childhood nickname. "Not here."

"Why the hell not? No one can see or hear us." They were hidden from view and the pounding of the waves would drown out anything they said.

She shook her head, gaze darting past him as though she expected someone to appear behind them at any moment. "Not now."

Irritation swept through him. "Then when? I'm tied up the rest of today, have no idea what time I'll be done, then I head out first thing tomorrow and won't be back until late Monday night." Why wouldn't she just *tell* him?

"I don't know." She pulled his hands away from her face and stepped back. "Look, just…it's nothing, okay? Just forget I said anything. It doesn't matter anymore."

"What the hell does that mean?" he demanded, setting his hands on his hips and blocking her from moving with his body. "Just tell me what's wrong. I hate this." He'd missed her so damned much and wanted to be with her. This wall she'd put between them made him insane.

"What's going on is you're confusing me," she fired back, eyes blazing. "What's with the weird vibe you've been giving off since I got here?"

He hadn't expected her to call him on it, but at least she'd noticed. "What vibe is that?"

"The…" She gestured between them with one hand. "You know. Last night."

He was going to make her spell it out. "Say it."

"Like you want to kiss me," she snapped in annoyance.

Oh, he wanted to do a hell of a lot more than that. And he liked that she'd called him out so boldly. Liked that she was willing to go toe to toe with him finally. "And if I did?"

Her eyes widened in shock, and she shook her head before blurting, "I'm seeing someone."

That was the last thing he'd expected her to say. Something dark and territorial lit up inside him. An uncontrollable, primitive response to this potential rival for her. "Who?"

"A guy," she said, trying to step around him.

He blocked her path. He wasn't letting her run from him. A fucking *guy*? "Who?" he demanded.

She made a frustrated sound and faced him, mirroring his stance with hands on hips. Christ, she was stunning, all fired up with her head lifted proudly. It took everything he had not to back her up against the rock wall behind her right now, pin her there with his body, and kiss her until her legs gave out.

"A guy from work. Not that it's any of your business," she added.

Oh, he was making it his fucking business. "For how long?" If it was serious he didn't think he could stand it.

"Why do you care?" she fired back.

Because you're mine. Gavin barely held it back as he met her angry stare, every possessive cell in his body howling in protest at the thought of her with someone else.

Before either of them could say anything else, Carly's voice called out over the wind. "Mom, I got your sunglasses!"

"Coming," she called back, and pushed past him.

Gavin set his jaw and sucked in a deep breath, letting her go. But only for the moment.

She was dating some asshole, and this was the first he was finding out about it? And she still hadn't told him the truth about what the real problem was.

To hell with this. They were hashing everything out tonight. Because there was no way in hell he was losing her now.

∼

TRISTAN REACHED the sand-strewn parking lot just as Gavin's SUV turned out of it. He pulled out his keyfob to unlock his truck, with Marley right behind him.

Wow. That happy little get together on the beach had not gone the way he'd thought it would.

Marley suddenly grabbed his arm, hauled him around to face her. "Okay, what the hell was all that?" she demanded, tucking a lock of wind-blown, dark auburn hair behind her ear.

"What?"

"Don't what me. You saw them. He carried her off like a sack of potatoes, disappeared around the corner to say who

65

knows what, and when Carly went over a minute later with her sunglasses, Autumn couldn't get them out of here fast enough."

Yeah.

"Gavin didn't say a single word the entire way back here. And they wouldn't even look at each other when they said goodbye." Her gaze cut to the back of Gavin's SUV as he drove away from them down Front Street, then to Carly and Autumn, who were already partway up the hill to the condo. "Autumn was acting a bit strange around Gav at the party last night, but just now she looked like she wanted to punch him in the face."

"I mean, can you blame her? I feel like that all the time."

Marley pressed her lips together and thumped her fist into his shoulder, frowning at him. "Seriously. Can you not tell something's going on with them?"

Of course he could. He and Gavin were literally two halves of a whole. Sometimes, he felt he knew Gavin better than his brother knew himself, so when something was off with him, yeah. He noticed. "He must've pissed her off somehow. I wouldn't worry about it. Whatever it is, they'll work it out."

Autumn had been their friend for more than twenty years, but she and Gavin had always been closest. Zero percent chance anything would change that. Well, barring some major, cataclysmic disaster, and Tristan couldn't think of anything like that.

Marley stared up at him with a mix of irritation and disappointment. "It's not like them to argue, let alone in front of us, and Autumn's only here a couple more days. I'm telling you, something's very wrong." She narrowed her eyes. "Do you know something? You do. You know something."

"I don't know anything. Other than I'm not gonna stick

my nose in their business or grill Gav about it because you know how much good that'd do." He and Gavin were tight and trusted each other completely. But that didn't mean he had the right to interfere in his brother's personal life. "They're both all grown up now, Marls. Let them be. They'll figure it out."

She shook her head, reached for the passenger door handle, and opened it. "I don't like it."

He didn't respond, since there was no good answer. But she was right. There absolutely was something going on between Gav and Autumn. And whatever it was, they were both pissed about it.

Marley was quiet until they were about five minutes from her and Warwick's place. "If you do find out anything, will you let me know?" Before he could open his mouth to answer, she rolled her eyes and snorted. "Okay, I realize the whole twin code thing comes first. It's just…whatever's going on feels way off. Autumn is as reasonable and levelheaded as they come. If she's this upset, it's for good reason."

Yeah, and Gav had a talent for pushing people's buttons. "If Gav wants to talk to me about it, he will."

"But you won't tell me if he does."

"I will if he's in trouble." Not unless.

Marley eyed him. "You two are so unbelievably frustrating sometimes, you know that?"

"Us?"

She huffed. Folded her arms. "Pain in my ass, both of you. *Still*, even at thirty years old."

He hid a smile as he turned onto her street. Being their mom and sister in one couldn't have been easy on her all these years, especially from age sixteen. But she had stepped in and stepped up when no one else in their life had. Without her, God only knew what would have happened to them. And he was well aware that she would always love them to death, no matter how much she complained about them driving her nuts.

Family, even a flawed one, was everything. So while he would keep a close eye on his brother. Whatever was going on between him and Autumn, Tristan wouldn't intervene until he needed to.

EIGHT

A pounding headache woke Autumn early the next morning. She rolled onto her back in Gavin's bed and stared up at the dimly lit ceiling, the pale light coming in around the edges of the blinds telling her it was just past dawn. One crystal clear thought hit her instantly.

I'm seeing someone, she'd blurted out to him yesterday.

It was a total lie, but Gavin didn't need to know that.

Jonas was a perfectly nice guy and had made it clear he was interested in being more than colleagues. He'd asked her out twice over the past three months, and both times she'd said no, using the excuse that they worked together. He had accepted it, but strongly hinted that he wasn't ready to give up yet.

She wouldn't be surprised if he asked her out again at some point during the conference. But her answer would still be no.

No surprise, she'd slept like shit, and when she finally had managed to slide under, she'd been tormented by restless dreams about a spectacular and disastrous end to her relationship with Gavin. And then there had been another featuring incredibly intense sex with him that left her whole body throbbing with an unfulfilled need that bordered on torture.

Yesterday's sharp turn of events on the beach made her feel like she was caught in a blender. With her conscience already weighing on her, Gavin's sudden announcement about never wanting kids had been a gut punch she hadn't expected. At first, she'd thought he was kidding as he liked to joke around, but then she'd realized he was being serious.

It was a hard thing to reconcile. While it was true it had taken him a while to mature and he still tended not to take life too seriously most of the time, she agreed with Marley that he would be a good father.

He was magic with Carly—although granted, their time together had been sporadic, and he got to be the hero all the time, never had to discipline her or be the bad guy. Were things good only because Carly came with no permanent ties or major responsibility? Would his feelings change for the worse once he found out the truth? Not that it was Autumn's job to manage his feelings. He was a grown man, his reaction was on him.

Telling him was the last thing she wanted to do now, but there was no way around it, though now she'd made up her mind to wait until after the conference. Preferably right before she and Carly got on a flight back home where they belonged.

The sound of dishes clacking softly in the kitchen made her drag herself out of bed. She found Carly pulling toast out of the toaster. Her daughter stilled when Autumn appeared in the entry, eyeing her. "Whoa, you look tired."

Shit. She really did look that bad. "Well, thanks a lot, I actually feel great. Might need a power nap later though."

Carly went back to spreading peanut butter on her toast.

"You'll feel better once you give your presentation at the conference. Want some toast?"

Autumn smiled, thinking for the millionth time what a miracle her daughter was and not correcting her assumption that she hadn't slept well due to anxiety over her upcoming presentation. "No, thanks. I'll stick to coffee for now. Want to work together for a while this morning?" That way she could monitor what Carly was accessing on the ancestry site and make sure she didn't do any digging that would give away the truth about who her father was. Because her daughter was quick and liable to figure it out on her own if she found the giveaway evidence.

"Sure, and then we can go down to Whale's Tale again? I still might buy that other book with the rest of my birthday money Gavvy and Trissy gave me."

Just the mention of his name twisted her stomach into knots. "Uh-huh, and you also want another treat from the bakery."

Carly shrugged as she screwed the lid back on the peanut butter jar. "I mean, it's in the same shop."

"Yeah, how convenient." She ruffled the top of Carly's hair, got her hand knocked aside and a warning glare that only a preteen girl could master. "Okay, let's both get showered and ready, then we'll put in a solid couple of hours and head down."

The morning flew by, and the focus on conference prep thankfully allowed her to put Gavin and their situation from her mind for a while. When she became aware of her stomach rumbling, she was shocked to find that nearly three hours had passed.

"You ready for a break?" she asked Carly, seated next to her at the island.

"Yes." Carly instantly snapped the lid of her laptop shut.

So far she hadn't looked up anything that worried Autumn, but given her daughter's innate curiosity and determination to find out something about her father, that was likely only a matter of time.

"How much did you get done?" Autumn asked her as they slid their shoes and jackets on. The day was bright and sunny, but the wind off the water was chilly.

"A lot, actually. Shouldn't take me much longer to finish the research, and then I can write my report."

"Good." She would check the progress later, keep steering Carly's attention away from her paternal side until she finally sat her down and told her the truth. After she'd told Gavin. "All right, let's go."

Warm, late-morning sunshine greeted them, the faint cry of seagulls carried on the steady breeze. A familiar figure appeared at the bottom of the sidewalk as they started down the hill.

"Well, hey there," Teagan called out with a big smile. "Where are you two off to?"

"Taking a work break," Carly said as they approached. "Wanna come get something to eat with us?"

Teagan raised her eyebrows at Autumn, her dark hair pulled back into a braid. "Yes, please come," Autumn said. She was curious about Decker's girlfriend and wanted to get to know her more. "I mean, as long as it works for you."

"I'll make time for you two."

"We're going to Whale's Tale," Carly told her.

"Good choice. Not sure what Poppy and her staff put in their food, but it's addictive."

"Might have something to do with butter and sugar," Autumn said, still trying to size her up. There was something utterly fascinating about her. Teagan and Decker's story was dramatic, but Autumn only knew little bits of it because

Gavin sucked at telling her the important parts. She'd have to get all the juicy stuff from Marley next time they talked.

The line for Whale's Tale was only a few yards out the door when they got there. Carly went into the bookshop to buy her book while Autumn stood in line for the café with Teagan, talking. Small talk, mostly, about work and Crimson Point. Nothing that alleviated Autumn's curiosity about the other woman.

"How did you and Decker meet?" she asked finally, unable to stop herself.

One side of Teagan's mouth turned up. "Ohh, that's quite a story."

Autumn was dying. "Oh, God, tell me. I need to know how you got under Decker's skin." More like armor. He was so different from the twins. Way harder, and remote. "I've known him almost my whole life, and he's still an enigma."

Teagan's teeth flashed in a quick grin. "Yeah, that's kinda what made me fall for him. I love unraveling a mystery."

Autumn took a sip of her iced coffee, riveted. Decker was the living embodiment of the strong, silent type, in a really grim kind of way. "Are you a reporter? Background in investigation maybe?"

Teagan arched an eyebrow at her, looking impressed. "Something like that, yeah. He saved me after I was taken hostage."

"No," Autumn breathed, fascinated. How the hell had Gavin left *that* part out? Now she was even angrier at him.

"Yep. Dove off a boat into the freezing ocean to save me from drowning."

"Oh, my God." *Decker, you dark horse.* Who'd have thought it?

Teagan smiled at Carly when they stepped back out onto the sunlit sidewalk. "You guys up for a short hike? Guessing you haven't been up to the lighthouse yet. It's worth a look, and the weather is cooperating today. The view from up there is incredible when it's not fogged in."

Carly turned to her, excitement glowing in her eyes. "Can we, Mom?"

It was plain her daughter was angling for any excuse not to continue work on her project, but Autumn could use the break too and wanted to get more out of Teagan. "Yeah, sure."

"Great. Follow me." Teagan led them to her vehicle and drove them across to the north side of town to a public parking lot close to the ocean. The landscape was more rugged here, rising dramatically out of the sea and reaching up to towering cliffs. "The trail entrance is just through there," she said, pointing to a thick band of forest near the northern edge of the lot.

Carly forged ahead of them on the trail, eager to explore. Autumn hung back with Teagan as they sipped at their coffees, waiting until Carly was out of earshot. The towering evergreens shielded them from the full brunt of the wind coming off the water to their left, long swaying branches overhead casting moving shadows on the pathway. The air smelled earthy, spiced with the sharp scents of cedar and fir.

"So," Teagan said before Autumn could restart their conversation. "How long have you and Gavin had a thing for each other?"

Autumn snapped her head around to stare at her in shock. "What?" Had Marley said something to her because of yesterday?

Teagan arched a dark eyebrow. "Come on. You really gonna deny it?"

"No, what did you mean?"

"The vibe you were giving off at the party the other night."

Hell.

She faced forward again, a bit thrown by the sudden turn of the tables.

"Come on, you can tell me. What's up?"

She didn't see the harm. "He's been giving me weird signals since I got here."

"Weird how?"

"Like he wants more than friendship all of a sudden."

"Yeah?"

"Yes." Every time she saw him, she felt a bittersweet pang deep in her chest. And every time he came close, her brain shut down, and her body went all tingly.

She hadn't tingled like that in… She didn't know the last time she had, and knowing he'd been about to kiss her yesterday was almost more than she could take.

All the guilty fantasies she'd had about him over the years were back, tormenting her in vivid detail. Imagining what it would be like with him now that he was an experienced man instead of the boy she'd known. About what it would feel like to have him on top of her. To feel that heavy, powerful body holding her in place while he satisfied every sexual need that had gone unfulfilled for way too long.

But she needed more than sex, and only wanted it from him.

"What, like you're not into him too?" Teagan snorted. "Girl, I was at the party. I know what I saw."

"Please. I was barely around him." Did she sound defensive? Teagan didn't know her, had no right to make assumptions or judgements.

"Yeah, that's exactly what I mean. The tension coming off you was noticeable."

How was she supposed to answer that? And she just knew Teagan would know if she lied. "I just...don't understand what's happening with him."

"You two have a history together?"

Oh, yeah. One night that still triggered a bittersweet ache in her heart. Along with a massive amount of regret for letting him go. "We've been friends since we were kids."

"That's not what I meant."

Autumn huffed out a breath and shot her a hard look. "What is your background exactly? Psychology? Interrogation?"

Teagan laughed under her breath. "I mean, in a way. But really I'm just more observant than the average person." She shrugged. "I see things most others miss."

This was so damned awkward, having her private hell exposed by a near stranger. "Did you bring me up here to talk about all this?"

"Yep." Teagan didn't look or sound the least bit apologetic.

"Did Decker say something to you?" Had any of the others picked up on her tension? "Or Marley?"

"Are you kidding me? Do you even *know* him? And no, Marley never said a word."

She relaxed a little. "I know him well enough. Well, I thought I did, until you told me he dove into the ocean to save you." Maybe Gavin didn't know all the details. Decker wasn't exactly the sharing feelings type.

"Then you know that even the thought of talking about that kind of stuff gives him hives. Which is why I'm talking to you. I like you, I love Gav, you've known each other forever, and from what I can see, you're good for each other."

"We're just friends." And she hoped they could remain at least that once they were on the other side of all this.

"You don't want more?" Teagan asked.

What she wanted was impossible at this point. Ridiculous, stupidly romantic little girl fantasies that should have died when he'd left home. And, oh, my God, why was this virtual stranger asking her all these uncomfortably personal questions?

"It's complicated." And unfortunately things were only going to get *more* complicated.

There was a long pause, and she felt Teagan's penetrating stare on her every second of it. "I understand all about having dark secrets. And since we just met, I get you not wanting to tell me."

Despite feeling a bit defensive at the moment, she still wanted to know Teagan's story. Desperately. "Did you say anything to Marley?" she asked instead. If she needed to do damage control, she wanted to know.

"Nope. But if you ever need to talk, about Gav or anything else, and you don't want to tell Marley, there's something you should know about me."

Autumn met her gaze, bracing herself. "What's that?"

"I don't tell secrets."

Autumn stared at her a moment, the deadly serious tone throwing her for a second, then couldn't help but laugh. "You know what? I believe you." Which was crazy, since they barely knew each other.

"Good." Teagan grinned and her intense demeanor vanished. "And, oh, man, I really hope I get to introduce you to Ivy while you're here."

"Who's Ivy?"

"A living goddess, as far as I'm concerned. She's engaged to Walker, one of the Crimson Point Security managers," she added when Autumn frowned. "And if I'm a human vault, she's the living embodiment of Fort Knox.

Wouldn't give up anything unless she wanted to, even under torture."

Torture? Holy. And something told her Teagan wasn't exaggerating. "What's she do?"

Teagan's admiring smile was feral. "Whatever needs to be done, but mainly hacking. Anyway," she continued in a lighter tone. "I hope things work out for you guys. None of them talk about the past much, but I know they all had it rough growing up. In all honesty, Decker probably had it easiest, since he left home first. Gavin says you and your parents were the stabilizing force in his life."

"He said that?"

"Mmhmm, his safe haven when things got hard."

Her parents had always treated him like the son they'd never had, giving him life advice and helping him the rare times he'd allowed it. And he and Tristan had always been welcome in their home. "Actually, I think Tristan has always been his stabilizing force. Marley nurtured them both as best she could after their mom died, and Decker provided what he could for them all even after he left."

"Yeah, they all made the best of a shitty situation. But that's still how Gav feels about you."

Oh. Damn. "He never told me."

"No, he wouldn't. None of them would. Too proud."

Yes. "Gavin was just part of the family. And my best friend, until…"

"Until he left."

Until I slept with him and let him go. "Yes. Then everything changed."

"Not everything." Teagan's tone was loaded, and Autumn seriously didn't want to go there again. "But I won't say anything more."

Thank you, Lord. "We almost there?" How far away was this damned lighthouse?

"Yeah, just around this next bend."

They were nearing the end of the forest path now. As the trees thinned, the path curved to the left, opening up at the cliff's edge.

At last the Crimson Point lighthouse came into view perched on the edge of the cliff, painted in thick red and white horizontal stripes. Up ahead, Carly stepped out of the shadows into the late spring sunshine, the sudden increase in wind blowing her red-gold ponytail sideways.

Her daughter laughed and looked back at them over her shoulder, the sheer joy on her face making Autumn's heart squeeze.

Oh, sweetie. How are you going to handle what's coming? No matter what, Autumn would make sure her daughter knew down to the marrow of her bones that she would always be there for her.

Thankfully, Teagan didn't bring up anything else uncomfortable the rest of the hike, but Autumn had to grudgingly respect her honesty and willingness to become friends. In fact, she liked Teagan. A lot. After their hike, they ate fish and chips on the beach, laughing like lunatics. By the end of their afternoon together, Autumn was sorry to say goodbye.

"Thank you for today," she said, pulling Teagan into a quick hug in the parking lot. "I didn't love how the hike started, but I honestly didn't realize how much I needed this."

Teagan patted her on the back. "It was my pleasure. Have fun in Portland, and I hope to see you guys before you take off back home."

"For sure. Maybe you can introduce me to Ivy."

"I'll see what I can do."

Carly was in high spirits on the walk back to their building, chattering away about Teagan and the others they'd met so far in Crimson Point, and how she couldn't wait to tell all her friends about everything when she got to school.

Little did she know she'd have something a hell of a lot more interesting to tell them than that.

"Speaking of school, let's get another chunk of work done on your project before we call it a day," Autumn said.

"Ugh, okay," Carly said, her excitement dimming. "It's interesting and all, but I kinda just want to be done now."

"Believe me, babe, I know the feeling." She checked her phone, which she'd silenced before the hike. Three missed calls and two texts from Gavin.

We have to talk.

And an hour later, *Please just call me.*

The please bit made her feel a little bad. She hadn't intentionally ignored him today but obviously wasn't going to call him in front of her daughter.

Was out with Carly and Teagan, she texted instead. *Heading back to your place now to finish some work.*

Meaning, she didn't have time to talk.

After a few minutes Carly took her laptop to her room to work, and Autumn settled herself back at the kitchen island with hers. She'd no sooner opened her presentation to go through it one last time when her phone rang. Gavin's number appeared on the display.

Drawing a deep breath, she decided to answer. "Hi."

"Okay, so at least you're not stonewalling me. Thanks for that," he said, the deep timbre of his voice making her insides flutter.

She didn't bother responding to the jab. She hated being at odds with him. "I'm just in the middle of prepping for the conference right now."

"I need to see you tonight so we can talk this out. Alone. No more excuses, Autumn."

Nerves fluttered in the pit of her stomach. She intended to hold him off until after the conference. "We can schedule a call for later."

"Nope. We're doing this face to face, tonight."

Her spine stiffened at his imperious tone. "I don't think—"

"Either you meet me somewhere private, or I'm coming over there. Your choice."

Wasn't much of a choice, but his tone made it clear he was serious. "Fine, you can come over here." It was his place. At least that way Carly could act as an oblivious buffer and give Autumn a good reason not to tell him yet.

"I'm in meetings until late. What time does Carly go to bed?"

"Nine-ish."

"I'll be there at nine-thirty." He ended the call before she could get another word out.

Autumn lowered her phone to the counter and ran a hand over her face, a gut-deep certainty taking hold that within the next few hours the trajectory of her entire life would change forever.

NINE

Keys in hand, Gavin paused a moment at the front door to his condo to gather himself. He was too amped up about finally clearing the air with Autumn. Work meetings had taken up his entire day, giving him only a few minutes to check his phone for messages, but she'd been on his mind constantly.

He wanted this situation between them resolved before he left for the security detail in the morning. Needed it behind them so he could focus and give his full attention to his job.

When he felt calmer, he twisted the lock and stepped inside. The scent of something toasty hit him.

He walked to the kitchen entry, his insides tightening when he saw Autumn sitting at the far end of the island with her laptop open, a half-finished pizza sitting on a baking sheet and a glass of wine in her hand. She glanced up with a taut smile, her sandy-blond hair loose around her shoulders.

"Hey," she said softly without getting up, when before this trip she would always have greeted him with a hug.

"Hi." He paused there in the entry a moment in uncertainty, glancing down the hall. Tris's bedroom door was shut, and he didn't see any light coming from under it. "Carly asleep?"

"In bed at least." She took a sip of wine and set her glass down, turning her body to face him more. And it was an insanely hot body. "How was work?"

"Busy." He crossed the kitchen, took a seat on one of the high stools along the wide side of the island. But he wasn't here to make small talk. "So, we need to clear the air here."

She squared her shoulders and lifted her chin, almost as if she was preparing to commence battle. "Yeah, we do. What's going on with you?"

He ignored her question for now, focused on what he was up against. "This guy you're seeing. Is it serious?"

She blinked, taken off guard. Good, because he didn't want rehearsed answers. But she hesitated a fraction too long before answering. "No."

An overwhelming wave of relief hit him. "How long have you been dating?"

"Not long." She crossed her arms over her breasts, looking him dead in the eye. "Now you answer. What's with you?"

He expelled a breath, relief still flooding his bloodstream. "Why are you acting like you're uncomfortable around me?" he countered.

She huffed out a humorless laugh, looked away, and ran a hand through her hair. "Seriously, Gavin? The way you've been acting since I got here isn't exactly making me more comfortable."

His patience was running thin. "Autumn. What's really bothering you? You said something had happened."

Her green gaze swung to him. Guarded. And it was like a punch to the gut. Since when did she not trust him? "I'll tell you after the conference."

A knot of worry formed in his chest. "Just tell me now."

"No. And as to the other part, what was with you yesterday?"

He lifted a shoulder, not about to apologize for what he felt. "I decided I'm done waiting."

"Waiting for what?"

"You."

She went dead still, her eyes widening. "Gav. What…"

"Do you have feelings for me?"

She blinked again, looking blindsided. Maybe even a little panicked, bright spots of color forming on her cheeks. "You know I love you. We've been friends for—"

"That's not what I meant, and you know it." He held her stare, refused to let her wriggle away from this. Away from *him*. Or their history. "That night we spent together. Did it mean anything to you?"

Her cheeks flushed darker. "Of course, it did. Why would you even ask that?"

"Why did you do it?"

To her credit, she didn't brush it away. Didn't get up and move away from him. "Because you were leaving."

"That's the only reason?"

"No." She paused a moment. "I wanted you to be my first."

Something like triumph surged through him, fast and hot like an electrical current. "Why?"

Now she did look away. "Because I was in love with you and wanted to keep that memory while you were gone," she admitted softly.

He thought his heart would implode. *Was* in love with him. "Why didn't you say anything?" Her admission gutted him. She'd been in love with him, had never said a damned word, and he'd left her behind thinking that night hadn't meant as much to her as it had him.

"Would it have mattered?" she countered, and the resignation in her face and tone hit him hard. "Would you have stayed if you'd known?"

No. "I couldn't. I'd signed a contract."

"Right. You were leaving no matter what," she continued. "And that's why I never told you. Well, that and because I knew you didn't feel the same way."

He resisted the urge to rub the back of his neck. Because she had him there. His feelings for her had been confusing as hell. Crushing on her, then back to just friends because he was sure he'd never have a shot with someone like her, rinse and repeat. "Maybe not back then."

Her gaze flew to his. Held at the unspoken implication hanging between them.

"But only because I was too young and stupid to realize it. And back then, I didn't think I would ever have a chance with you."

"What's that supposed to mean?"

"Our backgrounds. Your family was always stable. Mine wasn't. You guys had money. We didn't. You always had it all together, always knew what you wanted, and went for it. I didn't until I joined the Corps."

She stared at him. "Are you saying you didn't think you were good enough for me?" Her voice rose an octave.

He shrugged, that old defensiveness rising up. "I know I wasn't."

She shook her head. "That's such bullshit, but now this sudden shift from you makes even less sense. We barely saw each other while you were in the Corps, we—"

"I'm out now." He couldn't change the past. He could only move forward, and he wanted it to be with her.

Apart from his siblings, she had been the bedrock of his life. The one person he could always count on no matter what. He'd wanted her for years before that night and never allowed himself to act on it, had told himself that it must not have meant anything to her if she didn't want to even acknowledge it and had moved on so fast and easily with someone else right after he'd left.

"I don't understand any of this. You shipped out the morning after we slept together and never looked back."

Oh, *hell* no. She did not get to accuse him of that shit. "I called and wrote you letters. *You're* the one who never wanted to talk about it," he said angrily.

"Keep your voice down." She darted a worried glance behind him toward the hall.

With effort he reined in his temper, but the frustration was killing him. Bubbling away under the surface like acid under his skin. "I tried bringing it up multiple times, and you shut me down on all of them. And how was I supposed to know how you really felt when I heard you moved on to someone else right after I left?"

Her flushed face went pale, her mouth pinching. "You were gone and weren't coming back except when you got leave. So what did it matter?"

Because it fucking crushed me. He held it back, but only because he didn't feel like looking like a pathetic idiot. And she still hadn't told him what the problem was at the root of all this. "And what about now?"

To his horror, she sucked in a shaky breath and started blinking fast.

Shit. He reached toward her. "Hey, don't—"

"No. *You* don't," she accused, shooting to her feet and pulling away before he could touch her, glaring at him with tear-glazed eyes. "You don't get to come back years later and disrupt the life I built, then move clear across the country and suddenly change our entire relationship when it suits you."

He sat there in silence, absorbing her anger. He deserved it. And she deserved to have her say.

"I was right there, Gavin," she said, shaking her head in frustration. "Right there the whole time for the past twelve years, raising Carly on my own, and all of a sudden out of the blue now you decide you want me?" She shook her head, threw up her hands. "No. I've got a long day ahead of me. I'm going to bed." She started past him.

He was up and off the stool before she took another step, catching her by the arm and spinning her around to face him. Shock flashed in her eyes as he trapped her against the wall beside the refrigerator, his hands in her hair and the length of his body pinning her in place.

She stared up at him in stunned, breathless silence. The feel of her, all soft and curvy, had his blood pumping hot and fast, making him insane.

"You wanna know what's changed?" he said, heart hammering, muscles locked up with the primal need she ignited in him. He was sick to death of her shutting him out and fucking done with dancing around this. "When I came home and saw you last time, I finally realized what I've intuitively known all along."

"W-what?" she whispered, searching his eyes.

"That you're mine," he bit out, the need ratcheting higher, pushing him to the edge of his control. "That you've always been mine." She was right here with him finally, her sweet body cushioning his, pupils dilating in a way that couldn't lie. Whether or not she was ready to admit it, she wanted him.

That was all he needed to know for now. The final thread of restraint snapped, and he lowered his head to capture her mouth with his.

TEN

Autumn sucked in a breath and dug her fingers into his muscled shoulders, a thousand emotions colliding inside her as the initial burst of shock cleared. Was this real? Gavin kissing her, his hands in her hair, and his long, powerful body pressed to hers the way she'd fantasized about so many times.

And it wasn't a gentle, coaxing kiss. Nothing like the ones they'd shared that night so long ago. It wasn't a seduction or an apology.

It was a claiming, the raw hunger emanating from him leaving her stunned.

He broke the kiss to nip at her lower lip, flicked his tongue across it, and shifted his mouth before she could deepen the contact. "I wish I could go back in time," he murmured against the edge of her lips, his deep voice barely registering over the pounding of her heart in her ears. "Go back to that night and do it all differently."

Her head spun, her body on fire.

He sucked on her lower lip, slid his tongue inside to touch hers, then retreated, flooding her with molten heat. "I've thought about that night so many times. Wish I could have been what you deserved back then."

She shook her head to deny the self-loathing she heard buried in his tone. "No, don't say that."

He lifted his head just enough to stare down into her eyes, both of them breathing faster, their lips inches apart. He was so hot and hard all over.

She couldn't think clearly. Could barely breathe with the way he was looking at her, like he wanted to make a meal out of her. And she would let him.

"I've owed you for a long damned time, sweet thing. But I'm going to more than make it up to you now."

A hundred different erotic visions filled her mind. Him naked, all those mouthwatering muscles on full display for her, exposed to her gaze, her touch. Him holding her just like this but on a flat surface, his weight pressing her down into a bed. His strong hands commanding her one moment, then seducing her the next while his mouth took care of her every need and soothed the empty ache he'd left in her life when he'd shipped out.

"Say you want me, Autumn," he rasped against the edge of her mouth, the rock hard length of his erection pressed between her spread legs.

She whimpered in frustration and pulled his mouth back to hers, coming up on her toes to wrap one knee around the back of his thigh and pull him even closer. He made a deep, guttural sound that shot a thrill through her and rocked his erection against her core, hitting the spot that throbbed the worst.

Oh, God... She was dizzy. Couldn't catch her breath, her body transformed into a stripped electrical wire. She wanted him and what he was offering. Needed it so bad she—

The front door lock clicking open broke them apart. She

immediately ripped away from him, wiped her mouth with her hand and yanked down the hem of her shirt just as the front door opened out of view.

"Anybody home?"

Tristan. Shit.

Her gaze flew to Gavin, who stared at her with a clenched jaw, his cheeks flushed and his eyes still smoldering with unbridled heat.

"In here," she answered in a bright voice that sounded horribly fake, the terrifying hunger that had engulfed her moments ago suddenly extinguished.

Tristan appeared in the entrance to the kitchen, his easy smile fading when he saw them. He stopped short, eyeing them. "Hey." He looked at Gavin. "I texted to ask you to pick up a shirt for me, but you never answered, so I came to get it myself."

"Autumn and I were just talking about something," he said.

"Ah." Tristan's gaze moved back and forth between them, and Autumn wanted to close her eyes and groan. He had to know they'd been doing more than talking.

"Mom? Is Gavvy or Trissy here?" Carly called out from down the hall.

Wonderful. "Yeah, Gavin just came by to grab something," she called back, hoping her daughter wouldn't be able to tell what had happened.

A door opened down the hall. Then footsteps.

"Trissy! Gavvy!"

The tension in Gavin's face melted into a big, warm smile. "Hey, squirt." He opened his arms in welcome, and Carly rushed straight for him.

A hot rush of tears made Autumn spin away and head for the fridge, blinking fast. She couldn't handle watching them.

Couldn't bear to think how devastated Carly would be if things went badly after she told him.

She reached into the fridge and grabbed for the first bottle she found. A beer. Fine.

"I'll just…grab my shirt," Tristan said somewhere behind her. There was no way he wasn't picking up on the tension in the room. Zero chance he'd missed her tousled hair and the flush on her cheeks.

Without turning around she twisted off the top and chugged half of it, grimacing at the bitter burn. She hated beer. But it was either this or cry in front of everyone. Pausing only long enough to suck in a breath, she downed the rest of it.

"Wow. Thirsty, Mom?" Sarcasm dripped from Carly's words.

She put on a smile and looked over her shoulder at her daughter, her heart and body crying out for the man who stood beside her. The man she shared fifty-percent of her DNA with and had no idea. "Not anymore. But you should go back to bed."

"I'm not tired. And I'm just about finished my report. Can you read it and tell me if anything needs to be fixed?"

Her gaze strayed to Gavin. Locked with his and held, her pulse tripping and that hot throb reigniting between her thighs. Just his presence seemed to take up all the air in the room.

"I should go," he said when Tristan reappeared with a shirt draped over a forearm.

A flash of disappointment hit, immediately followed by a rush of relief. What had she thought, that Gavin would take her to his bed and fuck her into mindless oblivion while Carly was just across the hall?

She nodded and folded her arms, aware of how defensive

and stiff her posture was but unable to do a damned thing about it. "You heading out first thing?" she asked them both.

"On the road at oh-four-hundred," Gavin answered.

More disappointment. Which was ridiculous. Tristan's arrival had literally just averted disaster because she didn't think she would have stopped this on her own. "Drive safe. I hope the weekend is uneventful."

"Me too." Gavin smiled down at Carly, kissed the top of her head. "Be good for your mom, and good luck with the report."

"I'm always good," Carly protested, leaning into him.

Then he looked over at Autumn, and the intensity in his eyes made her stomach flip. "I'll see you Monday night, if not before." It wasn't a suggestion. "But think about what I said."

Between that and the forthcoming conversation she was dreading, it was going to be pretty much impossible to think of anything *but* him all weekend. "Good night."

"Good night. Sleep tight." The look in his eyes before he turned away made it clear he would have given anything to be staying the night in bed with her, and that neither of them would be doing much sleeping.

When the front door locked behind them she set the empty bottle on the counter and dropped her head back, praying for strength. Unbelievable as it seemed, things were so much worse than they had been an hour ago.

Gavin claimed to want her, but that might change once he learned the truth. She'd dodged a bullet when Tristan had interrupted them.

And she was very much afraid she wouldn't be able to dodge the next one when it came.

ELEVEN

Dan shuffled along in the breakfast line at the shelter, filled with a sense of excitement and anticipation he hadn't felt in forever. He hadn't been able to get a bed anywhere last night, so he'd slept in one of his preferred alternate spots under some trees behind a pawn shop a few blocks away.

Sleeping on the streets came with its own risks, and he was used to people treating him like shit stuck to the bottom of their shoe. Since becoming homeless, he'd been verbally and physically assaulted, robbed, and even pissed on by people because they thought he was that far beneath them.

Nobody gave a shit what happened to him, about how he'd wound up here or that he'd proudly served his country in two war zones. He'd been such a naïve fucking idiot back then.

Today, all that changed. He would send a message and take a stand against those who had put him here. People were fed up with the global establishment and ready to fight back.

He spotted TJ sitting at the end of a table across the room, hunched over his plate, and headed over. The guy was hard to figure out. Kept to himself, a real loner, but a fellow vet and one of the best guys Dan had met on the streets. He never had to worry about being attacked or harassed when TJ was around.

"Mornin'," he said, taking the chair beside him.

"Morning," TJ answered without looking up.

"You stay here last night?"

TJ shook his head as he chewed a bite of pancake.

"Me neither." He wolfed down half his scrambled eggs and potatoes, the ravenous void in his stomach easing. "You got another shift at the site today?"

TJ nodded.

Dude had a decent work ethic, he'd give him that. "Just so you know, you can make one-and-a-half times that with us over the weekend." He stabbed a bite of sausage, shoved it into his mouth. "Can't believe I'm getting paid for it. I'd fuck their shit up for free."

TJ didn't answer, just kept his head down and kept eating. Annoyed, Dan lowered his fork and gave him a hard stare. "I don't understand why you don't care. Aren't you pissed off? Doesn't it bother you that those hypocrite bastards are living the high life—on our backs—with their mansions and private jets, and now they're in our city to call the shots that wind up with more of us on the street? And that they don't give a shit so long as they get richer?"

Nothing.

"Look at this." He gestured around him at the shelter dining hall. Every table was full, and the lineup for food was out the door. It was like that every day. "It's not fucking right, and they never listen because they think anyone who's not a billionaire doesn't matter. It's up to us to teach them a lesson."

TJ's only reaction was to glance up at him for a second, then keep eating.

Dan shook his head. "Man, you piss me off sometimes." He plowed through the rest of his breakfast in silence while TJ finished his own meal and drank the last of his coffee. It was weird. They didn't seem to agree on some things, yet Dan couldn't help but admire him. TJ exuded a quiet, unshakable confidence Dan recognized as a leadership quality and wouldn't be surprised if TJ had been an officer.

That only made it all the fucking worse that he was on the streets now. People who served their country honorably should be taken care of when they came back home. Period.

TJ stood and picked up his empty plate. "See you."

"Yeah, but think about it, okay? Message me if you change your mind." Though he was pretty sure TJ wouldn't. "Hey," he added when TJ started to walk away.

TJ stopped, looked back at him.

If he wasn't going to be personally involved, Dan felt he should at least warn him about what was going to happen. "Watch yourself out there. Especially around sixteen-hundred-hours."

TJ stared at him a long moment, then gave him a nod and walked away. And even though Dan didn't understand him, he couldn't help but envy him a little. Despite everything TJ had gone through and the fucked-up hand life had dealt him, it still seemed like he had his shit together compared to the rest of them.

RYDER'S VOICE came through Gavin's earpiece as the vehicle he was riding in approached the downtown core. "Echo Two, what's your status?"

Seated in the front passenger seat of the SUV, Gavin took in the scene on the street as they approached the conference center and tapped his earpiece to respond. "Two minutes out. Route secure."

The mood was grim, a growing sense of hostility that continued to build as they got closer to their destination. A thin stream of protesters already lined the sidewalks up ahead near the south side of the conference center, but so far the heightened police presence on the streets seemed to be keeping everything under control.

Using the feeds their IT department had secured for them, he pulled up the center's security camera feeds on his phone and checked in with his brother, who was already there. "What's the situation out front?"

"Crowd's still growing, but so far the protest's peaceful and contained within the security barriers."

The feeds confirmed the same. "Copy that."

The city had doubled the police presence in anticipation of the protests to make a statement and to stave off violence as the weekend wore on. Having experienced combat, Gavin knew how quickly a situation like this could turn ugly, and no one on their team was taking any chances. This job was a big deal, and Crimson Point Security's reputation was on the line.

Behind the wheel, Cassie, another new agent, spoke. "We good?"

"All good." In the backseat, their Canadian diplomat VIP was in the midst of an intense conversation with his assistant and whoever they had on conference call. Gavin turned in his seat to look at him. "Sir, we're two minutes from the hotel."

The man nodded and continued speaking into his phone, not really paying attention. But that was fine. As his personal bodyguard for the weekend, it was Gavin's job to worry about and stay on top of all security concerns.

Up ahead, a cluster of protesters waving signs behind the security barricades containing the crowd saw the vehicle with its tinted windows approaching and surged forward slightly, hemmed in by the barriers. Gavin spotted a brick in someone's upraised hand.

"Incoming." A second later it slammed into the rear window and bounced off the bullet-resistant glass. The passengers in the back jumped and got quiet all of a sudden. Gavin kept his eyes on the crowd, watching for any sign of a serious weapon.

Unfazed, Cassie maintained their speed, slowing only at the last moment before making the turn into the hotel parking lot where police armed with rifles were stationed on either side of the entrance. A rock smacked into the back quarter panel a moment before they reached the entrance ramp to the underground parking garage.

Inside it, more police were stationed at regular intervals on each level, guarding the entrances to the stairwells and elevators. Others patrolled with bomb-sniffing dogs. All the VIPs were staying here. That made logistics easier, but also made the entire hotel a target as well as the conference center.

Cassie pulled up close to the elevator bank where Donovan, another Crimson Point Security agent, was waiting for them. The instant the vehicle stopped, Gavin stepped out and opened the right rear passenger door, scanning for threats while he escorted his charges into the open elevator.

"All clear," Donovan said to him and got in the elevator with them.

The ride up to their destination floor was quiet. They escorted the men to their suites, sweeping each to ensure they were safe before letting them in.

"All this for some meetings," the older Canadian said with a rueful smile. "We live in crazy times."

Gavin kept his opinions about that to himself. Whatever views he held about this summit or the people involved didn't matter. This was his first big gig since joining the firm. Personal feelings aside, he had been tasked with protecting this man for the weekend, with his life if necessary. That was the job.

"Unless you make changes to your itinerary, I'll be back to escort you downstairs at oh-seven-hundred," he said, all business. "Message or call if you need me before then."

The man nodded. "Good night."

"Good night, sir."

Out in the hall, he met up with Donovan. "You done for now?"

"Heading over to meet Callum and Ryder at the conference center. We'll send updates as we get them."

"Copy that. See you later." While technically still on the clock, his official duties had been fulfilled for the time being, so Gavin went to his own room one floor down. The shower was running when he walked in, and Tristan's stuff was already on the bed nearest the door.

Gavin toed off his shoes, removed his weapon and holster, and set them on the desk, then sighed in relief when he took off the sweltering combo of jacket and Kevlar vest and tossed them aside on a chair. It was surprisingly hot and muggy for the Pacific Northwest, the forecast calling for above normal summer temperatures throughout the weekend. Unfortunate, since bad weather would have been a natural deterrent and crowd control.

Crossing to the large window that overlooked the conference center plaza and most of the downtown core, he checked his personal phone for messages. Nada. Autumn hadn't responded to his text he'd sent first thing on the way to Portland.

Miss you, he'd told her.

She was busy at her own conference, he knew that. But he also knew she was using it as an excuse not to respond, and it drove him nuts.

Not knowing where they stood or what was going on with her had him on edge. And there was also that bit about her seeing someone from work. That was even worse. Although after last night he felt a lot better about it. If Autumn really was into the guy, she would never have kissed Gavin like that.

Resisting the urge to send another message, he shoved his phone back into his pocket and pulled aside the filmy white curtain to take in the full view. Portland was a scenic city, but right now protesters lined the streets in every direction, the crowds thickest in front of the main entrance of the conference center. Media trucks and their crews were scattered here and there, filming and reporting on the latest as more VIPs began arriving on site.

His gaze moved beyond all that, to the pale gray roof of Autumn's hotel several blocks away. It made him restless as hell that she was so close and he couldn't see her. Part of him wanted to show up there and wait for her to have a free minute, just so he could see her, but he was on duty until this summit was over and had to stay close to his VIP.

The bathroom door opened and Tristan walked out in a cloud of steam, toweling off his wet hair. "Hey. Arrival was uneventful?"

"Couple of dents in the SUV, but nothing major." He nodded at the growing crowd below in the plaza. "What's the expected number now?"

"Forecasts are for double this by morning. Maybe triple or higher by the afternoon. Walker and Callum said there's been some new intel about a big anarchist group recruiting from around the northwest. They're apparently busing people in now."

"Oh, awesome," he muttered, and looked back out the window. Mentally calculated what that size crowd would look like and how far it would spread around the hotel and conference center.

Unease trickled down his spine. That number of people could put Autumn's hotel in play if things got ugly. And Carly was there with her. "Triple or higher, huh?"

"Yeah." Tris pulled jeans and a T-shirt from his bag and tugged them on. "Maybe we should have Marley and Warwick come pick up Carly and take her back to Crimson Point," he said, saying what Gavin was already thinking. It was a twin thing, happened a lot with them.

"I'll message Autumn." Stating their concerns in a text would scare her, so he sent her a quick text asking her to call when she got a minute, adding that it was important. If she didn't answer him soon, he'd get Tris to try instead.

Tristan tugged his shirt over his head, then yanked back the covers on his bed and sat on the edge of it, watching him.

"What?" Gavin finally said.

"What's going on with you guys?"

"What do you mean?"

Tristan gave him an irritated look. "Please. I'm your fucking twin."

"I'm aware."

"So cut the bullshit. We both know I interrupted something when I walked in last night, and you've both been off since she got here. I stayed out of it, didn't say anything, but now I wanna know. What's going on?"

His immediate reaction was to deny it, but that was pointless. Tristan was literally his other half, knew him better than anyone, except maybe Autumn. But he wasn't ready to spill what had happened between him and Autumn on prom night. "The truth?"

"That'd be appreciated, yeah."

He lifted a shoulder. Said the only thing he could. "I love her."

Tristan started to laugh as though he thought that was hilarious, then sobered when he saw Gavin wasn't joking and shut his mouth, staring at him. "What?" he finally asked in confusion. "Like, *love* love?"

Gavin sighed. "What else you want me to say?"

A spark of annoyance lit his twin's eyes. "How about why the fuck I'm only finding out about this now?"

"I didn't realize it until recently."

"Since when?"

"Since we saw her back home last time."

Tristan shook his head, staring at him like he'd lost his mind. Or maybe more like he was disappointed. "Bro, what the hell are you *thinking*?"

Gavin blinked at his twin's heated tone. "About what?"

"You suddenly decided you're in love with her after all these years?" Tristan shook his head, his expression full of concern. "Have you even thought about the risks? Like what happens if you cross the line and then it doesn't work out after? You've been friends your entire lives. Are you seriously going to risk fucking that up forever?"

"Okay, calm down for Christ's—"

"I am calm. Of the two of us, I'm *always* fucking calm. And did you ever stop to consider it's not just you who stands to come out on the losing end if things go south between you? The rest of us love her too. And she's a single mom. Have you thought about Carly? About what it would do to her if you guys hooked up and then it ended?"

"I don't wanna fucking *hook up* with her," he snapped, his

temper surging. Tristan's reaction pissed him off—and fucking hurt, if he was being brutally honest. Everyone, even his own damned twin, still thought he was too emotionally immature to make a real relationship work.

What did it say about him that his own twin couldn't see how much he'd changed? Grown as a person. Matured. Fuck.

"You better not," Tris warned, and while Gavin got and appreciated his twin's protectiveness towards her, it still cut deep. Did Tris seriously think he would ever do something to hurt Autumn? He would fucking die for her.

"I said I love her, dipshit. You think I'm just looking to bang the woman who's meant more to me my entire life than anyone besides you, Marley, and Deck? I'm sick to death of everyone underestimating me." He wanted finally to be taken seriously. By Autumn, by Tris, his other siblings, and everyone else for that fucking matter.

"Have you told her all that?" Tris asked quietly.

"More or less."

"So, no."

"She knows." Deep down, she had to. Just like she had to know he would never risk their relationship unless he was deadly serious about her.

Even still, the thought of saying those three little words to her out loud lit up a deep, raw wound inside him that he didn't even want to acknowledge. But the vulnerability was there regardless, squirming around in his gut with cold fingers.

Being rejected by Autumn after holding out his heart to her would level him in a way he would never recover from. That's how much she meant to him.

Tristan watched him for a long moment, weighing everything he'd said, and all the annoyance faded from his eyes. "Does she love you back?" he finally asked.

Fuck. "I don't know." He was pretty sure she had feelings for him beyond friendship, and last night had proven that she wanted him. But that wasn't the same thing as being in love with him, was it? And her wanting him wasn't enough for him anyway.

So far, being in love pretty much sucked. He'd always heard how much it could hurt. This constant ache under his sternum was proof it was true. The uncertainty between him and Autumn was eating him alive.

"So what are you going to do?" Tris asked.

"Whatever I have to do to convince her to give us a shot." It was the only choice he had, same as he'd had to fight for everything else in his life anyway. Although nothing had ever mattered to him the way Autumn did.

Tristan nodded slowly, still watching him intently. But there was clear respect in his eyes now. "So you're all in?"

"Yes." He was willing to do whatever it took to make her his, including offering her his heart on a platter no matter how much it scared the shit out of him.

He couldn't force her to let him in. Couldn't make her take the leap he was asking her to. He needed her to do this willingly and because she loved him back. Nothing less would do.

"Good. Otherwise I'd be forced to break every bone in your face, and that'd be a damned shame since it's so good-looking." He patted his own cheek, eyes glinting with humor.

Gavin huffed out a reluctant laugh, the tension in his shoulders easing. It was a relief that Tris knew his intentions and backed him. He wanted his twin's blessing and support. Marley would approve once she knew how serious he was. And Deck...would come around in his own time like always.

No matter what, no matter what shit life threw at them, the four of them always had each other's backs. But if they didn't approve about him and Autumn, then he'd deal with it. It was his life, his heart he was risking.

"Not a word to the others about this, yeah?"

Tristan gave an insulted snort. "Seriously?"

He shrugged. "Since we're both being brutally honest with each other today, I just thought I'd make that clear."

"Yeah, okay." Tris grabbed his phone from the nightstand and stretched out on his back. "Wanna order room service? Company tab."

The last bit of tension eased from his shoulders. He and Tris were all good again. Now he needed to fix things with Autumn. "Yeah, I'm starving."

After placing the order he went back to the window, zeroing in on Autumn's hotel in the distance. She was so close yet so far away and not just physically. Nothing had been resolved between them, and the worst part was, he didn't know what it was going to take to convince her to give them a chance.

TWELVE

Capacity inside the large conference room was at standing room only by the end of the final session of the first day. Up at the front, Autumn's boss finished up his remarks and received a warm round of applause from the attendees. As everyone stood and began filing out the back of the room, he waved her over.

"I'll be honest, I haven't had time to look at the financials in your presentation," he said by way of apology.

Ugh. She'd sent them over a week ago and nudged him twice in the past few days because she needed his opinion before she presented.

"That's fine," she said, putting on a smile. "Will you be able to look at it tonight? I still have time to make changes if necessary." Not how she wanted to spend her night, but it was what it was.

He grimaced. "Can't promise anything. I've got a dinner engagement and then a meeting with some clients for drinks afterward. But I'll try." He gave her upper arm a friendly pat. "I'm not at all concerned. You're always on top of everything, and I'm sure what you have is perfect."

"I would really prefer not to present it without you checking it over first."

He blinked, as if he was surprised that she'd pushed back. "Oh. Well, yeah. All right, can you email it to me again? I'll look at it on my phone before dinner."

So he didn't have it saved? Or he had it on his laptop and didn't want to have to go get it? "Sure."

"Great. Have a good night."

"You too." She withheld a sigh as he walked away and got busy sending him the presentation again.

She liked Ross. He was fair and treated his people well, and a lot of CEOs weren't that way. The handful of times she'd met him in person over the past three years rather than over video or conference call hadn't changed that opinion. But asking her to present the pitch she and her team had been working on for the past seven months to their biggest client tomorrow without looking over everything made her angry.

It was she who risked looking like an idiot up there if something wasn't right, and while she supposed she should be grateful that he trusted her and had total faith in her ability, he needed to deliver on his promises and protect the reputation of the firm too.

"Uh-oh, what's that frown mean?"

It means I'm stressed, she thought with a mental sigh.

She glanced over at Jonas as he approached up an aisle then went back to finishing her email with a mental groan. The last thing she wanted was to have to fend him off again right now while her mental energy was running low. "Just some last-minute hiccups that need ironing out."

"What kind of hiccups?"

Work, social, *and* personal. But who was counting? Good times. "It's fine. All under control." He wasn't going away, so she slid her phone into the pocket of her suit jacket and faced him with a polite smile. "Conference going well for you?"

"Great."

He wasn't a bad-looking guy. Five-ten, brown hair, brown eyes, glasses. Nice enough, had always been kind to her.

But there were no butterflies when he looked at her. No hint of attraction. Only a mild annoyance that he kept trying. That was partly her fault though, as she hadn't come straight out and said it was pointless to spare him hurt feelings or embarrassment.

"The restaurants in the area are all booked up or closed due to the protests, but I managed to get a reservation at the steakhouse here at eight. Would you like to join me?"

She had to give him a few grudging points for perseverance. "I've got my daughter here with me."

"I can change the reservation to three people. Does she like steak?"

He really was trying hard. Including Carly would feel ultra creepy with a lot of guys, but she didn't get that vibe from him. "That's so sweet of you, but I promised her a quiet girl's night with room service and a movie."

"Ah." He did a decent job of masking his disappointment. "Another time then."

It was the perfect opportunity to shut him down completely, but they were coworkers, and she didn't need any awkwardness or hard feelings in the middle of the conference on top of everything else she was wrestling with. "Okay, well, I'd better get upstairs and finish my work so I can get to spending quality girl time with her."

"Okay. Want me to save you guys a seat at breakfast? The dining room filled up really fast this morning."

"That's all right, we'll just grab something when we're ready in the morning. Have a good night."

This time he wasn't as good at covering his disappointment. "You too."

The elevator banks were crammed. She took the stairs instead and heard the TV on when she walked into their suite.

She found Carly stretched out on her stomach on the bed watching TV with her laptop open beside her. "What are you watching?"

"The news." Her gaze stayed glued to the screen, where a reporter was covering the growing number of protesters gathering in the city center. *Local officials bracing for possible violence*, the headline read. "Is that really happening close to here?"

"Sweetheart." Autumn picked up the remote and switched the channel. A cooking show came on, and she waited for Carly to look at her. "The protests are blocks away from here, and the city has taken precautions. They have a lot of extra police here to help keep everyone safe."

"But Gavvy and Trissy are right there." Worry colored her voice.

She crossed the room, sat down on the bed beside Carly and stroked a hand over the crown of her head. Her situation with Gavin was unbelievably complicated, but she and Carly both loved them. "They're okay, baby. Their hotel and the conference center have police and other special security all around the building, plus their own team, who all have special training. And don't forget, Gavvy and Trissy were both Marines." Marley and Decker too.

"Still *are* Marines," Carly corrected her. "Once a Marine, always a Marine."

Autumn grinned at the protective note in her tone. "Yes, exactly. So they know how to look out for themselves, and the building they're in is very safe." The protests made her uneasy, but she didn't want to show that and make Carly even more anxious.

Carly seemed slightly mollified. "Okay. Will we get to see them this weekend do you think?"

"They're going to be really busy working, so I doubt it. But we'll see them before we go to the airport, promise."

Autumn kissed the top of her head. "Now, what do you feel like ordering for dinner?"

Forty minutes later, they were propped up against Carly's headboard, wearing matching terrycloth hotel bathrobes and slippers, watching a comedy movie while eating their room service dinner.

"This is the best vacation *ever*," Carly declared in between bites of her double hot fudge sundae.

Autumn laughed and took a spoonful of her own. To hell with the calories, she deserved this. "It doesn't suck, that's for sure."

Near the end of the movie Carly started to visibly fade, cracking several eye-watering yawns. Autumn gathered up the dishes and organized them on the delivery cart. "Bedtime for you, young lady. Go brush your teeth."

Carly grumbled but dutifully slid out of bed and went to do as she was told, evidence enough of how exhausted she was. Autumn turned off the lights, tucked her in and kissed her on the forehead. "Sleep tight. See you in the morning."

She closed the door to Carly's room and returned to her own where her laptop was waiting on her king-size bed. If her boss still hadn't looked at the numbers, she could at least go over everything one last time before crashing herself.

Sighing, she sat cross-legged with her computer in her lap and grabbed her phone where she'd left it charging on the nightstand. There was a message from her boss detailing one minor change. Along with three messages from Gavin.

Call me when you get a minute. It's important, the first one said.

He'd left it hours ago, right after she'd come upstairs from the final session. The most recent one had come in while she'd been watching the movie.

Part of her was dreading his response in case it had something to do with them, but she texted him back anyway. That kiss had changed things. A line had been crossed, and she had narrowly avoided obliterating it entirely.

Sorry. Was having girls' night with Carly. What's up? She hit send.

The message had barely been delivered when someone knocked on the door. She got up and pushed the room service trolley over to it, but when she checked the peephole, her pulse jumped.

She unlocked the door and pulled it open, staring up at Gavin in a dress shirt and slacks, the breadth of his shoulders and chest straining the crisp, white fabric.

"Hi," she said in surprise while her nervous system went haywire. "What're you doing here—"

"I can't stay long." He edged past her into the room. "You didn't answer my texts, so I came to talk in person." He glanced at the closed door between the bedrooms. "Carly asleep?"

"Yes." She closed the door and stayed beside it, afraid to get closer to him. Not trusting herself and feeling weird about being alone in the room with him wearing nothing but a robe. "Is something wrong?"

"Yeah." He turned to face her, and his serious expression made her heartrate kick up a notch. "I missed you."

Before she could get out another word, he gathered her up in his arms and pulled her against him. A deep groan rumbled in his chest as he held her close and rocked her slightly, his nose buried in her hair.

Every one of her senses sharpened acutely. She was hyperaware of the size and power of him, the clean, woodsy smell of his cologne that made her want to bury her nose in his neck and breathe him in. The feel of all those hard muscles surrounding her. Turning her on and making her feel so unbelievably safe at the same time.

This was a totally new side of Gavin, the one she'd secretly dreamed about for so many years, his intense, masculine energy and protectiveness focused completely on her. She'd wanted to keep an emotional and physical distance from him, but the hug undid her.

There was no point even trying to fight it. She had no defense against this genuine show of affection, the way he held her as though he'd been dying to all day and she was the most precious thing in the world to him.

Giving in, she looped her arms around his back and leaned into him, struck by the sense of safety and security on top of the punch of stark arousal that streaked through her. Was this a bad idea?

Maybe, but it was hard to care at the moment. He made her want to crawl inside him and stay there.

"How bad is it out there?" she managed to ask, making use of her few remaining functional brain cells. Protests could shift suddenly and turn violent, and she had Carly here.

He nuzzled her hair, pressed a kiss to the crown of her head, the pressure of his arms still tight around her, as though he couldn't bring himself to let her go. "Latest intel says the protest could triple by tomorrow afternoon. It's peaceful so far and they have barriers in place all around the conference center and hotel, but the security's pretty thin down here. Tris and I talked. Do you want me to have Marley and Warwick come take Carly back to Crimson Point?"

She lifted her head to look up at him, concern puncturing the warm, secure cocoon she'd been floating in. "Is that necessary?"

"Not at the moment. Just giving you the option in case it would make you feel better. I know you've got a lot on your mind right now."

More than he knew.

His expression was absorbed as he ran that intense green gaze over the length of her in a way that made her feel naked despite the robe. "To be honest, I just wanted an excuse to come see you."

He met her gaze again, and the breath stalled in her lungs, his closeness and raw masculinity making her feel lightheaded. For so long she'd only allowed herself to think of him as her friend. Now that he had suddenly changed the ground rules with their kiss, there was no way she could make herself believe the lie anymore.

"I can't stay," he said, his voice heavy with regret. "I'm on call twenty-four-seven and should still be at my hotel, but I had to see you. Had to just…"

Her skin began to tingle all over, a breathless anticipation gripping her as he lifted a hand and trailed his fingertips down the side of her face. A light, almost ticklish caress that raised goosebumps across her skin and made her nipples bead tight.

"Gav," she whispered, and it sounded like a plea. A plea for him to stop this now before they went to a place of no return, or to keep going and put out the fire he'd lit inside her. She wasn't sure.

One big, warm hand cupped her cheek, and he rubbed the

pad of his thumb across her lips. "Yeah." He leaned in, his pupils dilating until they obliterated the green irises.

She swallowed, fingers tightening on his back as she fought the urge to grab his face and kiss him until he couldn't see straight. She was weak where he was concerned, always had been, and was already teetering on the verge of doing something stupid. One more seductive touch from him, and the tenuous hold on her control would slip.

"I thought you said you can't stay," she blurted out in a breathy voice as anticipation curled through her, making her heart thud as liquid heat rushed between her legs.

"I can't," he murmured, his lips only a breath away from hers. "But I have enough time for this." He tipped her head back and lowered his mouth to hers in an all-consuming kiss that made her mind go instantly blank.

A wave of heat engulfed her, years of pent-up longing and empty fantasies fueling a need that bordered on desperation. She ignored the voice of protest screaming warnings in the back of her head.

There were so many reasons why she should stop this. The sane thing to do—the responsible thing—was to end this right now.

But she couldn't. Even if this was just temporary, even if they only had this one night together and her upcoming confession on Monday tore them apart for good, she would at least have this.

She wanted him. Needed him. *Only* him.

He suddenly broke the kiss, breathing faster, and caught her hand. "C'mere," he whispered, tugging her toward him. He led her backward, paused only long enough to quietly turn the lock on Carly's door, then drew her to her bed.

A half-dozen feeble protests formed in her brain, but she

couldn't get a single word out, the tidal wave of need inside her inescapable.

She expected him to push her down on the bed and climb on top of her, but he sat on the edge of it instead and drew her into his lap. One hand cradled the side of her face, guiding her lips to his.

This time, he kissed her slow and tender, his tongue teasing hers, coaxing, melting her, and making the ache between her legs worse. The kiss was beyond anything she'd imagined, so erotic that all her most intense fantasies paled in comparison with reality. Her toes curled when his free hand moved up and down her back, up her shoulder to the side of her throat.

His long fingers found the neckline of her robe and pulled it aside, opening a path for his mouth. Her head fell back as his lips and tongue caressed every sensitive spot on the side of her neck. Delicious shivers rippled through her, amplifying the heavy throb between her thighs.

Don't stop, she willed him silently, her fingers digging harder into the back of his neck.

He tipped her backward slightly, the strong arm around her back holding her upright, his other hand sliding down to cup her bared breast. His head dipped down.

The first touch of his tongue on her hardened nipple made her gasp. He stroked it harder, lips parting to close around the sensitive flesh.

She pressed her lips together to stifle a shaky moan, a thread of sanity still cognizant of Carly in the next room, the level of need he created in her skyrocketing. He held her steady while he pleasured her, sucking with slow, steady pressure, flicking his tongue across the tip until she was squirming in his lap, desperate to feel his hand between her legs.

He shifted her slightly and moved his mouth to the other nipple, wrenching another stifled moan from her. His fingers stroked a slow path down her midline, over her belly.

Her muscles tensed, her breathing suspended when he ran the pads of his fingers across the top of her mound, oh so close to where she was slick and aching. "Next time I'm gonna do this properly."

"Properly?"

He made a low affirmative sound. "Stretch you out so I can touch and lick you all over, watch your face while I make you come on my tongue."

Oh, holy shit. She made a garbled sound and hung on to his shoulders for dear life, her whole body taut, dying of anticipation, the image he painted pushing her to the verge of begging.

His hand eased deeper between her thighs and his big, warm palm cupped her, long fingers parting her slick folds. She arched, bit her lip to keep from crying out as he eased a finger just inside her, igniting hidden nerve endings that sizzled at the slightest contact.

"Baby, look at you," he whispered, his fingertips skimming up, up until they slid along the edge of her aching, swollen clit.

"*There*," she demanded. Or maybe she begged, she wasn't sure. Both.

He made a quiet sound of agreement and repeated the caress, watching her. His touch was scarily skillful, the pad of one finger gliding over the exact spot that made her mindless. "This is what it should've been like the first time," he murmured against her lips an instant before kissing her again.

She didn't care about that now. Only cared that he didn't stop, that he relieved this insane, almost painful need he'd ignited.

He groaned and broke the kiss, then dipped his finger back an inch inside her, making her back arch. "I've imagined you like this so many times."

He had? She brought his mouth back down to hers. Their tongues twined together, the kiss muffling the soft mewls and cries she couldn't stifle as his sure, skillful fingers stroked and explored, drowning her in pleasure.

He pushed her steadily higher, higher, until he had her trembling all over, balanced on the precipice of release. With a pleading sound, she grabbed his wrist to anchor his hand in exactly the right spot and rocked shamelessly against it, riding the fingers buried inside her while his thumb rubbed her clit.

Stars exploded behind her closed eyelids when the orgasm hit. She clenched around his fingers and cried out into his mouth, caught in the vortex of pleasure.

He slowed the movement of his hand, drawing it out, coaxing every second from it possible until gradually it faded into gentle ripples. Breathless and weak in the aftermath, she pulled her mouth from his and dropped her head onto his shoulder, shaken.

Oh, God. That had been even better than she'd dreamed of. But now the ache inside her had moved to her heart.

Gavin made a low, guttural sound and wrapped both arms around her, squeezing her tight. "Goddamn, Autumn."

She was suddenly acutely aware of the rigid length of his erection pressed hard into her bottom, wanted to rub against him like a cat.

"I wish I could stay. I'd give goddamn near anything to lay you back on this bed and hear you scream my name while I'm inside you."

A tremor ran through her, her temporarily sated body already wanting seconds. And thirds.

He sat her up to kiss her one more time, gentler now, then ran his gaze over her, still splayed across his lap, robe gaping open to reveal her breasts and the flushed, slick folds between her legs that still pulsed with aftershocks. "Do you really have to go?" she whispered.

He groaned. "Yes. Fuck." He gave her one last swift kiss, pulled the halves of her robe back together and slid her off his lap onto the bed before heading to the sink in the bathroom.

She drank in the sight of him standing there, all broad-shouldered and powerful, a flush of arousal across his cheekbones, the solid ridge of his erection straining the front of his pants. In that moment, all she wanted was to sink to her knees in front of him, unzip his pants, and treat him to the same level of pleasure he'd just given her.

He turned to face her and stopped in the bathroom doorway. She lifted her gaze to his, the deep, masculine sound of hunger he made along with the mix of lust and tenderness on his face making her heart and belly do a sudden cartwheel.

"I would just about kill to feel your mouth on me. But if I don't leave in the next five seconds, I won't make it back to my hotel tonight, and I'll get my ass fired. So hold that thought, sweet thing." He stalked toward her, paused to tip her chin up and give her one more fierce, sizzling kiss, then pulled away. "I'll call you tomorrow when I can. Message me if you need anything."

You. I just need you. "Okay. Be safe."

He paused in the act of opening the door. One side of his mouth tipped up, making him so damned sexy she had to restrain herself from leaping up to drag him back to the bed. "Always."

Then he was gone.

She flopped onto her back and threw her forearm over her eyes. "Oh, *shit*," she whispered into the empty room, shaken.

He was doing and saying everything she'd dreamed of for years, and now she was terrified. Because it could all be taken away just as fast on Monday night when she told him he was Carly's father.

THIRTEEN

"All right, everyone gather 'round." Ryder said to their assembled team.

Gavin moved in closer to the main computer monitor with his twin and the rest of the CPS team surrounding him for the early morning briefing. Everyone was here except Decker, who was liaising with other security personnel at the conference center. A lot had changed overnight, none of it good.

"This is the itinerary for the day," Ryder continued, running a hand over his short-trimmed beard as he talked them through the information on screen, mostly timelines and locations. "Everyone knows their individual assignments, but we have new intel to brief you on. Callum?"

Standing on the other side of the monitor with his arms folded, Callum Falconer was an imposing presence in the room. The former Delta operator was revered as a god-like figure among everyone who worked at CPS. He had left the military years before and was now married with two young kids, but he'd seen more combat than all of them combined, and a couple years ago he'd led a rescue mission into

Afghanistan after the US withdrawal to extract Nadia, the woman who would become his wife. Fucking legend.

"The Feds are now forecasting at least triple, possibly quadruple the number of protesters we saw yesterday," Callum said in his deep, booming voice. "This group is highly organized and motivated, recruiting people from all over and busing them in from up and down the West Coast. Local officials have made the call to bring in a riot force to add an extra layer of security and deter violence."

Or, you know, it could also backfire and trigger violence.

Gavin kept that thought to himself, however. Portland had been chosen specifically as the site for this conference because one of the billionaires in charge lived in the area and had wanted to showcase the region, but Gavin bet the organizers were wishing they'd rethought that and chosen somewhere more remote.

"Riot squad is en route, ETA fifty minutes. We'll update you on their position once they're on scene, but they'll be stationed north of the external security perimeter."

"Meantime, we're going to review the existing contingency plans and security updates from the local authorities and other security units in charge here," Ryder added, pulling up maps and floor plans on screen. "As we all know, jurisdiction becomes an issue in operations this size."

Yep, plus there were less than a dozen CPS members on this detail. The situation outside was fluid and beyond their control. All they could do was mitigate the risk for their own people and the VIPs they were tasked with protecting.

Gavin followed along as Ryder and Callum detailed the contingency plans. If shit went sideways, they would evacuate the conference center only as a last resort and had the capability to call in helicopters to extract the VIPs from the conference center rooftop if necessary. But unless the center was in imminent threat of being breached, they would instead gather everyone up into one of the large ballrooms as a safe room, and the whole shebang would go into Fort Knox mode and the National Guard deployed.

"If that happens, it's full-on lockdown," Ryder told them. "So you need to make sure you get your VIPs and anyone else into the ballroom before that happens. We clear?"

A murmur of affirmatives went up. He thought of Autumn, a hint of worry creeping in. Her hotel wasn't a target, and it was far enough away from the conference center that it should be safe.

Still. He needed to give her a heads up so that she was aware and able to judge the situation on her end. She was a fierce mom, would do whatever she had to in order to keep Carly safe. And so would he, because he adored the kid.

"All right, that's it for now. Any questions?" Ryder asked, looking around the group. No one said anything. "Good. We're getting our own updates from Walker and Ivy back at HQ, so we'll update you as needed. Anything comes up in the meantime, let us know." He nodded once. "Dismissed."

The team dispersed immediately, some to other areas in the conference center to coordinate with other security organizations, and others like him and Tris back to the hotel to escort their VIPs to the first session of the day. On the way down the hall, Gavin pulled out his personal cell to send a text.

"You updating Autumn?" Tris asked.

"Yep." Her big presentation was first thing this morning. She hadn't wanted to evacuate Carly last night but needed to know the situation in case security at her hotel wasn't updating them.

More protesters expected than originally anticipated. Riot police on the way. Stay in your hotel until the streets are cleared and the situation has been contained. Will message you later. Love y—

His thumb paused, then deleted the last bit. It was too soon, she wasn't ready to hear that.

Even though it was the truth.

∽

HOLY SHIT, this was actually happening, and the ticking clock was almost down to zero.

Dan wandered through the protest staging area with a renewed sense of purpose and excitement. *Finally*.

The government he had faithfully served through years of military service, repeatedly putting his own safety and mental health on the line in combat overseas, was finally going to get a little taste of payback. Payback he would dish out personally.

There was a definite buzz in the air, a contagious sense of camaraderie and united anger. The people gathering here with him were grim-faced, determined, and ready for action.

"We're done letting them control us. We're done talking. We're here to send them a message, and we won't back down!" someone standing on a stage shouted into a bullhorn.

"We won't back down!" the assembled crowd roared in approval, everyone punching their fists in the air. All around him people were waving signs or holding banners with slogans across them.

You're either part of the solution or part of the problem.

Get out.

Beware of politicians.

Fight today for a better tomorrow.

People from all walks of life were here, including a few highly visible groups of fellow veterans wearing leather jackets with patches on them and carrying flags. More and more people flowed in from the surrounding side streets every minute, supplied by a steady convoy of buses and other vehicles dropping passengers off blocks away around the city center.

"Hey, man. You serve?" a young guy wearing an organizer shirt asked him, nodding to the tat on Dan's exposed forearm.

Semper Fidelis. "Fourteen years."

The guy smiled at him. "*Oorah*. I bet you can still handle yourself."

"Damned right, I can."

"Excellent, we need guys like you to lead the way." He clapped Dan on the shoulder. "Follow me."

Filled with a pride and purpose he hadn't felt in way too damned long, Dan went with him to another staging area set up several blocks away, out of sight down a back alley he knew well.

The crowd here was younger, almost all males, and there was a palpable change in vibe. An edgy, darker feel while they muttered to each other in low voices in the shadows and passed around balaclavas.

"How do you feel about sending a message with more of a…punch," the young guy said to him.

Dan saw a group of men emerge from the back door of the building with noticeable bumps under their jackets. Nodded. "That's exactly the kind of message I'm interested in delivering."

"Awesome. This way." The young guy gestured up the short set of steps.

Inside, Dan found more young men gathered around boxes and tables, forming an assembly line of sorts. Bottles. Piles of rags. Booze.

One of them nodded at him. "Hey, man. You know how to make these?" He held up a bottle with a rag sticking out of the end.

Dan smiled. "Brother, I can make 'em with my eyes closed."

"Great, then give us a hand."

He gathered up some supplies and joined the assembly line. Within twenty minutes, they had both tables covered with rows of Molotov cocktails.

"It's almost time," the organizer said from the open doorway. "You ready?"

"Ready," one of the guys working with Dan said. "Come and get 'em."

Dan helped distribute the devices and pairs of thick gloves to the steady stream of young men coming through the door, then tucked two bottles into the waistband of his jeans and tugged the hem of his hoodie down to hide them. At the door, the organizer thanked him and handed him a black balaclava.

He pulled it on and checked his phone one last time. No messages. For a moment, he considered texting TJ, but decided there was no point and put it away.

"All right, let's get this party started," one of the others said from outside where everyone was gathering, and the others shouted their agreement.

Dan was put near the front of the group, right behind the organizers. Fifty or so strong, they walked to the end of the alley and turned onto the main street. His heartrate sped up.

Before him was a sight to behold. Hundreds of people were flowing into the main street from the side routes, dozens of little streams spilling into a river. Feeding it. Creating a tide that flowed right through the downtown core, heading for their target at the end of the street.

He couldn't see much ahead of him, not the police or whatever other security that must be on scene by now, just that sea of bodies all marching together. Couldn't hear much over the shouting and whistles that came from all directions, drumming and chants blending into a continuous roar.

A unified chant lifted above the noise. "End corruption now!"

Dan joined in, throwing his fist into the air on each word. A half-block ahead, the crowd suddenly slowed. Almost seemed to stumble.

"They called in the fucking riot squad," someone out front cried.

Dan slowed with the others and craned his neck to see over the crowd. Sure enough, a long black line came into view a couple blocks up the street. A wall of cops in black uniforms and ballistic gear, helmets and visors obscuring their faces, batons and shields at the ready. As he watched more filed in on both sides, blocking the entire width of the street and barring their way.

Their column slowed more. Stopped. People bitched and grumbled, the whole crowd growing restless, a seething mass of resentment and rage building higher with each passing second.

A powder keg waiting for a single spark to ignite it.

Dan clenched his jaw and shook his head in silent rage. Calling in the riot squad was a fucking stupid move. Now things would get even uglier.

"This way!" The guy who had enlisted Dan for help with the devices shoved his way back to the center of their group and turned to wave everyone on, his voice slightly muffled by his balaclava. "Come on! We're not backing down, we're going to show those bastards what happens when they betray us!"

A loud roar went up, raising the hair on Dan's arms and neck. His group began marching forward. The crowd ahead parted, the more peaceful protesters moving aside, watching in awe as Dan's group pushed their way through, moving toward the front of the column that stretched right up to where the riot cops were standing. Dan kept in step with his group, heart thudding, flooding his system with adrenaline.

His gaze locked on the line of cops. His gut tingled the way it had just before a firefight.

The riot cops saw them coming through the ranks. Started banging their batons on their shields in cadence, and took measured, menacing steps toward them. Moving forward to engage.

Someone in the crowd near the front lines threw something. It bounced off a cop's shield.

"*Now!*" Dan bellowed.

Everyone launched their projectiles in unison. The cops raised their shields to deflect the incoming barrage.

Dan's focus narrowed on a group of cops directly in front of him, the sights and sounds taking him right back to his combat days. He couldn't believe he had to fight like this on the streets of an American city to make himself heard.

With the first volley over, the cops took another step forward, shields up.

"Charge!" someone yelled.

A battle cry erupted all around him. Chills raced down Dan's spine. He opened his mouth to join in, howling like a demon as they broke into a run, going straight at the line of cops blocking the way to the conference center.

Someone lobbed a lit device. It smashed into the ground a few feet in front of a cop and burst into flames. The crowd hurled rocks, bricks and bottles at the cops. They huddled together under their shields, sheltering from the storm.

As he ran, Dan noticed groups of men along the sides of the street, smashing cars and flipping them over. Torching one close to the cops would push them back.

He pulled out one of his devices, lit the end of the rag and hurled it toward an overturned car. He missed, and it flew into a wooden art installation attached to the façade of a hotel on the corner. Instantly it burst into a small blaze, the flames racing up the tinder-dry wood.

He cursed under his breath, slowed and lit his second one. This time when he threw it, he had the satisfaction of seeing the flames engulf the vehicle moments before he swept by.

Just ahead of them, the line of cops wavered, moved away from the burning car. The momentary lapse opened a gap in front of them.

Yes.

Dan raced through it with the others, screaming in triumph as they breached the line and ran for the conference center with the full force of the crowd coming right behind them.

FOURTEEN

"As you can see, this campaign is expected to generate the most impact and attention from your target demographic groups and overall audience." Autumn paused to bring up the next image in her digital slide show on the large projection screen at the front of the room, detailing their projected numbers in reach and earnings using various graphs and charts.

The boardroom was silent, fifteen sets of eyes trained on her during the most important presentation of her career. This account was worth twelve million dollars for her small but upcoming advertising firm. Her boss had given her free rein to gather everyone and everything she needed or wanted to make this campaign a success.

Now it was up to her to sell the pitch. "And here's why," she finished after a meaningful pause to give the audience time to absorb the information.

Her assistant hit the lights, and she unveiled the advertisement package she and her team had been working on for the past seven months in preparation for this pitch. The owner and entire senior executive team from their biggest client, a luxury car brand, watched intently while she played the video of the ad.

Twenty-nine-point-three seconds, just under the thirty-second mark that copious amounts of industry research had shown was the most effective length for an ad. It had a dark, mysterious vibe to it, but with an elegant polish designed to appeal to both male and female high-end buyers, and a clever little hook at the end that their focus group data showed captured viewer interest. The overall feel was sleek and sexy without being pretentious, aimed at appealing to a wider demographic than the company had targeted before.

The lights remained off for just a few seconds after the ad finished for maximum impact, then her assistant turned them back on. The grins and interested expressions Autumn saw around the long table had her giving a mental fist pump. It was the edgiest ad they had designed for the campaign and therefore a bit of a gamble, but she'd felt in her gut it was the right one for this pitch.

"And there you have it," she finished with a satisfied smile. "Any questions?"

Seated at the head of the table, the CEO shook his head slightly. He was several years younger than Autumn and already a billionaire after inheriting the business from his grandfather several years ago. "I fucking love it." Everyone laughed at his colorful response.

"I do too," their forty-something COO echoed from beside him. He was the common sense partner in their upper management, the voice of reason and experience. The brakes, whereas the CEO was the gas, all ideas and energy and fire all the time. They balanced each other out and worked together well. "Damn, now I really can't wait for mine to roll off the assembly line next month."

At more than a hundred grand for the base model, it

wasn't a vehicle Autumn and most other people would be owning in their lifetimes, but this ad would create a buzz amongst a wider demographic for the company. Increasing profits were what business was all about, after all. Her firm was small by advertising standards.

If they got this contract, they would not only have a record year to celebrate, but hopefully more record years from campaigns with this company and others like it going forward. Word of mouth was key in this industry. Buzz generated by this deal would have other companies coming to them directly.

No pressure.

"We love it too," Autumn said, bringing it home, "and given the data generated from the feedback collected from our sample groups, we're confident this will reach a thirty-percent broader base than your previous ads."

"I'm sold. I'm fucking *pumped*," the CEO exclaimed, still grinning as he looked around at his team, then back at Autumn. "Can we see it again?"

"Absolutely." Her assistant hit the lights, and she played the video again.

Ten seconds in, however, the fire alarm suddenly blared through the room, ripping her out of the moment. No one moved, everyone looking at each other.

She looked over at her boss, seated in the back corner, the shriek of the alarm a stark reminder of the trouble brewing down on the streets below. False alarm hopefully?

Moments later the conference room door opened and a uniformed security officer stood there. "I'm going to have to ask you all to leave this floor immediately and take the stairs down to the lobby. We're evacuating the building."

Her boss stood. "Is there a fire?"

"I don't have any further information at this time. Please leave quickly."

"Is this related to the protests?"

"I don't have any further information to give, sir. Please evacuate the building immediately." *Or I'll make you*, his set expression said.

Her boss turned to face everyone. "Okay, we'll pick this up again as soon as we get back. After you," he said to the CEO.

Autumn grabbed her bag and followed the others out of the room, exiting last with her boss. "I need to go get Carly," she told him as they headed down the hall with a stream of other people headed for the nearest stairwell.

"Of course. I'm sure this is just a precaution. I'll meet you outside, and hopefully we can get back in here soon and finish up. Fantastic job, by the way. Almost makes me want to yank a chunk of my retirement savings out to buy one of those things. Almost," he repeated with a wink, not seeming alarmed in the slightest.

But she was. Being evacuated outside right now while there were protests happening nearby didn't ease the anxiety humming in the pit of her stomach. But if there was a fire, they had no choice.

The lineup slowed as the funnel of people narrowed as it moved through the emergency door. Through the open space she could see more people coming down from the upper floors.

Carly was in their room four floors up. She didn't have the cell phone she'd been bugging Autumn for since last fall, so Autumn couldn't message or call her except by calling the room directly, and she didn't see a house phone anywhere in the hall. Though she had a feeling Carly would stay put until she came for her, she dialed the hotel to speak to reception and have them connect her with their room.

An automated voice answered, putting her on hold as she finally reached the stairwell. Autumn waited her turn, struggling to curb her impatience while soothing music played through her phone.

She pushed her way through the line of people descending the stairs, hugged the railing as she started climbing the stairs, her progress hampered by everyone coming toward her, bumping and jostling her and slowing her down. But when she reached the next floor, a security guard stepped in front of her to block her path.

"You can't go up, ma'am. You have to—"

"My daughter is upstairs in our room, and I can't reach her by phone." The music kept coming through her phone. "I have to get her," she said, and angled her body to get past him.

He grabbed her upper arm and stepped in front of her again, stopping her. "Staff members are checking the rooms on the upper floors one by one and evacuating everyone. I can't let you go up. You need to leave the building now."

She ripped her arm free and faced off with him, a burst of panic shooting through her. "I'm getting my daughter." She pushed his shoulder, tried to step around him.

He set his jaw, seized her by the shoulders and turned her around to face down the stairs. "Go. Now. Or I'll have to take you down myself."

"Get your hands off me!" She whirled and shoved him, hard, instinct driving her. Her daughter was upstairs in their room waiting for her, and there might be a fire. This asshole had no right to—

"Hey." Another officer appeared out of nowhere and grabbed her left arm.

She pivoted and swung at him without thinking. He reared his head back just in time to avoid her fist in his face. Part of her was shocked. She'd never hit anyone in her life. But she'd fight anyone who tried to stop her from getting to Carly.

"Ma'am," the other one snapped, and trapped her arms against her sides. "*Enough*. Let's go."

"No! Let me *go*! My daughter's up there alone. You have to let me get her!" She bucked and kicked as he practically carried her down the stairs. Her phone fell out of her hand, immediately vanished from view under the people streaming down the steps. "My phone! I need to talk to my daughter!"

Someone behind them bent to retrieve her phone and handed it to the officer. The screen was shattered.

"Someone on staff will escort her out of her room," the officer snapped. "Now calm down before I have to charge you with assault."

She struggled and argued with him all the way down the last three flights of stairs to the lobby. He muscled her through the doors into the lobby, shoved her busted phone at her and handed her off to another guard with a gruff, "Watch her. Make sure she doesn't get back inside."

Autumn immediately tried to duck back inside but the guard grabbed her, frog-marched her through the front entrance and out onto the street. It was chaos outside the main doors.

A large and growing crowd milled around close to the building in confusion, blocking her view of the main cross street and impeding the rest of the hotel occupants from exiting.

Guards posted around the area were shouting and trying to force everyone farther away from the hotel. When she tried again to veer back inside the one closest to her held out his arms and moved in front of her to prevent her from getting past him.

"My daughter's still in there up in our room," she yelled, frantically looking for a way back in. She didn't see any smoke. Maybe it was actually a false alarm, but she wasn't taking chances with Carly. "I have to get up there."

"No way, lady," he said, and dragged her farther away from the entrance.

"Goddammit, let me go!" She ripped free, retreated out of range and checked her phone.

Through the spiderweb pattern on the shattered screen, she could just barely make out a text message from Jonas.

Is Carly in your room? I'm still upstairs. I can get her for you.

He had sent it just two minutes earlier.

She tried to type a response but couldn't get the keypad to work on the damaged screen, and the guard wasn't interested in helping her, too preoccupied by the chaos unfolding around them. Scanning the crowd anxiously, she picked out her boss standing with some coworkers over by a large concrete planter, slowly being edged farther out into the street by the growing mass of people.

"Ross!" She pushed her way through the slow-moving crowd between them, heart hammering. "*Ross!*"

He turned, spotted her, and pushed through the crowd to wrap his arm around her shoulders and shepherd her toward the others, his much larger frame shielding her. "I need your phone, quick," she blurted. "Do you have Jonas's number?"

"Yes." He unlocked it, handed it over and kept guiding her away from the hotel while she pulled up the number.

There was no point trying to call him. It was way too loud out here. She'd never hear him. *This is Autumn. Carly still in room,* she texted back, struggling to stay calm. *I'm outside.*

They wouldn't let me up and won't let me back in. Please get her!

Three dots appeared, then a message. *I'll get her don't worry. What room?*

Oh God, she could kiss him right now. *Seven-one-nine*, she answered. *Our code word is Taylor Swift.*

He responded immediately. *Got it. Meet you outside in a bit.*

She clutched the phone to her chest and closed her eyes, relief sliding through her. "Thank you, thank you, thank you," she breathed.

"Everything okay?" her boss asked.

She nodded but kept hold of his phone. When she was calmer, she edged away from the others, staying even with the doors so she could see the crowd filing out. The people who had been herded toward the main cross street were stalled in a big mass by the far side of the building, something clearly preventing them from going farther. The protests?

She texted Gavin, knowing his number by heart.

It's Autumn. Phone broken so using my boss's. Just evacuated our hotel due to fire alarm. Unsure if false alarm. Coworker bringing Carly down b/c they wouldn't let me up to get her. Do you know anything?

She hit send and went back to scanning the exiting crowd. A warm breeze ruffled her hair, bringing the scent of the air freshener from inside the lobby—

And smoke.

Fear jolted through her. She whirled to face the far side of the building, the reason for the crowd's reluctance suddenly and terrifyingly obvious.

The hotel really was on fire.

FIFTEEN

Carly sat on her bed, unmoving as the fire alarm blared out in the hallway. Her school did fire drills all the time. Was this a drill? Or maybe a false alarm?

The alarm kept going, and her anxiety grew. Her mom was downstairs somewhere at her conference. Should she leave the room and go down the fire exit?

Her inner voice told her to stay here, certain that her mom would come and get her. She didn't want to get lost if there really was a fire and not be able to find her mom.

She jumped when a sharp knock came at the suite door. "Carly?" A man's voice called out.

She didn't answer, heart tripping as she sat frozen on the bed. Who was it? What did he want?

"My name's Jonas, I work with your mom. We've met once before at the Christmas dinner last year, do you remember?"

She had a vague memory of him, brown hair and glasses. But she still didn't answer. Her mom had taught her never to answer the door when she was alone.

He knocked louder. "Carly? I just talked to your mom on the

phone. She's been evacuated, and they won't let her back in the building, so she asked me to come get you and take you outside to meet her. We have to leave now. I hear you like Taylor Swift?"

That was her and her mom's secret code. He wouldn't know it unless her mom had told him.

Carly jumped up and hurried to the door, checking the peephole first. It was him. She undid the safety chain and opened the door a few inches.

He smiled down at her. "Hi. You okay?"

She nodded, the pit of her stomach buzzing. "Is there a fire?" She didn't smell or see any smoke, and he didn't look worried.

"It's probably just a drill, but we have to leave now just in case. The staff is evacuating everyone. Do you need to grab anything?"

"My laptop." She backed away from the door, quickly got her backpack and slipped it on as she made her way back to him. She was still a bit scared but trying to hide it.

"It's okay," he told her. "We'll be outside in just a few minutes, and your mom is there waiting for you."

Carly nodded and stepped out into the hall. He set a guiding hand on her shoulder and steered her toward the stairwell entrance at the end of the hall. It was practically empty except for several staff members they passed on the way.

"Everyone out of that room?" one woman asked them in a brisk tone as she unlocked another door to check for occupants.

"Yes." Jonas pressed the metal release bar on the steel door, shoved it open and held it for Carly. He stepped inside the stairwell behind her, and they joined the line of people moving down the steps. They went down one flight of stairs. Turned to go down another.

Just before they reached the bottom, she smelled smoke.

Fear jolted through her, and she looked up at Jonas, who looked worried now. Was there an actual fire? How bad, and how close? Would they be able to get out in time?

Other people around them must have noticed the smoke as well because they started murmuring in concern and darting nervous glances around. Carly swallowed and moved closer to Jonas.

He squeezed her shoulder and gave her a reassuring smile that did nothing to stop the hot buzzing in her stomach. "It's all right. Almost there, keep going."

But they weren't.

Before they reached the next floor the smoke was already so thick she could hardly see the people at the bottom of the stairs, stinging her eyes and throat. She coughed, put a hand over her nose and mouth.

Jonas pulled the collar of his shirt over his lower face and increased his grip on her. "Keep going."

She did, but it was slow because of all the people stuck in front of them. At the next landing security was there. "This way, folks," the man said in a booming voice, directing them through the door and down the hall to the stairwell on the opposite end.

But once they got there the smoke was almost as bad and only thickened as they made their way down the stairs. Jonas grabbed a handful of Carly's unicorn hoodie and held on tight.

She coughed, pulled the collar of her hoodie up over her nose and mouth. They still weren't at the bottom, and she didn't know how many more flights they had to go.

The smoke thickened as they neared the lobby. They got stuck inside the stairwell doorway at the bottom, a mass of people ahead of them blocking their way to the main exit and the street beyond.

"Crouch down." Jonas pushed on her shoulder, urged her into a crouch in front of him, and she realized he was trying to avoid the worst of the smoke.

Anxiety shot through her. Why wouldn't the people in front of them move faster and let them out?

Through the smoke Carly could just make out the open exit doors almost straight ahead. But no one was moving.

They stood there trapped in the stairwell while the seconds ticked by and the smoke continued to get worse. Everyone was coughing, an almost electric sense of panic crackling in the air.

Several people started pushing forward against the wall of bodies hemming them in. A heartbeat later, a mini stampede ensued, fear and desperation driving people to mow down whoever was in their way of the exit.

Oh no—

Jonas suddenly yanked her to her feet, pulling her close to the front of his body to try and protect her from the crush. One second they were okay, and the next they were being flattened from all sides. The sense of claustrophobia increased as they remained trapped in the stairwell without any forward motion, their path ahead still completely blocked.

Carly huddled in front of him, and she could feel his fear.

"Let us out!" Jonas yelled.

"We can't fucking breathe!" someone behind them up the stairs shouted. "Move!"

It was like a powerful wave slammed into them from behind, crushing them even harder into the people ahead of them. Screams and scuffles broke out as people fought to free themselves. She and Jonas were trapped in place, unable to move while the smoke thickened.

Panic crawled up her spine. Jonas shoved backward against the force behind them, fighting to hold his ground.

A high-pitched scream rent the air.

Pandemonium broke loose. Everyone started pushing and shoving. Knocking others down to get past them, only to wind up trapped just inside the doorway, making the blockage worse.

Carly cried out and shrank closer to Jonas. They couldn't stay here. They'd be trampled. Their only chance was to force their way outside.

Jonas pushed her toward a small gap that opened between some people struggling ahead of them. "Go, go," he yelled over the mingled shouts and screams, propelling her forward.

She struggled through the gap, got stuck right after that but managed to wriggle through another. She looked over her shoulder for Jonas but couldn't stop, the force of the people behind her shoving her forward.

Jonas was too big, couldn't get through the same gap. He shot a hand out, grabbed for the strap of her backpack so he wouldn't lose her.

It slipped off her shoulders, leaving him holding a fistful of nylon. A heartbeat later he disappeared from view, as if swallowed alive by the roiling mass of people all fighting their way to the only exit available.

After what felt like an eternity later, Carly finally made it through the restriction. She squinted and coughed, though the smoke seemed thinner here. Disoriented, she tried to push her way through the unmoving crowd filling the sidewalk to find some space.

She pulled the hoodie away from her nose and mouth, blinked to clear her eyes. Her stomach lurched when she saw what was happening. A tide of protesters charged up the street right in front of her, yelling war cries that made the hair on her neck stand up.

Cars were overturned and burning, broken glass glinting in the sunlight. Everywhere she looked there was chaos. People were massed together in large groups, trying to flee in all directions to get away from the danger, caught between the fires and the protesters.

And everywhere she looked, there was no sign of her mom.

She whirled around in a circle, scanning frantically for her or Jonas. They couldn't be far away. Her mom had to still be somewhere nearby, she wouldn't have gone away from the hotel without her.

But the crowd swallowed her up again, forced her to keep moving away from the hotel entrance. "Mom!" Carly tried to spin around, an icy wave of fear breaking over her.

She was lost and being dragged right into the middle of the protests.

SIXTEEN

The stream of people exiting the hotel stalled around the front entrance, prevented from going any farther by the tightly packed crowd gathered outside. There were too many people between Autumn and the entrance for her to see it clearly and the wind had just changed direction, blowing the worst of the smoke straight at them.

She squinted and covered her mouth and nose with her forearm to try and block it out, struggling to wedge her way through everyone milling around the entrance in confusion. Sirens blared. People were shouting, but she couldn't tell if it was the protesters in the street or due to the fire.

She shot an anxious glance up at the far end of the building. Black smoke drifted into the clear summer air, tongues of orange and yellow flames licking out from around the corner.

Heart hammering against her ribs, she looked back at the entrance and kept fighting her way closer. Did Jonas have Carly? Had they made it out, or were they still trapped inside? She didn't know how extensive the fire was at this point, but it was already terrifying and would spread quickly if the fire crews didn't get here fast.

The phone in her hand hadn't buzzed, but she checked it for the dozenth time anyway. Still nothing from Jonas or Gavin.

The growing crowd pressed in tighter and tighter around her until she could hardly move, the sense of claustrophobia adding to the panic churning inside her. There was no sign of Jonas or Carly, and she now realized that trying to fight her way to the entrance through this mess was pointless.

She pivoted and pushed back through the crowd the way she'd come. The sirens stopped suddenly, signaling that the fire crew was finally on scene.

She felt like a fish trying to battle its way upstream as she slowly made her way toward the far edge of the swelling crowd until she had enough room to move. The fear kept building, the frantic need to find Carly a constant scream in her head.

Skirting the perimeter, she headed for the far side of the crowd, scanning the entire time for any sign of her daughter. And when she got close enough to see the scene unfolding on the street, her stomach clenched.

It looked like a war zone. The responding fire trucks were stuck down the street, unable to get any closer to the hotel because of the chaos. A wall of angry protesters rushed past the burning hotel carrying what looked like Molotov cocktails, heading in the direction of the conference center.

"Autumn!"

She whipped around. Through the shifting sea of bodies, she spotted Jonas's head for an instant before the frightened crowd swallowed him back up.

"Jonas!" She raised her arm, waved it frantically as she began shoving her way toward him. A flash of red-gold hair appeared off to the right. Her heart leapt, then sank when she realized it wasn't Carly.

Jonas reappeared. He must have spotted her because he raised his arm and started in her direction. They met near the far edge of the crowd. Her daughter wasn't there.

Cold tentacles of fear slid through her. "Where's Carly?" she shouted over the noise, shoving down a burst of panic. Maybe he'd put her somewhere safe to wait rather than risk pulling her into the crowd.

The look on his face turned her insides to ice. He opened his mouth, hesitated before answering. "We got separated inside. I—"

"You *what*?" She spun around, an icy wave of terror breaking over her. No. No. This wasn't happening. "Carly!"

"She was ahead of me," Jonas shouted behind her. "I saw her get outside, but I couldn't get to her."

Autumn didn't respond, couldn't even if she'd wanted to, fear all but choking her as she scanned the area. Her baby was alone somewhere in this chaotic, dangerous mess.

Her gaze landed on a police officer off to one side trying to direct people away from the burning building. She rushed at him as fast as her rubbery legs and the packed crowd would allow her. He spotted her, must have seen the panic on her face because he stopped and faced her.

"My daughter's missing," she blurted out when he was within earshot. "Twelve years old, strawberry blond hair. She made it out of the hotel but—"

"Ma'am, I need you to keep moving—"

"My twelve year old is missing!"

A scuffle broke out beside her. She got a flying elbow to the middle of her back. "Hey!" The cop immediately shoved past her to intervene.

She almost grabbed him to yank him back around and make him *help* her, so frustrated she was on the verge of screaming. Instead she whipped up the phone and dialed 911 while she kept scanning the area.

A faint busy tone droned in her ear. "Come on," she snapped, and dialed again. The lines couldn't possibly all be busy.

This time it connected, but she couldn't hear what the operator was saying and plugged her other ear, straining to understand. "I can't hear you," she said into the phone, and without waiting quickly detailed what was happening.

The mass of people around her suddenly shifted. The quick change in momentum knocked her off balance. She stumbled, grabbed for the person closest to her and managed to catch a fistful of shirt to slow her momentum and keep from doing a face plant in the midst of the dangerous crowd.

Her knees hit the pavement with a painful thud and the phone fell from her hand. Before she could grab it, the crowd moved again, this time in the opposite direction. Cursing under her breath, she made one last attempt to snatch it between all the moving feet, missed, and hurriedly surged to her own feet before she got trampled.

It was like she'd been trapped in a washing machine. She was bounced back and forth, jostled from every side until she lost all sense of direction. She fought to hold her ground, but the momentum of the crowd was too much.

The shrill screech of police whistles punctuated the mingled shouts, drumming, and shuffle of thousands of panicked feet, adding to the unbearable tension inside her.

Carly! Where was she? Autumn had to get free of this, had to find her daughter before she was carried away on this human tide.

A hard weight knocked her forward, then plastered tight against her back, flattening her against the person in front of her. With an enraged cry, she shoved against the man's back to fight the crushing pressure, battling to stay on her feet as the crowd swept her along in a powerful, inescapable current.

SEVENTEEN

They never should have held the damned conference here in the first place.

Gavin stood grimly beside his twin and the rest of the team in the security room, watching the incredible scenes unfolding in the few blocks surrounding the conference center on the video monitors. Despite the city's and organizer's security implementations, all hell was breaking loose outside.

The cops were on the verge of losing control, and the protesters were gaining ground, their numbers swelling. If they breached that line of riot cops, only two more security barriers stood between them and the hotel and conference center.

"We're going to security plan Charlie," Ryder announced to the silent room. "The Feds have teams moving in, with reinforcements on the way. Sniper teams are giving live intel from their positions."

"What about the National Guard?" Gavin asked. Some of the guys in Crimson Point were Air National Guard PJs. If activated, they might fly rescue and extraction missions.

"The governor has alerted them. Members have been called to base."

"Locate and secure your VIPs at the hotel and escort them to the safe room here," Callum told them. "We'll coordinate with on-site security and RV with you."

Copy that. It was go time.

Tris exchanged a look with him before they turned and quickly left the room with the other CPS personal protection team members. Government security contractors were responsible for the overall security of the conference site. Gavin's team was responsible for the VIPs under their charge.

"This shit's gonna be ugly if they breach the external perimeter," he muttered as they ran for the emergency exit protected by guards carrying semi-auto rifles. These guys weren't fucking around.

"Oh, yeah," Tris answered, right beside him. "You hear from Deck?"

"Nope." Decker was somewhere onsite with another element from CPS, but not involved with VIP personal security.

And now Gavin was worried about Autumn and Carly too. He'd left Autumn a message but hadn't heard back from her yet. He just hoped they were safe inside their hotel and would stay there.

He dialed his VIP as he ran. "Where are you?" he said the moment the man answered.

"In my room. Why?"

"Security situation outside is deteriorating rapidly. We're evacuating everyone into the conference center immediately. I'm on my way to you now, ETA four minutes. Be ready to move when I get there."

The man cursed. "Is that absolutely nec—"

"Be ready." Yeah, it was fucking necessary.

"All right, understood."

He and Tris reached the entrance to the hotel, also manned by heavily armed guards. They tore up the stairwell together, their rapid footsteps echoing off the concrete walls.

The hallway was thankfully almost empty when they got to their floor. Gavin ran to his VIP's room while Tris rushed to his and rapped sharply on the door. "It's me. You ready?"

The door opened only a moment later. The sixty-something diplomat looked a little rattled as he came out with his briefcase, shrugging into his suit jacket, his tie undone around his neck. "Yes."

"This way. Stay close."

"Okay. What's happening outside?"

Chaos. "The protesters have set fires and are attacking the police."

"Oh, shit."

Gavin didn't answer. There was no threat here, only an urgency to get this man into the more secure conference center as quickly as possible. Tristan and his VIP were a short way ahead of them up the hall.

They quickly hustled their charges down the stairs to the lower emergency exit, pausing at the door to check with Callum in the control room. "Tris and I have our VIPs at exit delta. We clear to move into location bravo?"

"Affirmative," Callum answered.

He nodded to alert Tris. "Let's go." He hit the release bar.

Tris swept past him with his own VIP. Gavin followed a moment later, grabbing his VIP's right shoulder with his left hand and grasping the man's belt with his right in a two-handed body-control technique. Maneuvering his VIP with two hands from behind gave him the advantage of control, but would hamper him if he needed to draw his weapon, leaving the VIP exposed to threats from the front. Hopefully it wouldn't be an issue.

The corridor was empty, but he remained on high alert, rushing the man through the tunnel to the conference center entrance. Tris paused at the far door to check in with Callum. "Clear," he called back to Gavin.

A moving mass of people greeted them on the other side. Gavin immediately swiveled, grasping his VIP's arm to bring the man behind him. He moved through the crowd quickly, his height and size giving him an advantage as he followed his twin while watching for any threats.

They moved fast, muscling their way through knots of people when necessary while ignoring the angry retorts, concerned only with getting the men into the safe room on the second floor.

Armed guards were stationed inside the center at regular intervals, and there were undercover FBI agents mixed in as well. The uniformed Feds guarding the main ballroom saw them coming and opened the double doors to the ballroom.

Gavin followed his brother in, taking in the scene with a single sweeping glance. Hundreds of people were already inside, gathered along the front of the room where the stage was, their hushed, nervous voices creating a low buzz that filled the air.

Gavin took his VIP to the far side of the room and released him. "This room is locked from the outside. No one gets in without authorization. You'll stay here until the situation has stabilized. I'll contact you when we get the all clear."

The man nodded, looking a little pale. "Got it."

Gavin met Tris in the center of the room and strode for the double doors. The new security plan called for them to assemble inside the main entrance lobby and help reinforce the interior security barricades if necessary.

He picked out Callum's red-gold hair instantly as he stood with some of their team at the RV point. Beyond the huge, tinted glass windows along the front of the entrance, he could see the melee. On a shit-scale of one to ten, the situation outside looked about a solid nine.

People were running back and forth in confusion behind the barricades. More tactical officers were deploying. Beyond all that, he could see the mass of people moving up the street toward them all.

In the past twenty minutes, the line of riot cops had been pushed back almost a hundred yards, and the crowd kept growing. At this rate, in under thirty more minutes the cops would be up against the first security perimeter barricades.

If that was breached, Gavin and the rest of his teammates would have to wade into the fray to form a last line of defense and protect everyone inside this building.

"Listen up," Callum said to them. "We're going to coordinate with the teams at the internal security barrier and review the contingency plan." He waved them all forward, nodded at the guards to let them through, and the doors opened.

An instant wall of noise assaulted them. Gavin stayed beside Tristan on the short walk to the internal perimeter barrier, his gaze on the crowd coming up the street and the line of tactical cops blocking their way only a few hundred meters away from Gavin's team's current position. He talked to several security contractors, getting up to speed, then stood back as they conferred with Callum and their own team leader.

He kept his attention on the mob coming their way as he waited. And his heart sunk when he saw a stream of people coming through the line of riot cops in the distance.

"Shit." He hurried over to Callum. "The riot squad line's been breached in at least one place."

Callum shook his head. "They're letting through groups of innocent bystanders mixed into the crowd. Apparently they were evacuated from their hotel and got tangled up. Incendiary device started a fire."

Foreboding swept through him. *Autumn and Carly.* "Which hotel?"

Callum named the one they had been evacuated from.

He swore and rushed back to where Tris was monitoring the situation in front of them, dialing her number. "Autumn and Carly's hotel was evacuated due to a fire. They could be out there." He nodded at the churning mass coming up the street as he put the phone to his ear.

"Oh, Jesus," Tris muttered, and quickly moved away to talk to someone.

Autumn's voicemail picked up. He ended the call and shot her a text, could have sworn he heard his name from somewhere in the crowd. A second or two later, he heard it again.

"Gavin!"

His head jerked up, his gaze snapping toward the direction of the faint voice. He didn't see anyone he recognized at first, but then through a small gap in the tightly packed crowd between the riot squad and the second security perimeter barriers, he spotted Autumn, arm waving over her head.

Seeing her trapped in the midst of that fleeing mass of innocent people triggered something deep and elemental inside him. He lunged forward without thinking, vaulted the first set of barriers and raced toward her, ignoring the shouts from his team.

He didn't care if he'd been ordered not to leave his post. Didn't care that he might get fired. All that mattered was reaching Autumn and Carly and getting them to safety.

The guards posted at the second set of barriers spotted

him and moved together as if they were going to try and block him. "*Move*," he yelled, waving them off before racing past them and vaulting the second barrier.

He crashed straight into the people crowded up against the barricade, twisted and shoved his way through the mass of bodies between him and Autumn. He was barely aware of the elbows and shoulders battering him, his gaze locked on Autumn as she kept disappearing and reappearing in the moving human tide.

Moments later he spotted her again, and the frantic look on her face twisted his guts into knots. By the time he reached her, his chest and back were soaked with sweat, his heart hammering. Without a word he grabbed her, locked his arms around her torso and twisted his body to take the brunt of the impacts as people repeatedly knocked into them.

"Where's Carly?" he shouted.

"She's missing."

He looked at her sharply. Took in the tear tracks on her cheeks, the stark terror and grief in her eyes.

A group of people plowed into them from the left before he could answer her, knocking them sideways. He grunted, barely kept his footing but managed to keep hold of Autumn.

She was saying something to him urgently, but he couldn't hear her over the combined chaos of the crowd and the roars of the protesters closing in on the cops standing in formation behind them. He did a quick scan around them, couldn't see Carly anywhere and made a snap decision.

They couldn't stay here. He needed to get Autumn inside where it was safe and find out what the hell had happened so he could help find Carly.

He spun Autumn around in front of him, applied the same two-handed technique he'd used on his VIP and steered her toward the far edge of the street where the crowd was thinnest. The guards at the external perimeter let them approach, helped him get her over the line of concrete barriers.

"Hurry," he urged her, propelling her forward. If Carly was lost out here by herself, every moment counted.

He lifted Autumn over the second set of barriers, didn't stop to look for his brother or the others, and rushed toward the guards manning the front of the hotel, who let them inside. The doors shut behind them, instantly blocking out most of the noise.

He maneuvered her behind a concrete pillar at the right side of the entrance and swung her back around to face him. "What happened?"

"There was a fire," she gasped out, shaking and pale, that haunted look in her eyes fueling another rush of adrenaline. "I couldn't get to her. A coworker was supposed to bring her outside, but they got separated. I couldn't f-find her. I—"

He tapped his earpiece. "Tris, I'm taking Autumn to the ballroom. Get your ass there now. Carly's missing."

"On my way," his twin answered. "Be there in two minutes."

Gavin glanced back outside, determined they had only a few minutes more than that before the line of riot cops might be breached. He grabbed Autumn's upper arm, started for the ballroom.

She dug in her heels. "No, I need to—"

"It's not safe here. If they get past that line of cops, the first barrier will be breached a minute or two after that. I'm taking you to a safe room. You'll stay there while Tris and I go look for Carly."

"No, I—"

"You have to stay here so I know you're safe. You can't

go back out there." He hurried her down the corridor and up the carpeted steps to the ballroom doors.

Just as he was about to nod at the guards guarding the room to open the doors, Autumn put on the brakes and spun to face him, grabbing the front of his shirt with both hands, hard enough that he heard stitches pop. "You have to find her."

"I will. Don't worry."

She swallowed, staring up at him with fear-drenched eyes. "God, I didn't want to tell you like this."

He looked past her at the guards, waved for them to open the ballroom doors. "Tell me what?"

"She's yours."

His gaze jerked to hers. He stared at her in silence, his brain taking in that stricken look on her face as it tried to compute the words and what they meant. And when her meaning became clear, everything around them funneled out.

"What?" His voice was low. Deadly.

"I just found out the day we flew here. That's what I've been upset about—"

"What the fuck?" It wasn't possible. They'd used protection.

She winced, shook her head. "I didn't know, I swear, but it's true—"

"Hey," Tris called from behind them.

Gavin glanced over his shoulder, reeling, struggling to accept what he'd just been told. He found his voice. "Carly's still out there somewhere. They got separated outside their hotel."

Tris's gaze shot to Autumn, his expression taut. "Where was the last place someone saw her?"

"Exiting the front of the hotel." She looked up at Gavin.

He jerked her hands from his shirt, turned her by the

shoulders and gave her a push toward the guards at the door. "Go. *Go*," he repeated when she opened her mouth to argue. "I'll find her."

He couldn't look at her, couldn't think straight right now, but there was a completely new level of urgency and fear spreading through his gut as he faced his twin while removing his weapon holster. Carrying it into the mess outside was just asking for trouble. He had to leave it behind.

Tris mirrored his actions.

Carly was out there alone, and they had to get to her. Nothing else mattered. "Ready?"

"Yeah."

Without a word he left Autumn standing there and took off running back down the stairs with Tris hard on his heels.

EIGHTEEN

Autumn's hands flew up to cover her mouth as she watched Gavin and Tristan run back toward the stairs leading to the lobby. She was shaking, sick to her stomach. Her baby was out there somewhere lost in the midst of that violent mob, the twins were about to wade straight into harm's way to find her, and she had just dropped a bomb on Gavin.

She swallowed hard, fighting back tears. What the hell was she supposed to do? She couldn't just sit here doing nothing while Carly was out there.

Gavin had given her the option to remove Carly from this situation last night. Not only had she made the wrong call there, she'd selfishly focused on herself and her own needs instead of her daughter's safety.

Gavin's reaction to her confession just now was everything she'd feared. The look on his face, the betrayal… It was another knife in her guts.

She stood unmoving outside the ballroom while dozens of people swept past her, the security team herding everyone through the double doors. She couldn't go in there. Couldn't stand the thought of being locked down inside it when Carly was still outside.

She wanted to throttle Jonas for losing her, and those security guards for manhandling her and preventing her from getting her daughter instead of helping her. But mostly she was furious with herself and sick with guilt.

Carly was *her* responsibility. She should be out there looking for her.

"Autumn."

She whirled around, blinked the scalding tears back and found Decker striding toward her. She rushed straight for him, grabbed him tight.

He caught her in surprise, took her by the shoulders to look down at her with a frown. "What's wrong?"

"Carly's missing." Her voice wobbled. "The twins just went out there to try and find her." While she was trapped in here being useless.

His gaze moved past her toward the stairs. "How long ago?"

"You j-just missed them." No way was she telling him about the rest of it. He'd find out soon enough.

He steered her toward the ballroom. "Go inside, they're going to shut the doors anytime now. Cassie," he said to someone off to the side, and for the first time she noticed the tall, woman with silver eyes and short, black hair standing nearby.

"Autumn, right?" Cassie gave her a friendly smile. "Come with me." She put a hand on Autumn's back and urged her through the ballroom doors.

Autumn opened her mouth to protest, but when she glanced back, Decker was already running in the direction the twins had gone. Her shoulders slumped. Now three quarters of the Abrams family was in mortal danger in their mission to rescue Carly, and this whole disaster was her fault.

"Come on," Cassie urged, pushing harder between Autumn's shoulder blades. "You can't stay out in the hall, and they're not going to let you out of the building now."

"I can't just sit here while—"

"They'll find her. And in the meantime, we can help find her from here."

Autumn looked at her sharply. "How?"

"By identifying her on video so we can direct them where to go." She had her phone out, hit a button and put it to her ear. "Hi. We've got a new situation. I've got Autumn with me, her daughter is lost in the crowd outside. The Abrams boys need virtual backup finding her. Can you help?" She paused a moment. Nodded. "Great. One sec." She lowered the phone so Autumn could see the screen, turned it sideways.

A woman's face appeared. She looked a little bit older than Autumn. Brunette. Hazel eyes. "Autumn, this is Ivy, our secret IT weapon," Cassie said.

Ivy. The woman Teagan idolized.

Ivy nodded, her expression calm and all business. "Hi, Autumn. What's your daughter's name?"

The woman's I-got-this demeanor took Autumn's anxiety down several notches from DEFCON one to a one-point-five. "Carly. I called 911 to report she was missing but the phone got knocked out of my hand, and I couldn't retrieve it. It's crazy out there and I have no idea where she is…" She clamped her lips together, drew in a shaky breath as new tears flooded her eyes. This was something out of her darkest nightmare.

"I can imagine. But we're going to find her." Ivy was so

calm, no hint of judgement. "Can you give me a description of her?"

She nodded, hurriedly wiped her face. *Get your shit together.* "She's twelve. Long, light red hair. About five-three." She was going to be so tall. Thanks to Gavin.

"What was she wearing?"

"I'm not sure. She was still in her pajamas when I left her, but she usually wears her pink unicorn hoodie."

"Okay, all great information." Ivy's gaze was on something else off screen, her arms moving slightly as though she was typing. "I'm bringing up various security camera feeds outside the conference center. Where was she last seen?"

Autumn had no idea how she had access to all that remotely. "Right outside our hotel." She gave the name and address, plus the cross streets.

"Excellent." She focused back on Autumn. "Are you up to this? The scenes outside are going to be stressful."

"Yes," she answered without hesitation. The security guards were shutting the doors to the ballroom. She pushed down a bubble of panic at being physically barred from getting to Carly, focusing on the task at hand. "I'll do whatever you need me to."

"I'm going to start with the feed right out front of the conference center to start. I'll sweep over the area slowly. It's chaotic out there, but Carly's hair color is a definite bonus to help us spot her."

Autumn nodded, hope swelling deep in her chest. "I'm ready." *Hurry, hurry.*

Ivy did something on her end, and Cassie's phone switched to the video feed out front. The situation hadn't calmed at all since Gavin had brought her inside. She watched the crowd intently, scanning from left to right and back to front, looking for any sign of Carly's red-gold hair.

Ivy changed cameras several times, giving them different angles. "There's Decker," Autumn said, pointing off to the side of the shot where he was hopping over a security barrier. Moments later he was swallowed by the shifting crowd. She didn't see any sign of the twins.

"One more time," Ivy said, and began all over again.

Autumn's eyes stayed glued to the screen, fighting against the fear and despair that threatened to drown her. "I don't see her." Several red-gold heads, but none of them Carly. Would she have her hood up?

"All right, I'll start moving north up the street. We'll work our way toward your hotel, circle it, and then come back south. And we'll keep looking until we find her."

Ivy's confidence calmed Autumn a little more. "Okay."

She sat in the chair Cassie indicated and took over holding the phone, angling it so they could both see along with Ivy. With the three of them monitoring the video feeds, plus the twins and Decker on the ground outside, Carly had six pairs of eyes looking for her.

It would be enough, she told herself.

It had to be enough.

∼

THE LEVEL of chaos in the street was something Gavin had only witnessed in places like Kabul or Aleppo, and both those cities had been under siege at the time. It was surreal that this was happening in Portland.

Holding up his ID, he shouted at the security agents outside the conference center to let him through. They stepped aside, and he turned sharp left, racing for the thinnest part of the crowd on the far side with Tris right behind him.

The riot police were still being pushed back from their

original position. A group of violent protesters had breached the line in one spot and were currently stuck in the midst of the crowd, swirling between the reforming cops and the more peaceful protesters trapped against the outer security perimeter. Trying to find Carly in this mess was a logistical and personal nightmare.

He was still reeling from Autumn's announcement, couldn't afford to get caught up in his head and lose focus out here, but it was damned near impossible to stop thinking about it. Carly could be anywhere between here and their hotel, which was still burning. There were tens of thousands of people in the streets, the peaceful and violent all mixed up together in a roiling, confusing mass, with pockets of violence and destruction happening all over the city center.

"Abrams, what the hell's going on?" Ryder's stern voice said in Gavin's earpiece.

He didn't reply because there was nothing he could say that would justify what he was doing. Nothing except that he was on a mission to rescue his daughter, and as he'd just found out five minutes ago and was still struggling to comprehend it, he wasn't ready to announce it to anyone else.

Moving at a dead sprint, he waved an arm in warning and shouted at the people ahead of him at the first concrete barrier to get out of his way. They backed up slightly, creating a small gap, and stood wide-eyed as he vaulted the barrier and plunged past them into the crowd.

It was like hitting a brick wall. He slammed into several people at the same time, gritted his teeth as he found his footing and kept pushing forward. Even here on the perimeter of the crowd it was tight. He was going to have to fight his way through the shifting mass with every step, and he had no idea where he was going, other than toward the burning hotel.

"Gav, slow down," Tris yelled behind him, his voice

nearly swallowed by the collective noise engulfing them from every direction.

He couldn't slow down. Didn't so much as spare his twin a backward glance as he kept plowing onward while scanning the area for anyone that remotely resembled Carly. She was so little, could so easily be crushed or trampled out here.

"Hey!" someone shouted in objection when he shoved them aside, and threw an elbow.

It slammed into Gavin's shoulder, glanced off his jaw, hard enough to snap his head back. He grunted and stumbled sideways onto one knee, knocking over two people in the process.

"Fuck you, asshole," another guy yelled at him, grabbing him by the front of his shirt while Gavin was busy deflecting a boot coming at his head.

He braced for the punch, his hand balled into a fist to return the favor. Before the blow landed, the hand gripping his shirt was ripped away, and the man was thrown backward.

A strong hand locked around the shoulder strap of Gavin's vest and yanked him upright. He glanced up to find Decker holding him, his face a hard mask. "You good?"

"Yeah," Gavin said, looking around. "Where's—"

"Right behind me."

Gavin glanced past him and saw Tristan battling his way to them. But there was no time to stop and regroup. "Let's go."

"We'll never find her in this together. We need to split up and fan out, cover more area," Tris said, breathing hard as his head swiveled around.

He was right. But that also meant they would all be that much more vulnerable wading through this shit show alone. "Okay. We split up and go as far as their hotel. We'll RV there if we haven't found her before then," Gavin said.

"Yeah, copy," Decker muttered, his tone and expression making it clear that while he didn't like it, he agreed it was the best chance of finding Carly.

"I'll take the east side of the street," Gavin said. It was the riskiest location, involving him fighting his way through the angry mob clear across the street to get there. But Carly was *his* responsibility.

He went in that direction, leaving his brothers to go in theirs.

"Gavin, you copy?"

He was surprised to hear Ivy's voice in his earpiece. She wasn't part of their team this weekend, although maybe Walker had brought her on unofficially. "Yeah, go."

"The crowd's thinning to your two o'clock, eighty meters or so."

Might as well be a mile away in this mess, but he was grateful for the help. Ivy must have eyes on the security feeds in the area. "Roger."

"I've got Autumn and Cassie helping me search for Carly on the video feeds, but I'll direct you as you go."

He was glad Autumn was involved in the rescue effort. Now that the initial shock of her news had worn off, he was operating on pure instinct. He couldn't imagine how hard it was for her to be locked inside when Carly was out here alone, somewhere between here and the burning hotel.

He tried to imagine how a twelve-year-old would react to the situation, what Carly might do. Had she tried to look for Autumn, been swept up in the crowd and carried forward into the street with the momentum? Or had she managed to hang back close to the hotel somehow to wait for her?

Either way she had to be fucking terrified right now, and Autumn was distraught. And as someone who had just found out he was a parent—Jesus, he was a father—he was experiencing a whole new level of fear.

He had to find Carly and keep her safe, no matter what.

The battle to reach the far side of the crowd was exhausting. He was only ten meters or so from the edge of the street when the crowd suddenly surged to the left, knocking dozens of people off their feet and taking him with them.

A body under him cushioned his fall. The woman's scream nearly pierced his eardrum.

Cursing under his breath, he scrambled to his feet and threw out a forearm to protect them both, blocking an elbow strike from the person flailing next to him. Someone else bounced off his back as he turned and aimed for the spot Ivy had indicated.

Something heavy glanced off his right upper arm and clipped the edge of his lower lip. He tasted blood. A second later, another projectile grazed his eyebrow as it flew past his face, slicing it open.

He wiped the blood out of his eye, didn't stop. Wouldn't stop until he found Carly and got her to safety.

She was his. As incredible as it seemed, Carly was his daughter.

I'm coming, squirt. I'm coming.

He would save her or die trying.

NINETEEN

Carly darted a fearful glance around her, heart pounding so hard against the inside of her ribs it made her feel sick. She was trapped in the moving mass of people surging into the street, unable to stop or get free.

All around her, people were yelling and pushing and shoving. Cars and piles of trash were burning on the street, filling the air with smoke that blew in her face when the breeze shifted.

She coughed and squinted, couldn't see what was in front of them or where they were going, only knew that she was slowly being swept farther and farther away from the hotel and her mom.

Instinctively she pressed close to the people in front of her, a group of adults who all seemed as confused as she felt, huddling there and making herself as small as possible. It scared her that no one seemed to know what was happening, that they were all afraid too, and no one was in charge. Even the police couldn't make it stop.

She had lost sight of the man—Jonas—who had come to

her room to get her almost as soon as they had reached the bottom of the staircase in the hotel. She'd looked everywhere in the crowd for her mom or him, but the police had forced everyone away from the hotel because of the fire.

Another burst of fear ripped through her, triggering the burn of tears. How was she going to find her mom now?

An arm looped around her shoulders. She looked up to find a lady frowning down at her in concern. "What are you doing out here by yourself? Where's your mom or dad?" the woman yelled over the noise. A mix of angry voices, drums, whistles, and shouts that came from every direction.

"I don't know," Carly said, her voice wobbling as a huge lump filled her throat.

She was so scared. Being stuck out here in this huge, unstable crowd felt more dangerous than being back in the hotel even with the fire. Smoke from it continued to drift through the air, stinging her eyes and throat.

The woman pulled her closer and craned her neck to look around. "There's a policeman over there," she said, then turned to yell at the others around them as she moved Carly slightly to the right. "There's a little girl here. Let us through!" She turned them and tried to guide Carly to the right. "It's okay, sweetheart. I'll get you to the policeman, and he'll help you find your parents. Okay? Now hold on tight and don't let go."

Carly nodded and pressed herself close to her, clenching the woman's waistband so tight her fingers ached. Several more adults near them tried to stop and put their arms out to block people behind them and give them room to move, but were quickly shoved forward by the force of the crowd.

Carly and the woman stumbled. Someone caught Carly by the back of her hoodie and pulled her upright before she hit the ground. She staggered forward a step and choked back a sob, struggling to hold onto the woman's waistband, afraid that if she lost her grip she would never get out of this.

She wanted her mom. Wanted this nightmare to be over right *now*.

"It's okay," the woman repeated over the din, but Carly didn't believe her. "Let us through!" she yelled, the shrill edge of fear in her voice making Carly's stomach cramp.

She wanted to shut her eyes but was too scared to risk it, ducked her head instead because looking around just made everything seem worse.

Before they'd moved more than a few feet, a loud roar went up from somewhere nearby in the crowd. Then high-pitched screams ripped through the air. Carly tensed, then the tightly packed mass of people moved around them like a whirlpool, swirling and shifting, sucking them in deeper toward the center.

Carly hid her face against the woman's back, struggling to stay upright, gritting her teeth against a scream of terror as she was mashed from behind and both sides. Panic exploded through her, a bone-deep terror that she was about to be crushed to death.

Big arms wrapped around her from behind, breaking her hold on the waistband and jerking her away from the woman. "Get on my shoulders, quick!" a man shouted.

He boosted her up before she could argue. Carly grabbed hold of his shirt as he struggled to get her seated on his shoulders, his hands wrapped around her legs to hold her steady.

She crouched over his head, looking around frantically. She could see over the crowd now, but the view before her made the lump stuck in her throat swell.

A sea of people spread out as far as she could see in every

direction, everyone caught in the confusing, disorganized mass. Some were fighting. Others were trying to flee. All of them were trapped like her.

"Do you see a cop close by?" the man shouted up at her. The woman who had helped her was somehow still beside them, one hand on Carly's leg, eyes full of fear, her mouth pinched.

"That way," Carly shouted back, pointing to the left to the only officer she could see. He wasn't close by, but he was on a horse off to the side of the street. She couldn't be sure, but he looked trapped too, except the crowd seemed to melt away when the horse moved into it.

The man carrying her turned in the direction she indicated and began fighting his way through the crowd while she clung to the fabric of his shirt to keep her balance. She was still afraid, terrified she would fall off and be trampled, but with her eyes locked on the mounted policeman, she felt a burst of hope. If she could just get to him, maybe he could help her find her mom.

∼

DAN'S PULSE pounded in his ears as he took in the rapidly deteriorating situation around him. A thin rivulet of blood trickled down into his eyes from a cut beneath the balaclava.

He ripped it off, wiped his bleeding forehead and kept pushing forward with grim determination. The city center was a veritable war zone. He and the other protesters were showing those bastards just how much contempt and rage they had for them and their narcissistic, elitist agenda.

But at some point over the last few minutes they had begun to lose their momentum. Their headlong charge toward the line of cops had been brought almost to a halt by another line moving in behind the first at the last second.

They had stalled, were now at risk of being driven backward at any moment if they didn't punch through the lines before the cops could reform farther south, between his position and the conference center.

"Gas! Gas!"

He saw the cannisters arcing into the crowd. Puffs of tear gas rose up from the ground. Cries echoed around him as the crowd suddenly halted and tried to scatter, retreating in blind panic.

Dan sucked in one last clear breath. He closed his eyes and leaned his weight forward onto the balls of his feet, hands outstretched in front of him in an attempt to hold off the wave of humanity now coming back at him and the others.

"We're not stopping! Come on!" the young guy that had led their charge bellowed from just ahead of him.

Dan kept pushing. Held his breath as long as he could, then risked opening his eyes a fraction. Shit, a thin veil of gas hung in the air. There was no avoiding it.

Pain seared his eyes as the gas made contact with the moisture there and in his nose. Then his starving lungs finally gave out, and he was forced to suck in a breath. Fire scorched his throat, his lungs tightening.

He doubled over, coughing, wiping at his streaming eyes. People were still trying to scatter. He could feel the tide turning around him. But he had been gassed plenty of times in the military and refused to back down now. He wasn't a fucking coward.

Through burning, tear-drenched eyes, he saw the blurry line of cops waiting ahead with their shields and batons and the handful of protesters who were still trying to push forward. The tear gas was thinning now. He just had to grit his teeth and hold on until the worst was over. If they got past the cops, the air would be clearer.

Dan focused inward, letting all the bitterness and rage he'd carried all these years settle deep in his gut. It was fuel. Nourishment for his anguished soul. The time had come for him to lead.

The hair on the back of his neck stood up. He opened his mouth, let out a war cry, and blindly rushed forward, cutting through the retreating crowd. Tears continued to stream down his face, blinding him, intensifying the pain.

But he wouldn't stop. Would never stop until they made him.

Others joined in on his left and right, heading for the enemy line standing between them and their ultimate goal.

More of the crowd merged with them, enraged by the tear gas. The line of charging protesters ahead of him crashed into a wall of shields and batons, seemed to melt as men ducked and raised their arms over their heads to protect themselves. Dan clenched his jaw and punched through a slight gap that opened in the line where cops were busy beating at other protesters.

"Go, go!" someone yelled behind him, planting a hand in the middle of his back to help propel him forward.

Dan put on a burst of speed, struggling to see, gagging from the gas. Another group of riot cops appeared in front of him out of nowhere, blocking his path.

He skidded to a halt, unable to move left or right through the retreating crowd. Seeing the new line of cops, the men around him turned and fled, leaving him standing there alone.

Before he could move, in unison the cops zeroed in on him and started forward.

Cold slid down his spine as he tried to take a step back, only to be stopped by a river of people rushing past him. He was trapped. About to be beaten like a dog in the street and dragged away in cuffs.

Blinking fast, heart and mind racing, he glanced around, desperately searching for a way out.

Above the sea of moving heads behind him, he spotted his chance in the form of a young girl perched on someone's shoulders.

TWENTY

"At your one o'clock, eighty meters," Ivy said.

"How sure are you this time?" Gavin panted.

They'd hit so many dead ends already and he couldn't keep going on like this, constantly battling his way through this angry, panic-stricken mob. He had no idea where his brothers were now, but they'd been out here fighting through the masses for almost forty minutes without a single positive ID on Carly.

He was soaked with sweat, his lip still bleeding, and the cops were deploying tear gas. Clouds of it drifted on the air, mixing with smoke whenever the breeze shifted.

It hadn't reached him yet, but it would soon enough, and then every mucous membrane and every single inch of sweaty skin would feel like a flamethrower had opened up on him, making it damned near impossible to breathe or see.

He only had a few minutes before it happened, if that. They had to find Carly before then.

"One o'clock," Ivy insisted.

He shoved aside the sense of hopelessness starting to creep into the back of his mind. Fuck that. He would keep battering his way through this crowd until he dropped from exhaustion, and then he would fucking crawl on his hands and knees to get to Carly if need be.

"Copy."

He spun around once again, shouldered through a cluster of several dozen people huddled together between him and the location Ivy had just indicated. Beyond them through the shifting smoke and crowd ahead he spotted a flash of red hair, but when he got closer saw that it was a young woman.

"It's not her," he said, breathing hard, disappointment hitting.

More pockets of gas appeared amongst the groups of protesters still filling the street. The area he and his brothers were trying to cover wasn't that big, but the density of the crowd along with the fires and the protesters battling with cops had turned it into a nightmare. Every meter he gained felt like a hundred.

"Copy."

This wasn't working, and they were almost out of time. One shift of the breeze, and he'd be practically blind. If they hadn't had a single sighting of her yet, then it likely meant she hadn't reached this point yet. "She's got to be farther north."

"Gav!"

He twisted his head around to see Tristan wading his way toward him. They both moved for the edge of the crowd where the concentration of bodies was thinnest. Trying to fight through the thick of it was slow and exhausting, like moving through quicksand with weights on his feet.

"Where's Deck?" Gavin asked.

Tris shook his head, soaked with sweat and trying to catch his breath. "Dunno. But the gas is gonna be a bitch."

"Yep," he said grimly. The thought of Carly out here

somewhere, alone and terrified, was like a knife in his guts. He drew in a sharp breath, felt a burn at the backs of his eyeballs that had nothing to do with tear gas. "Fuck. Fuck."

Tris did a double-take, stared at him. "Hey, we'll find her."

It's not that.

He shook his head, clenched his jaw, struggling to keep a lid on all the emotions roiling inside him. Tris was literally his other half, the person who understood him the best, and the one he trusted most in this world. But he didn't know.

Gavin had to say it, or explode.

"She's mine, Tris," he rasped out, his voice barely carrying over the barrage of sound engulfing them.

Tris frowned at him. "Who?"

"Carly. Autumn just told me."

"What the *hell*?" Tris said, throwing out an arm to block a punch meant for someone else when a scuffle broke out next to them. They were both already pummeled to hell, would likely have been nursing broken ribs if not for the Kevlar vests under their dress shirts. "Are you for real? Is that even a possibility?"

"Yeah." On both counts. Forty-five minutes ago he would have said no way. Autumn had seemed completely convinced, but was there any way she could be wrong?

Tris shot him a quick, are-you-fucking-shitting-me look, then went back to scanning the crowd. "When did she tell you?"

"Outside the ballroom."

"Holy fuck."

Gavin didn't answer. Felt like he was still in shock as he looked across the seething sea of humanity between them and the burning hotel still two blocks away. Flames were shooting from the east side and roof, the fire crews only just beginning to deploy now that the crowd had finally been moved far enough away to let them work.

Gavin's stomach sank. There were tens of thousands of people out here, too many of them bent on violence. If Ivy couldn't spot Carly on any of the video feeds, how in hell were he, Tris, and Decker supposed to find her on the ground in the middle of this shit storm?

"Come on." Tris grabbed hold of his upper arm, started towing him back toward the edge of the street. Everywhere he looked, people were running around in complete chaos with no idea what was happening and nowhere to go. It was fucking insane. "When the hell did you guys get together?" Tris demanded, still scanning.

He'd held the secret inside for so long, but now he was bursting with it. Trying to make sense of what had happened, while simultaneously scanning for any sign of Carly and hoping for more direction from Ivy. "Prom night. It was a one-time thing, and we never talked about it again."

They were forced to stop and fend off three guys coming at them with bricks. With a few well-aimed elbow strikes, he and Tris knocked the bricks from their hands, then kicked their feet out from under them, sprawling them on their asses before quickly moving past. The violence these pricks had started had unleashed this entire thing.

Tris kept heading for the side of the street. "What about the guy she said was the father?"

"I don't know." He had so many questions. Wanted answers to every single one, but— "We have to find her, Tris." He would have given his life to protect Carly even before he'd found out. Now… He wanted to burn down everything and everyone keeping him from her.

"We will. We won't stop until we do." Tris spotted someone, lifted an arm in greeting. "There's Deck."

Gavin followed his twin's gaze to find their elder brother angling his way through the crowd toward them. "Not a word to him, Tris. I don't want anyone else knowing until we get Carly back and I straighten everything out with Autumn." Their family dynamic wasn't exactly traditional. Deck saw himself as the head of the family and a father figure rather than a sibling and was a total hardass. Gavin couldn't take a lecture from him right now about Autumn on top of everything else.

"Yeah, course," Tris promised.

The three of them met near the edge of the crowd, moving to a moderately secure spot to look around from their new vantage point. "Nothing more from Ivy?" Deck asked, his chest heaving, face streaked with smoke, blood, and sweat.

Gavin shook his head, battled to hold it together as he imagined Carly crushed in that volatile crowd, or trampled while she choked on the gas, blind and unable to breathe as she cried for Autumn. *Fuck.*

"Ten o'clock, sixty meters," Ivy suddenly said.

Gavin's head snapped around, his gaze zeroing in on the location Ivy mentioned…right in the middle of the worst of the crush.

Pockets of gas drifted up and dispersed among the crowd, people staggering around covering their face and hands as the riot cops pushed the wall of people steadily back. His heart hitched. "Can you verify anything about the target?"

"Red hair in a ponytail, and she's wearing a pink hoodie. Someone's got her on their shoulders. Autumn's sure it's her."

Raw adrenaline punched through him. He'd seen Carly wearing her favorite pink unicorn hoodie just two days ago when they'd flown the kite at the beach. "Copy. Moving to intercept." He surged forward without stopping to consult with his brothers, not wanting to waste even a second, pulse thudding hard as he forced his way back into the churning crowd.

Less than ten meters in, a slight gap opened up in front of him and he spotted a red ponytail and the unicorn on the back of her hoodie. "Carly!"

She disappeared behind a cloud of smoke, pockets of gas drifting all around her.

A superhuman burst of strength punched through him, electrifying his tired muscles. He plowed through the crowd like a bulldozer, mowing down everyone in his path. Oblivious of the knocks and blows he sustained. Unaware of where his brothers were, his focus narrowed to the spot where he'd just seen Carly.

The veil of smoke lifted slightly, revealing the complete scene before him. His stomach plummeted like a concrete block as he realized Carly was now trapped between the second line of riot police and the violent mob attacking them.

TWENTY-ONE

Carly's fingers were numb from being locked around fistfuls of the man's shirt. The violence happening all around them was getting worse, they were still trapped, and the police were too far away to help her.

A loud pop ahead made her jump. White smoke drifted up from the ground.

"Shit. Honey, close your eyes and cover your nose and mouth with your sweatshirt. Don't open them until I say," the man told her, spinning around hard to move away from the smoke.

The stress in his voice sent a new streak of terror through her. People near the smoke were screaming and coughing, and some looked like they were choking before they fell over.

Before she could force her frozen fingers to release his shirt, she spotted another man nearby in the crowd. Bearded, dirty face. He was coming toward them fast, and the frightening look on his face, the way he seemed to be staring right at her, sent a chill down her spine.

She slammed her eyes shut, let go of her rescuer's shirt with one hand, and pulled the neck of her hoodie up over her mouth and nose, covering it with her forearm for good measure. But the smoke must have gotten to the man carrying her because he started coughing and doubled over.

She stifled a shriek as she began to tip forward, opened her eyes without thinking. The strange man emerged out of the crowd and grabbed her. Yanked her off the man's shoulders before she fell.

Carly grabbed onto him, at first thinking he was trying to help her. But then he whipped her around so that her back was plastered to his chest, locking one arm across her chest and the other around her throat.

She tried to scream, but the smoke got into her eyes and mouth. It burned like hot pepper juice, way worse than the time she'd accidentally rubbed them with jalapeno-stained fingers after making salsa.

She bucked and thrashed her head back and forth, clawed at his arms, trying to escape the man and the choking smoke. But his arms across her throat and chest were like iron, the pressure relentless, making it impossible to breathe.

"Stop it," the man snarled, jerking her harder against him as he tried to force his way through the crowd.

She couldn't see, kept her burning eyes shut as tears poured down her cheeks, coughing spasms ripping through her. She couldn't breathe. Couldn't think, the panic taking over, her body writhing.

The man suddenly stilled, his whole body going rigid.

"Let her go, Dan," a muffled voice called out close by.

Through stinging eyes, Carly squinted at the blurry outline of someone wearing a gas mask standing in their way.

DAN FOUGHT TO hold onto his young insurance policy as TJ blocked their way. The girl was skinny but putting up one hell of a fight, even after being dosed with a bit of gas. The ongoing effects from his own exposure were making it even harder to maintain his grip on her.

His eyes still burned like hellfire, every breath like sucking hot fumes into his lungs despite the air clearing. The cops were only a short distance behind him and getting closer every moment. He had to act fast, get the hell beyond their reach and then dump the girl so he could disappear.

Escape was gonna be even tougher now that he'd taken off the balaclava, but he knew guys down at the docks who would help him. He just needed to buy a bit of time, stay off grid for a while, maybe up in the mountains until the heat was off.

But first he had to get past TJ, who was standing between Dan and his freedom. His face was hidden by a gasmask but that hard, clear stare pinned him through the lenses of the goggles.

"Let her go," TJ repeated without budging.

"Get outta my way, man," Dan warned, pivoting to move around him, his skin prickling in warning.

He liked TJ. Didn't want to fight him, and didn't plan to hurt the girl. She was merely a means to an end to help him escape. But he wasn't fucking around, didn't have time for this, and would do whatever he had to in order to protect himself.

"Let her go. She's an innocent kid caught up in this shit."

Dan couldn't let her go. Not yet. She was his only currency to keep the cops at bay if they kept coming after him, and they were way too close. They had been trying to nail him for something for a while now.

"I don't want to fight you, brother," he warned, quickly moving a step or two to the right. "But I need her, because I'm not letting them take me."

TJ didn't move.

Desperation began to take hold, making him twitchy. He could feel the fucking cops bearing down on him, closing in. His nerve endings crawled with it, his inner radar screaming that he had to bug out *now*. "Fucking *move*!"

"Not until you let her go." TJ spread out his arms as if to corral him, and took a menacing step forward.

Blinking his watering eyes, Dan gritted his teeth and balled his right hand into a fist, planting his feet in preparation to take a swing. If he had to throw hands at TJ here and now to get clear, then so be it.

A tear gas cannister landed less than ten feet away.

Oh, shit— He spun away, bracing for another wave of pain. Stumbled over someone's foot.

An instant later, TJ slammed into him like a fucking linebacker. Dan flew sideways from the impact, lost his grip on the girl as he automatically threw out his hands to break his fall.

She was ripped from his grasp even before he hit the ground. He shot to his knees, tried to push to his feet and run for it, but the gas was already swirling through the air.

He choked. Rage exploded through him with the pain. Fucking pigs! He struggled to his feet. Blindly staggered several steps before strong hands seized him from behind.

"Get on your knees, now!" a deep voice boomed. A cop.

Dan refused to go down without a fight. He lashed out with his remaining strength, threw an elbow and slammed his boot into a leg, battling for his freedom.

A hard blow across the back of the head made him bellow in mingled fury and pain. His knees hit the pavement, and then they were all over him, pinning him on his belly and mashing the side of his face into the pavement as they wrenched his hands behind his back.

"Fuck you," he snarled through bared teeth, tasting blood as he strained under the weight holding him in place.

The cuffs went around his wrists. Plastic flex ties digging deep.

He went rigid as mingled shock and denial slammed into him. Struggling to comprehend that this was really happening. That he had lost, without even getting within striking distance of the conference center.

His vision blurred. He struggled to breathe through the fiery pain in his lungs as they yanked him upright and began dragging him away. He hung in their grasp like a deadweight, knowing any further resistance was futile and wanting to make their job as difficult as possible.

They kept dragging him away, battered and bleeding. Broken inside.

The bitter, ironic laugh that bubbled up turned into a suffocating coughing fit. He bucked and twisted as it tore through him, but the cops never slowed their steps.

The corrupt government had won yet again. And once again he was the loser.

But the ultimate irony was that at least behind prison bars, he would have a bed and three meals a day while he served out his sentence, courtesy of the corrupt government he'd served so faithfully until today.

TWENTY-TWO

Rage punched through Gavin. Some asshole had grabbed Carly in a fucking chokehold and was using her as a human shield to evade the cops coming at him.

His heart and lungs felt like they were about to explode as he plunged through the panicking mass of people preventing him from getting to Carly, his gaze locked on her small figure as she flickered in and out of view through the swirling, tightly-packed crowd.

"Gav, you got him?" Ivy said in his earpiece.

"Yeah." The fucking coward was still holding her in front of him. Carly was fighting like hell to get away from him. Gavin was going to break his face for it.

It looked like most of the violent protesters were on the run now, but the cops continued to lob more tear gas cannisters into the seething mass anyway, pushing everyone farther back. Gavin's chest tightened as one of them detonated near Carly.

He put on a burst of speed, his thighs and arms burning as he shoved and pushed people aside, bulldozing his way to

Carly, bracing for the moment the gas hit him. "Carly!" She was still fighting the guy, trying to get free.

The asshole stumbled. Went down.

Gavin was less than fifty feet from her when suddenly a guy in a gas mask grabbed her and took off in the opposite direction. "No!" Gavin shouted, his voice drowned out by the wall of noise surrounding him. His eyes began to burn suddenly, his vision blurring from the tear production.

He cursed and swiped at his eyes, squinted to try and minimize the effects of the gas, but it was useless. He lost visual on her. *Fuck!* "Ivy, you got her?" They couldn't fucking lose her again. Not now, when he was so close.

"Looking for a different camera. Stand by."

He couldn't afford this holdup, Carly was—

"Suspect moving north, northwest. Thirty meters from you and gaining."

Gavin's watery gaze panned over the crowd as he struggled to focus his view. "Got him." He locked his jaw, watched in helpless frustration as the man cut through the crowd carrying Carly.

They vanished for a moment, then appeared through a gap that opened. The man jumped behind a concrete barrier with her and disappeared from view completely.

Hot, blinding rage swept through Gavin. He flung people out of his way, grunted at every blow that rained down on him from rocks and bottles and whatever else the protesters were hurling at the cops.

After an agonizing delay, he finally made it to the thigh-high concrete barrier. In one move, he planted his palms on the top, vaulted it, and landed on both feet on the other side, prepared to chase the bastard down and pummel him.

Instead, he jerked to a stop so sudden that he stumbled and had to catch his balance. Blinking his burning, tearing eyes, he took in the scene before him. Dozens of people were taking shelter against the barrier, including the man who had taken Carly.

The stranger was lying prone as he stretched out on top of her, his arms curled protectively around her head. Literally shielding her with his own body. His gas mask was gone, replaced by a bandana over his nose and mouth that would do nothing to mitigate the gas. He squinted up at Gavin through red, swollen, and watery eyes, unmoving.

The end of Carly's red ponytail trailed out across the pavement beneath him. "Carly!"

Her head jerked up. The gas mask hid her face, but her muffled response was clear. "Gavvy!"

Gavin lunged over, dropped to his knees as the guy sat up on his haunches to let her up, and grabbed Carly. He wrapped her up tight in his arms, crushed her to him and shut his eyes, burying his face in her hair while coughs wracked him.

Fuck. Just…holy fuck.

Her thin little arms were wrapped around his neck. He fought to get his shit together, ordered himself to calm down. "Hey, squirt."

She hugged him harder, and his heart nearly imploded.

Mine.

The protective, primal thought triggered a rush of goosebumps all over his body, the tidal wave of relief that crashed over him so powerful it left him dizzy.

"Gav, you're out of range, I don't have a visual on you. Do you have her?" Ivy said.

"Yeah. I got her." And goddamn that felt good to say. "She's okay."

"That's great news. What's the plan?"

"Gimme a minute." He took another moment to hold her

tight, then eased the pressure and shifted her in his hold. "You okay?" he asked close to her ear.

She nodded and kept clinging, little coughing spasms wracking her. She didn't seem hurt, but the gas would be burning her like a bitch, and he wasn't going to remove the mask to check her face for injury.

He glanced around them, taking in all the frightened people huddled behind the line of concrete, too afraid to move. And the guy who had carried Carly over here was gone.

Gavin scanned the vicinity. This spot was better than being in the middle of the crush, but it still wasn't safe enough. He needed to get her inside the security of the conference center until this was over. And that meant battling his way back the way he'd come while carrying her.

Tris hopped the barricade with Decker. "Hey." The two of them came to stand guard over them, breathing hard, eyes red and streaming. "She okay?" Tris asked, wiping an eye with his shoulder.

Gavin stroked a hand over the top of her head. "Think so." Physically, hopefully fine once the gas wore off. Emotionally and mentally, likely not. God, what she'd been through today.

"We can't stay here with her," Decker said, glancing around in concern. "Still way too unstable."

"I know." He eased Carly away from him.

Tris knelt down to smile at her. "Hey, Carls. How are you, kid?"

Carly flung her arms around his neck in answer. While Tris cradled her, Gavin quickly ripped off his dress shirt and removed his Kevlar vest beneath it, leaving him in only a white T-shirt.

"Just gonna put this on you to protect you more, okay

squirt?" He slid it over her head and the gas mask, did up the Velcro straps as tight as they could go, but it still hung off her little frame.

She sat still as a doll, her fear palpable. "Do we have to go back through there?"

"It's not safe here, sweetheart. We're going to take you to the conference center where your mom is waiting for you. And this time you've got all of us to look after you."

"That's right," Tris said with a reassuring smile, giving her ponytail a gentle tug. "All three of us as your very own personal security detail. People pay us big bucks for that kind of protection, but for you we'll do it for free."

Gavin tapped his earpiece, mentally gearing up for this next part of the mission. "Ivy, we're taking Carly to the conference center. Can you get us help?" The three of them gave her a decent level of protection, but law enforcement might be able to make the return trip a lot easier if they knew they were coming.

"On it."

He checked the vest one last time, giving the Velcro tabs another tug. It was way too big but better than nothing, and would at least protect her torso and internal organs if anything hit her. He would protect her head with his arms. "You ready?"

Carly hesitated a second, but nodded. He bent and scooped her up, pushing to his feet with Tris's help. "Just close your eyes and hold on, we'll have you inside with your mom in no time," he told her, bringing her to his chest and urging her legs around his waist.

She immediately locked her ankles at the small of his back and wound her arms around his neck, burrowing in close. His heart squeezed painfully. *Sweet baby.* "All right, let's get outta here."

He slid over the barrier, kept his back to the crowd as he edged his way along the perimeter. His brothers stayed glued to him, Deck out front like a human icebreaker slicing a path through the mob, and Tris protecting his right side.

A few bottles and rocks pelted them. Gavin angled his body to shield Carly more, set his jaw as they slammed into his unprotected side. But he'd take the pain gladly as long as Carly was safe. He would protect her with his last breath.

She didn't move, didn't lessen the grip of her arms and legs and kept the gas mask buried in the crook of his neck while he carried her. "It's okay," he told her, pain streaking along his ribs.

"Feds know your situation," Ivy said. "They've alerted the riot squad and will look for you."

Good. "Copy. Cops know we're coming," he told his brothers.

"Almost to them," Decker called out. "Thirty meters."

Gavin caught something flying at him in his watery peripheral vision an instant before it slammed into his ribs. He grunted, sucked in a breath as pain streaked along his side, hunching over Carly more. Mother*fucker*.

"Cops are coming to us," Tris announced.

Thank Christ.

Twenty seconds later, a wall of tactical officers surrounded them, forming a protective canopy with their shields. Their moving shelter escorted them as far as the first security barrier, more projectiles bouncing off their shields.

Gavin was sweating and sucking in air by the time they finally reached the heavily guarded entrance to the conference center, his side throbbing from the deep bruise forming there.

Callum and Ryder were waiting for them at the doors, armed with bottles of water. Gavin staggered past them and carried his precious bundle inside with a profound sense of relief and gratitude that she was safe now and the worst was over.

The moment the doors closed behind them his adrenaline level ebbed.

"It's all over," he told Carly, pausing to remove the gas mask from her face. When those red-rimmed green eyes startlingly like his own focused on him, he gave her a reassuring smile, his throat tight. "Hey, squirt."

Safe. This was his baby girl, and she was safe.

"*Carly*!"

They both looked up. Autumn was racing toward them down the wide corridor, blond hair streaming behind her, her face a tortured mix of emotions as she ran straight for their daughter.

TWENTY-THREE

Autumn flew across the polished tile floor, her heart racing a million miles an hour as her entire world narrowed down to only her daughter.

Gavin set her on her feet, and Carly ran toward her. "Mom!"

Autumn grabbed her and lifted her off her feet, clutching her as close as possible. Relief crashed over her so hard her knees went weak. She sank to the floor and sat there on her knees, burying her face in Carly's hair as she rocked her baby back and forth.

The dam that had been holding back the tears finally burst. They poured out freely, shaking her whole body with the force of her sobs.

Carly was okay. Against all odds, Gavin had brought her back safely, but when Autumn thought of how close she'd come to losing her…

She shuddered, felt like a giant fist squeezed her heart when she registered the feel of Carly's arms locked around her shoulders. Carly wasn't a clinger, had been pulling away more and more recently, didn't want to be cuddled or hugged much, so this told Autumn just how scared her baby had been.

"Oh, God, thank you. Thank you, thank you," she breathed through her tears, struggling to get a grip on herself.

"We need to wash the gas off her," a huge man with red-gold hair said, kneeling beside them. "Tip your head back, sweetheart," he said to Carly, who did as she was told and closed her eyes.

While Autumn held her, he carefully poured the water over her face several times, then used a cloth to wipe at her eyes, nose, and mouth. "Better?"

Carly nodded, blinking as Autumn helped dry her face.

"Need to do your hands too, and then you have to change your clothes, okay? And have a shower as soon as you can to wash your hair and make sure you get any residue off you."

"'kay," Carly said, holding out her hands for him to pour water on. Autumn helped clean them, vaguely aware that out of the corner of her eye Gavin, Tristan and Decker were all rinsing their faces too.

"Okay, you're good to go, young lady." The big man squeezed her shoulder and stood.

Autumn hugged her close, resting her cheek on the top of her head. A moment later, strong hands slid under her arms from behind. "You both need to get back into the ballroom now."

Gavin. He helped lift her to her feet, steadied her when she wobbled under Carly's weight.

Shit, she was still shaking all over, her nervous system's violent reaction to the whiplash of emotions coursing through her. But she wasn't letting go of Carly for anything.

Her body was on autopilot as he turned her and ushered her down the hall. "It's okay," she said to Carly between sniffles, but maybe it was more to herself.

The guilt and fear over what might have happened were still eating her alive. She should never have entrusted Carly's safety to someone else. She should have stood her ground and fought tooth and nail against the hotel security until she made it up to their room to get her herself. "It's okay now."

Gavin hurried them up the carpeted stairs, practically lifting them both on the way. Autumn kept Carly locked to her, a wave of dizziness making the staircase tilt as her heart finally began to slow. She was in a kind of daze, felt a sense of surprise when all of a sudden they were standing in front of the ballroom and the guards were opening the doors for them.

A hush fell over the crowd when they entered. Ignoring all the curious stares inside the packed room, she made her way over to a clear spot and set Carly down, kneeling in front of her to cup her daughter's face in her hands.

Carly's face was so pale the freckles across her nose stood out sharply. Her eyes were red and swollen, still watering, and her skin was streaked with smoke. The elbows of her hoodie and knees of her jeans were torn, her skin scraped and bleeding underneath. But miraculously she didn't seem to have suffered any worse injuries.

"Are you hurt anywhere, sweetheart?" Her voice was rough.

Carly shook her head. "No, I'm okay, Mom. Really."

Autumn heaved out a deep breath and took her daughter's hands, squeezing tight. "Good. I'm so sorry, baby. So sorry." Only then did she clue in that Carly had a tactical vest strapped over her torn hoodie.

Hands reached down to undo the Velcro. Autumn looked up and focused on Gavin for the first time as he gently lifted the vest over Carly's head.

His face was streaked with smoke and blood, his right

eyebrow and the corner of his mouth still bleeding. He wore only a white T-shirt soaked through under the arms and across the chest and back with sweat, and smeared with grime and blood. Tristan and Decker stood a short distance behind him, looking much the same.

"Gonna need this back," Gavin said to Carly, and Autumn's heart clenched when she realized that he had put it on Carly to protect her, leaving himself completely vulnerable in the midst of that terrifying mob.

Of course he had.

His gaze shifted to Autumn, the angry red of his irritated eyes making the green irises twice as vivid. "We have to go." His expression was impossible to read, and while he didn't seem angry at her, she understood that their moment of reckoning was still to come.

Just as she also knew that things had already changed between them forever.

"Thank you," she said even though it felt completely inadequate, resisting the urge to fling her arms around him and hold on tight. He was every bit the hero she'd always imagined, had just risked his life to go after Carly and then protect her on the way back here. And so had the others.

"All of you," she said to Tristan and Decker.

"Glad she's back with you safe and sound," Tristan said with a smile. Decker didn't respond, but she hadn't expected him to. Praise or thanks of any kind made him uncomfortable.

Gavin reached out and ran a finger down the length of Carly's nose. "Okay, squirt, you stay here with your mom."

"Where are you going?" Carly asked, her face pinched with anxiety.

The soft, unguarded smile he gave her melted Autumn's insides. Did he believe that Carly was his? Could he see the resemblances now too? "Have to finish my job, squirt, but I'll see you later."

"You promise?"

"Promise." He spared Autumn a quick look, then left with his brothers.

"They'll be okay, right, Mom?" Carly asked in a small voice.

Autumn pulled her into a hug and rubbed a hand up and down her back to soothe them both. They had both been traumatized today, though in different ways. It would take a long time to get over this, and Carly would definitely need therapy. Autumn might need some too.

"Yes. They'll be fine now." She hoped.

From the moment she'd seen Gavin carrying her through the front doors, Autumn had been floating on a cloud of gratitude and relief. But now, watching Gavin walk out those doors with his brothers to confront more danger and put himself back in harm's way to protect others, there was a new weight in the pit of her stomach.

She loved him. Loved him so damned much it hurt, and it hurt even more to know that she might already have lost him forever.

TWENTY-FOUR

"You believe this shit?" Tris said to him as they stood in the main plaza of the conference center watching the Air National Guard Blackhawks flying across the city. Decker was elsewhere with his own detail.

It was mid-afternoon. The VIPs were safe. The entire CPS team on site was currently on standby waiting to find out if they were needed to assist with more rescues before taking their VIPs to a private airfield close to the city.

"Nope," Gavin said.

This whole thing felt surreal, their worst-case scenario models acted out in real time. His ribs throbbed where he'd taken a direct hit earlier, but at least there was no more tear gas in the air, and his eyes and lungs were fine again. Most important, Carly was safe. That was all that mattered.

People had the right to protest—peacefully—and this had been anything but. Innocent people had been hurt or killed in this fucking mess, and Carly had almost been one of them. Gavin had no sympathy whatsoever for the people responsible for the violence. The governor had made the right call in deploying the military.

The riots had finally been contained almost three hours ago. Numbers were still uncertain and changing by the minute, but so far hundreds of people had been arrested and removed from the area. An unknown number had been injured and at least three had died, two of them trampled in the densest part of the mob when the tear gas had been deployed, and the other from a baton blow to the head.

Now every emergency crew in the region was working alongside the military to mop up the mess. A column of dark smoke continued to rise into the clear blue sky from the roof of Autumn's hotel. The fire was still burning, the delay in response caused by the protests allowing it to spread to three floors on the east side. Four crews were on scene battling it.

"Wouldn't have believed it if I hadn't seen it with my own eyes," Tris said, shaking his head.

"Heads up," Ryder's voice said over their radios. "The charter jets have arrived, flight plans filed, and have been cleared for departure. All teams move your VIPs there immediately. Update us with your movements and ETAs."

"Copy that," Gavin answered. He let out a deep breath, winced, and put a hand to his side. His right eye was swollen almost shut, and his lower lip throbbed.

Tris had patched him up a few hours ago with some butterfly bandages. The skin around the eyebrow was thin, so he might eventually need some stitches to hold the wound together and stop it from bleeding. But he'd deal with that tomorrow back in Crimson Point if need be.

All in all, he was lucky it wasn't worse.

Tris glanced at the hand pressed to his side. "You gonna get that looked at?"

"Nah, just a bruise. Brick caught me in the ribs." He had zero regrets about taking his vest off and putting it on Carly.

They headed back into the conference center together. A

little more than an hour ago, they'd gone up to their VIP's rooms and hurriedly packed whatever was inside in anticipation for the green light to leave.

Given the number of protesters who had flooded into the city center in spite of security measures and the level of violence unleashed by some of them, the organizers of the conference had pulled the plug. Rumor was they were apparently making plans to reschedule it in a smaller, richer and more exclusive city like Vale or wherever.

"What are you gonna do about Carly and Autumn?" Tris asked him.

He'd been thinking about them nonstop since leaving them in the ballroom. "I dunno. I need to talk to Autumn, figure all this out."

He'd made it clear that he wanted a relationship with her, and Autumn knew how much he'd adored Carly before finding out the news. But he had no idea what she wanted now, or how she felt about suddenly finding out he was Carly's father.

He didn't even know *how* she'd found out. He needed answers to all the questions that had been circulating in his brain since she'd told him.

"Carly does look like you, bro."

"You mean she looks like both of us."

Tris's mouth lifted. "Yeah, but I never rode the bony express with Autumn." He grinned at the dark look Gavin shot him.

"The bony express? Where the hell did you even hear that one?"

"Come on, it's funny as shit." He sobered. "No way she would lie about something like that."

"No," he agreed. And she never would have told him if she hadn't been sure. "I think it was a shock to her too."

"She say how she found out?"

"No. But it explains why she was so twisted up when she got here." Had she ever suspected at all? Even a tiny part of her? Or wondered maybe? She'd always seemed so convinced it was the other guy.

"How do you feel about it?"

"I'm…still absorbing it."

"But you love Carly."

"Fuck, yeah, I do."

"And you still love Autumn too."

He nodded. He'd been angry and in shock at first, thinking she'd hidden it from him all this time. Now that he'd had time to process it more and wasn't in the middle of a life-and-death situation, he knew she would never do that.

"I know what you said on the beach, but Marley was right. You'd be a great dad. Will be a great dad. For what it's worth. And I'm already her favorite uncle because I'm fucking awesome, so…"

Shit, Gavin could still barely compute the dad part.

Of course, he'd thought about what his role with Carly would be like if he and Autumn entered a romantic relationship. But he'd assumed it would be like it already was, and supporting Autumn through the ups and downs of parenthood without having a ton of input since Autumn had done all the work up 'til now and Carly was her child.

All that had changed now, and the reality was hitting way differently. "Thanks," he muttered. "Now leave it alone, okay?"

"Sure."

Guards let them back into the building. They walked back to the stairs that led up to the second-floor ballroom. Inside, fewer than a hundred people were there waiting for further instructions.

"See you back on the coast?" Tris said to him.

"Yeah. Later, man." Gavin alerted Cassie that he would be leaving the conference center in the next few minutes, then picked up his VIP and escorted him out to the tunnel connecting the center to the hotel parking lot.

Cassie pulled the SUV up mere moments after they emerged through the steel door. Only two routes were currently open to traffic leaving the city center.

Cassie turned out of the underground parking and drove toward the second one, heading east away from downtown. Gavin shifted stiffly in the front passenger seat as they turned onto a feeder route, the shoulder strap of his seatbelt rubbing against his sore ribs.

The military had checkpoints set up all along the route. Their vehicle cleared the first one on the way out of the city center and another before reaching the highway. Both sides were lined with a combination of military and police vehicles in each direction.

Gavin looked in his side mirror as Cassie merged into the long line of traffic leaving the city and crawled along. Behind them, Portland's heart lay in ruins, plumes of smoke punctuating the skyline.

He and Cassie didn't speak during the drive. In the back seat, their VIP made a series of consecutive calls to other conference members. Gavin tried to block out what he was saying, not wanting to listen.

He was exhausted. Had just found out he was a father. Had almost lost his daughter. Didn't know how this was going to affect him and Autumn. Not to mention he was battered and bruised.

More than anything at the moment, he wanted this detail to be over with so he could get back to Crimson Point, have a long, hot shower and something to eat so he could settle his mind before going to talk with Autumn. He held off texting her, not knowing what else to say, and because it would be unprofessional while he was officially still on the clock with the client who had paid a shit ton of money for this detail.

Heavy traffic delayed their arrival at the private airport several miles outside of town by almost forty minutes. Gavin shoved down the impatience riding him, ruthlessly squashed the frustration that threatened to manifest itself in some road rage. Finally, they reached the turn for the airport.

Cassie drove right onto the tarmac where the Learjet was waiting with its cabin door open. Gavin stepped out of the vehicle, covering a wince and a groan as every bruise and aching muscle protested.

Maintaining his professional demeanor, he escorted his VIP to the bottom of the jet's lowered staircase. "Have a safe flight, sir."

"Thank you." The man stopped him, reached back to dig in his back pocket, and pulled out a leather wallet. Gavin watched in disbelief as he withdrew a wad of hundreds and pressed them into his hand.

Gavin yanked his hand back, feeling dirty. "That's not necessary."

"Please, take it. You went through hell out there today, went above and beyond for me, and I'd like to show my appreciation and respect for the job you did."

"Thank you, but no." He stepped back before he could make another attempt. "Safe flight."

"Then I'll be sure to send your boss a glowing review of your conduct and recommend your firm's services to my colleagues."

Yippee. "Thank you, sir." As soon as the VIP boarded, Gavin heaved a mental sigh of relief that the job was over.

He got stiffly back into the vehicle. "Not feeling so hot, huh?" Cassie said.

Honestly his mental and emotional turmoil were way worse than the rest. He'd meant what he'd said the other day at the beach.

What the hell did he know about being a father? With his military service, training courses, and deployments he'd only been around Carly sporadically throughout her life so far. He was Uncle Gavvy.

How the hell was she going to take the news? That worried him more than anything.

"Been better," he admitted.

"Here." She opened the center console armrest and took out a bottle of ibuprofen. "They're extra strength. Take three."

He made a face, decided suffering for no reason was stupid, and swallowed them with half a bottle of water.

"Ready to get the hell outta here and back to the coast?" she asked.

"Fuck, yes. Drive this sucker."

"My pleasure," she said with a sly smile.

They drove in silence to the I-5 and the turnoff for the coast, no talking or music. Gavin's brain was stuck in a loop. Him. Autumn. Carly.

It went round and round in circles in his head, going nowhere. So he shut it down and let his mind go blank as he stared out the window instead.

Cassie was a good driver, confident and experienced. Gavin leaned his head back and let his eyes close. He dozed, then slipped under at some point, waking when the vehicle took a pronounced curve in the road.

"Time is it?" he muttered, blinking his good eye. The

swelling in the right one seemed to have gone down a bit, because it was now open a slit.

They were on the coastal highway heading south. He could see the ocean, the setting sun hovering above the horizon as it threw glowing rays of orange and pink over the sparkling water.

"Almost nine. We'll be back in Crimson Point in about twenty minutes." She glanced over at him. "Everyone's meeting at the Sea Hag for a bite and a beer. You gonna come?"

He checked his phone, saw the message from Tris with the invite. Nothing from Autumn, but she was no doubt busy taking care of Carly. "Yeah, I could eat." He needed food, then the long shower before he saw Autumn.

When they arrived at the Sea Hag, the lot was full of company SUVs. Inside, the rest of the team was already there. Someone, probably Callum or Walker, must have paid the owner to close the place for them.

"'Bout time you two showed up," Ryder called to them from the bar, holding three bottles of beer between the fingers of each hand.

"Saved you guys a seat," Tris said, waving them over to a table near the plate glass windows at the back that overlooked the rolling waves as they crashed onto the beach.

Gavin went over, noticing the way his twin eyed Cassie as he pulled out a chair for her. She and Ivy were the only females in the place.

"Well, thank you," she said. "Such a gentleman."

"Welcome." Tris sat beside her, and Gavin sat across from them. "You good?" Tris asked him.

"Yeah, fine."

The other tables got up and mingled around the bar. Everyone started shooting the shit about the riots. Gavin refrained from joining in, too caught up in his head and not wanting to think about Carly trapped in that dangerous mass.

Then Ivy slid into the chair beside him, her eyes searching his in a way that made him feel like she was assessing him. Gavin wasn't exactly certain what her story was, had only heard that she was a major badass with training that would put theirs to shame. He wasn't close enough to her or Walker to know the details, but he would be lying if he said he wasn't curious about her, and Teagan absolutely revered her.

Although everything he'd seen from her was enough to convince him that the rumors were probably true. "You look better than I thought you would."

"Yeah?"

She nodded. "You were impressive out there."

He shook his head. "Couldn't have done it without you. Thanks."

She made a face, waved it away. "No need to thank me. Just glad Carly's safe."

"Me too." He was pretty sure he was going to have nightmares about losing her in the volatile crowd.

Ivy gave a nod, and there was something a little eerie about the way she continued to watch him. A bone-deep certainty that she suspected the true connection between him and Carly.

Which was nuts, because only Autumn and Tris knew so far, and he was sure Autumn wouldn't have told her.

"You sure were great with her. She trusts you completely. And you went out there to find her without hesitating," she said.

"So did my brothers."

"But you led the charge."

He shrugged, growing uncomfortable under her scrutiny.

"Known her since she was a baby. Of course, I went after her."

Ivy nodded thoughtfully, took a sip of her drink before continuing. "You know, life is funny. I didn't know shit about kids before I came here. I'm pretty much the least maternal person you'll ever meet, and yet here I am the stepmom of an amazing teenage girl. And not to toot my own horn like an asshole or anything, but I'm totally killing it, by the way."

Gavin grinned, amused but unsure why she was telling him this, and starting to seriously wonder if she actually did know about him and Carly. He'd heard that she noticed things others didn't. Maybe she'd figured it out on her own? "Yeah? I'll have to ask Shae what letter grade she'd give you next time I see her."

Ivy snorted. "A-plus, all the way. Anyway, as someone with a fair amount of personal experience where teenage girls who have suffered trauma are concerned, I promise you they're a hell of a lot more resilient than you might think."

Gavin stared at her, picking apart her words, including the underlying, unspoken confession he sensed she'd just given him. Ivy was notoriously private, and even Teagan didn't know the details of her past. Yet here she was basically telling him that she had suffered some sort of trauma as a teen. Why? And what was it?

Ivy gave him an understanding smile. "Take it from me, Carly's gonna be just fine." She set a hand on his shoulder. "And so are you," she added, standing and giving his shoulder a squeeze before walking away.

"What was that about?" Tris asked, leaning toward him.

He honestly had no clue. "She was just asking about Carly."

Tris nodded, eyeing Cassie again as she talked nearby with Donovan and Walker, who curled his arm around Ivy's waist. Walker was former intelligence. A logistical wizard, keeper of secrets, and an expert at extracting them. Maybe that's why he and Ivy had clicked so well.

Tris finally noticed Gavin watching him watch Cassie. Gavin raised his eyebrows in silent interest, flinched when it felt like the right one might split open again.

Tris lowered his beer a bit and blinked at him blankly. "What?"

"You tell me, bro."

"Nothin' to tell." But his gaze was on Cassie as she came toward them.

"Hey. Any update on Carly?" she asked as she pulled up a chair between him and Tris and sat down.

Gavin shook his head. "She's at our place with Autumn, probably crashed out by now." Marley and Warrick had come to get them in Portland and drive them back to Crimson Point hours before he and Tris had left with their VIPs.

"Tucked all safe in a nice warm bed, thanks to you." Cassie smiled and clapped him on the back. "You were amazing today." Her gaze slid to Tris. "You too."

Tris flashed her a grin, practically fucking blushed. Jesus. "Thanks."

"How long have you guys known Autumn, anyway?"

"Forever," Tris answered. "Since we were five or six."

"Five," Gavin corrected automatically. He remembered the exact moment he'd first laid eyes on her.

He and Tris had been new to the area, new to the school and knew no one. On the first day of kindergarten Autumn had walked into the classroom with her long blond hair in a braid down the middle of her back and sat at the desk beside his. At lunchtime, he and Tris didn't have anything to eat, having wolfed down their bananas and yogurt Marley had packed them at recess.

When he'd come back to class, there was half a ham sandwich and a cookie sitting on his and Tris's desks.

He'd bristled, embarrassed that someone had noticed them not having any lunch and felt sorry for them. Autumn had returned to her desk and stared straight ahead at the blackboard, but he'd caught her darting a sideways glance at his desk to see if he'd taken the food.

He'd known it was her. But he was hungry so he tucked the food away in his desk for after school and ate it on the way home. She walked beside him, a secret little smile on her face that told him he'd been right. But he decided he didn't mind.

"Want to be friends?" she'd asked.

Just that easy. He'd understood even then that people's actions showed who they were. Not their words.

She was kind. Had gone out of her way to be nice without making a big deal out of helping him, been mindful of embarrassing him. "Okay."

And the sweet little smile she'd given him in reply made him feel like maybe he wasn't so out of place after all.

A chair scraped over the scarred, dark hardwood floor, pulling him out of the memory as Decker spun it around and straddled it. He scanned Gavin's face briefly, then said, "What was the story on that guy who got Carly behind cover?"

"Been wondering that," Gavin said.

"We can ask Ivy to see if she can get a good shot of the guy on video," Cassie said, shoving another couple of fries into her mouth. "I'm dying to see her work her magic in person, actually." She lifted an arm to wave her over.

Ivy sauntered back toward them. "You called?"

"We were wondering if you could get us a good look at

the guy in the gas mask who pulled Carly from the hostage-taker," Cassie said.

"Let's find out," she said, whipping her phone out of her back pocket and taking the empty chair. She pulled up something, did whatever forbidden, hackery shit she had up her sleeve, and two minutes later they were all watching footage of the riots from the security camera feeds around the entrance to the conference center.

"There she is," Ivy said, tapping Carly's little red head poking above the crowd as she rode on someone's shoulders.

Gavin sat motionless, his gaze locked on the screen as he watched more tear gas get deployed near Carly and the man carrying her. The guy stumbled, and that protester bastard grabbed her, holding her in front of him.

He was aware of the tension in his muscles, aware of the rage building again, realized he was holding his breath as the guy in the gas mask appeared in the background. He had on what looked like a vest from a construction site.

A tense standoff between the two men followed. Gavin had missed that part when it had happened. And their body language during the interaction was telling. "They knew each other," Gavin said.

"Sure looks that way," Tris agreed.

"Hundred percent," Ivy said.

More tear gas deployed near them. The asshole holding Carly fell. The newcomer grabbed her, immediately spun around and rushed in the opposite direction, one hand reaching up to pull off the gas mask.

He had to be a protester. Why else would he be there, let alone with a gas mask on? He'd come prepared.

"There," Gavin said the moment the mask left the guy's face, the video showing the back of his head. "Can you get a different angle?"

"It gets spotty from here," Ivy said. "There are only a couple of blind spots in this area, and he finds one of them. There's an ATM on the corner there. Just a sec." She tapped the screen, typed a bunch of commands into whatever program she had, accessing other feeds. "Maybe this one…"

The new feed captured the unlikely rescuer carrying Carly toward the concrete barriers lining the west side of the street but only showed the back of him. Most people in his situation would have panicked and gone into self-preservation mode, worried only about saving their own ass.

Instead, this guy had protected Carly. There was zero hesitation in his movements. He had reacted instinctively to the situation, making the decision not only to confront the other protester and rescue Carly, but then immediately take her to safety behind cover. Law enforcement training? Military?

"Whoever he is, he knows what he's doing," Cassie commented, snatching a fry from Tristan's plate. He twitched but didn't protest, and it spoke volumes. Tristan had a thing about people taking his food, probably something to do with going hungry as kids sometimes, but whatever.

Turning his attention back to the footage on Ivy's phone, Gavin was sure their good Samaritan had professional training.

Ivy tried a couple more angles, but they couldn't get a good view of his face. "What's that on his vest?" It looked like a symbol of some sort.

Ivy worked her magic, narrowing and tightening the focus until it became clearer. "P, I…S?"

Gavin punched it into his phone along with the word Portland, and found the symbol within moments. "Pacific Industrial Solutions. It's a commercial construction company based in Portland." He looked up at the others.

Decker swallowed a sip of beer, set his bottle down on the table. "One of us should go talk to him."

"I volunteer as tribute," Cassie said. "I'm heading back there in the morning anyway. I can find out where the jobsite is and take a look around, see if he's there before I head back."

"I'll go with you," Tristan announced.

Cassie looked at him in surprise. "Really? Ryder and Callum don't need you here?"

He shrugged. "The guy risked his life to protect Carly. I wanna find out who he is and thank him. It's the least we can do."

"Plus, he knows the guy who put Carly in a chokehold," Gavin said. "I want a name to give the cops." And make sure that bastard got what was coming to him.

Decker nodded in approval. "Damned right."

"Okay then." She pushed her empty plate away and stood, looking at Tris. "I'm leaving at oh-six-hundred. Want me to pick you up?"

"I'll meet you at HQ."

She lifted an eyebrow. "What? You don't want me knowing where you live or something?"

"I'm staying at Marley's tonight." His gaze shifted to Gavin. "What about you?"

"Not sure yet." Depended on how things went with Autumn. He shot off a quick text to the temporary burner phone he'd bought her.

In Crimson Point. Will head over in a bit to check on you guys.

She had been through a lot today too, had to be exhausted, and hashing things out with him was probably the last thing she wanted right now. But they had to talk, and it couldn't wait. This was too important. There was too much at stake.

Decker rose. "I'm heading home. See you guys tomorrow night?" he said to him and Tris.

"Sure." Gavin stood as well, stretching his sore muscles before saying goodbye to the others and heading for the door.

Outside, the salt-tinged sea breeze whipped over him, clean and refreshing, clearing his head. He stepped to the edge of the building when Tris waved him aside. "Give her a chance to explain everything," his twin said quietly.

There was no mistaking who he was talking about. Gavin nodded. "Course I will."

"I mean, this is what you wanted all along, right?"

He inclined his head. But he'd imagined it happening a lot differently. "There's no guarantee she's going to give me a shot."

"She will. Message if you need me. Otherwise, good luck, and I expect a full debrief in the morning. And remember what I said earlier about the dad thing. You got this, asshole." Tris clapped him on the side of the arm and started for his vehicle.

Gavin stood there alone for several minutes, staring out at the restless, rolling ocean, trying to get his thoughts together. He wanted answers to the zillion questions racing around in his head. Wanted Autumn and Carly worse.

Turning away from the water, he started up the hill for the CPS building where he'd left his truck, mentally gearing up for the most important conversation of his life.

TWENTY-FIVE

"Didn't I tell you Ivy is incredible?" Teagan said as she took another cracker and piece of cheese from the platter between them on the living room coffee table. She'd come over to Gavin and Tristan's place not long after Autumn and Carly had arrived back in Crimson Point. To keep her company, lend moral support, and probably to make sure Autumn felt safe.

It was working. Without her, Autumn was sure she would have gone crazy being alone for so long after all that had happened today. Talking about everything—well, not *everything*—with Teagan had helped a lot in terms of decompression.

Autumn nodded and swallowed the sip of wine. She'd already had two glasses to settle her nerves, but anxiety continued to grind away in the pit of her stomach. Waiting to find out what Gavin would say was taking its toll. "You did, and she definitely is. I have no idea how she accessed all those feeds so fast. I need to meet her before Carly and I leave, to thank her in person."

Teagan tossed her dark hair over one shoulder. "I'll invite

her over tomorrow." Her deep brown eyes lit with interest. "I mean, unless you think you'll be busy doing other stuff. Or… some*one*."

Autumn gave a nervous laugh and leaned back against the sofa cushion, letting out a deep breath. "You should have seen the boys out there today. Especially Gavin."

"I can imagine. They're all protective of Carly."

"Yes, but especially Gavin." He'd plunged into danger to find Carly without hesitation, and Autumn was convinced he would have done it whether his brothers followed him or not. She was convinced from the look he'd given her that the news had taken his protectiveness to a whole new level. A father's instinct to save his child.

"Gavin give you a timeframe of when he'll be here?" Teagan asked as she got up to carry the empty platter to the kitchen.

He had texted not long ago to say he was coming over without specifying a time. "No. He's probably got a lot of things to tie up first."

Teagan came back into the living room. "Deck just texted to say he's on his way home now, so I would imagine the twins have both wrapped up everything too."

She'd no sooner said it than they both heard a key turning the front door lock.

"That's my cue," Teagan said, pausing to hug Autumn. "Call or message me if you need anything, okay? I'll talk to you tomorrow."

"Thanks. And thanks for coming over." She was amazed her voice worked at all given how tight her throat was all of a sudden.

"Yeah, of course. Anytime."

Autumn sat back down on the sofa to wait, her pulse thudded in her ears, stomach muscles tight as she awaited the confrontation she'd been dreading from the moment she'd read that email.

She heard Teagan's and Decker's murmured voices in the entry, then the front door shut. A few moments later, Gavin appeared in the threshold to the living room.

Her heart clenched at the sight of him. Tall and built and still as gorgeous as ever despite his bruised and swollen right eye and the cut on his lower lip. His auburn hair was damp as if he'd just showered.

"Hey," he said quietly, watching her, maintaining his distance as though he wasn't sure of his welcome. But she was equally wary, not knowing what to expect from him. Thankfully he didn't seem angry anymore, which was a huge relief.

A bit of the tension in her stomach eased. "Hi. How're you feeling?"

"Fine." He glanced over his right shoulder, down the hall. "Carly asleep?"

"Yes, she was worn right out after she ate and showered. I had to carry her to bed."

He nodded, faced her once again and finally entered the room, coming over to the couch and lowering himself onto the end of the sectional next to where she was seated. His sexy, masculine presence had her heart knocking against her ribs. She met that vivid green stare, her hands tightening on her knees.

She had loved him most of her life. Couldn't bear to lose him now that he knew the truth.

"I talked to my parents," she said, the spike in anxiety making her stall and delay the inevitable as long as possible.

"That's good. I'm sure they would have been worried otherwise."

"I'm pretty sure they would have been on the first flight

here in the morning if I hadn't called. I told them we're both fine and we'll still be flying home in a couple days. And they don't know, by the way. About Carly."

He nodded but didn't say anything else, watching her. It was impossible to forget what it had felt like to be held in those strong arms.

She wanted to crawl into his lap right now so badly and wrap her arms around him, snuggle up and kiss every mark on his face and body and know that he still loved and wanted her. That he didn't blame her for what had happened.

He'd sustained every single mark on him to rescue and protect Carly, and that made her love him even more.

He leaned back against the cushion, his stiff movements telling her he was in more pain than he was letting on.

"Are you hurt?" she asked in concern.

He shook his head. "Few bumps and bruises. I'm good. How're you doing?"

"Good now. But…it's been a day." She gave him a sardonic smile that made the edges of his lips twitch.

"It's been memorable."

The heavy silence that followed pulled her insides into a hard knot and set all her nerves on edge. She had never seen Gavin this quiet and contained, his stare boring into her with an intensity that made her heart hammer.

The unbearable tension grew until she couldn't take it a moment longer. There was no avoiding this. Might as well get down to it. "So. What do you want to know?" He must have lots of questions, and she would answer every one she could.

"You're sure she's mine."

He phrased it as a statement, not a question or an accusation, but she flushed automatically anyway, defensiveness rising hard and fast. "Yes."

"We used a condom."

"Apparently not properly."

He frowned slightly. "What do you mean?"

Her cheeks grew hot, reminding her why she'd never wanted to talk about this with him before. "It was my first time. I'd never put one on anybody before, so I might have done it wrong, and I didn't check after to see if it had broken. Did you?"

"No. It was my first time too."

She stared at him for a moment. "It was?"

He frowned. "Yeah."

"I thought… I mean, I'd heard that you…"

"No. And I can't believe you believed the rumors."

Of course she had. Even back then Gavin had been sexy as hell, with most of the girls in their class falling all over themselves to get his attention. She couldn't believe she'd been his first. "Well, then… There's our answer. Neither one of us knew what we were doing. Either it leaked, or it broke. I'm not sure. But it failed."

He seemed to weigh her words. "And the timing lines up?"

She licked her lips, reminded herself to be patient. He wasn't calling her a liar or accusing her of anything by asking the question. He didn't know any of this because she'd never explained it to him before. Had never thought to.

"I had a light period soon after, about two weeks or so. I didn't think anything of it at the time since I was never all that regular, but it was probably implantation bleeding. And as far as proof goes…"

She retrieved her laptop from the coffee table and clicked on the tab she'd loaded when she'd put Carly to bed. "Carly's been working on bits and pieces of the family tree assignment for her seventh-grade capstone project over the past couple months. She's always been curious about who her father was, but I didn't have much information to give her. So when she asked me if she could have her DNA analyzed to find out more about his side, I said okay. I got the email about the results the morning we flew here."

Gavin sat up slowly and leaned forward to look at the screen as she turned it toward him.

"His surname didn't come up anywhere in the results or when I searched for it in the database. So then I clicked on DNA matches, and…" She hit the button and waited for it to load, watching his face.

She knew the moment the results populated because of the flare of surprise in his eyes. "Marley."

"Yes. She must have done a DNA test with this same company. And as you can see, she's a twenty-five-percent match with Carly, meaning she's her biological aunt. You're welcome to do a test yourself to confirm, but… The science says she's yours."

He leaned back again, his gaze shifting to her. There was a warm light in his eyes now, and his voice was gentle. "Does Carly know?"

"No." She gave a humorless laugh. "And I don't know how I'm going to tell her, especially after what she's just been through."

"We'll tell her together." He shook his head. "I hate that you faced all of it by yourself at that age. Being pregnant, giving birth, raising her on your own. And damn, I can't tell you how many times I cursed whoever her father was." Another head shake. "Turns out it was me."

That gave her pause because she hadn't expected the admissions. It seemed like he believed her and had accepted that he was Carly's biological father. The knot in her gut eased a little more. "Okay, we'll tell her together." This was all good news. Better than she'd dared hope for. But how did he feel about it? It was so unlike him that she couldn't get a read on him. He was masking everything from her. Why? "Is there anything else you want to know?"

"Yeah." He seemed to weigh his words.

"Just say it."

"Okay. The guy you hooked up with after I left. The one you thought was Carly's father." The hurt was there in his eyes again. "Who was he?"

"No one important. I never saw him again because he lived in another state. I tried to contact him initially after I found out I was pregnant, but he never responded. I decided then and there that I wasn't interested in chasing him down." She shrugged. "I wouldn't have wanted to share her with him anyway."

Gavin held her gaze, his expression weirdly calm. "I was your first, and you waited until the night before I shipped out. Why?"

She'd dreaded the question for the past thirteen years. It was time to be honest about it. "Because I knew everything was about to change. Because I knew that was all I could have of you."

"Bullshit." Anger flashed in his eyes—or was that regret? "I tried to talk to you about it after, and every time you shut me down."

"Yes, because you were away living a brand new life that didn't include me."

"You think I would have abandoned you?" He sounded almost insulted.

"Gavin." She shook her head sadly, all the years of hurt, of hiding her feelings and regret swirling between them like ghosts. "Even if we'd both known the truth back then, can you honestly say you would have been ready for us? At eighteen right after you'd enlisted in the Marines?"

His jaw tensed, annoyance burning in his eyes. "No," he finally admitted in a gruff voice.

"No," she agreed. "If you'd known, you would have done the honorable thing and tried to make it work with us throughout your military commitments and deployments because of our history and because you cared about me. But you weren't in love with me back then, and you know it. So it never would have worked. You would have wound up resenting Carly and me in the end, and broken my heart for a second time."

His jaw worked, but he didn't argue. "You're saying you were in love with me back then?"

There was no point in denying it. "Yes."

Confusion flickered across his face. "Then why him? If you loved me, why go to someone else less than a week after I shipped out?"

She expelled a breath. Baring her soul to him right now made her feel hideously vulnerable, but she had to tell him everything if they were going to work through this for Carly's sake. "I was heartbroken after you left and worried sick that my dad was going to die from cancer. I met him at a friend's party a few days later. I was drunk and lonely, missing you, scared, and… He reminded me of you. And I was eighteen."

There it was, in all its pathetic honesty. She had gotten drunk and slept with a total stranger less than a week after Gavin had left because he'd looked a little like him. And worse still, she had pretended he was Gavin the whole time.

Gavin expelled a hard breath. "And you thought he was the one because…"

"We didn't use anything." It was totally unlike her. It had been incredibly stupid and irresponsible, and she had always regretted it. Being drunk was no excuse. "That's why I was convinced it was him and never questioned it."

Gavin didn't respond. Just watched her with that penetrating, X-ray stare that made her insides quiver.

She averted her gaze. "Look, the point is, I didn't know the truth until the other day either, so I'm just as surprised as you. I realize you weren't expecting this, and you made it clear at the beach that you don't want to be a father. But I want you to know I don't expect any—"

"Stop. Just stop." He reached out for her hand. Gripped it tight.

She looked at him again as she tried to rein in the torrent of emotions swirling inside. Her breath caught at the look on his face. His expression was no longer distant.

There was pure fire in his eyes, heat and determination and raw hunger. Her heart stuttered.

"That was then. Things are different now," he said in a low voice that made her insides flip.

She swallowed, heart tripping all over itself, hope and an answering wave of heat suffusing her. "Because of Carly?"

"Because that little girl is mine." His voice dropped, a mix of desire and tenderness in his eyes that turned her inside out. "And, sweetness, so are you."

TWENTY-SIX

A riptide of hunger and possessiveness swept through Gavin as he stared into Autumn's worried, pale green eyes. He wanted to wipe that look away forever. Prove to her once and for all that she could trust and count on him as her lover and partner no matter what.

"But you—"

"I told you what I wanted the other night. Nothing's changed for me. If anything, this just solidifies everything." He reined in his impatience when she looked skeptical. He remembered her reaction in the kite store, the way she'd paled when the woman thought he was Carly's dad. Then her expression later when he'd said he didn't want kids. "I know what I said on the beach, but I also told you I love you, and in case you hadn't noticed, I've changed a lot. Matured."

She nodded, looking contrite. "Yeah, you have."

"And you know I love Carly to death." He'd been waiting for months for her to come out here, trying to come up with a plan to confess his feelings and then prove to her that they were meant to be together. He'd wanted them to be permanent. Had never dreamed that she and Carly were already connected to him forever.

Another nod. "But then why did you say that about not wanting kids?"

This wasn't a comfortable admission, but he had to be honest with her. "Because I don't want to find out I suck as a father by messing a kid up."

Her expression softened. "You can't really believe you would be like him."

His hands balled into fists on his lap to keep from hauling her off that couch and kissing the breath out of her. If he touched her, there was no way he could stop, and they needed to talk this out. "You know there's nothing I wouldn't do for either of you, and Carly's half grown now anyway. I might never have expected this, and I might still be worried that I'll screw up as a parent, but I'm ready for it. For both of you. There's no way I'm letting either of you go, no matter what mistakes we made in the past."

Autumn blinked fast, tears glistening in her eyes. "Do you mean that?"

"God, yes, I've never meant anything more in my life." He reached out a hand, palm up, his throat thickening. "Just give me a chance to prove it to you. I won't let you down, I swear. Either of you."

She gave him a tremulous smile, then squeezed his hand in return. Sealing a silent pact.

God.

Suppressing a groan of relief, Gavin tugged her off the cushion and pulled her into his lap, ignoring the pain in his bruised ribs as he wrapped his arms around her and held her tight. He buried his nose in her soft, clean hair as he closed his eyes and just breathed her in. This felt like a miracle.

"She's ours, Autie." He still couldn't believe it. Everything he'd ever wanted was coming true.

"I know. Isn't that crazy?" Autumn whispered. She felt like heaven, all warm and soft in his arms, giving him her trust.

The hunger inside him rose sharply. He needed her. Needed her to believe in him. Needed her love. "She's ours, and I love you both so damned much."

She lifted her head, cupped his face between her hands to search his eyes. "Gav…"

No more talking. His hand slid around the back of her neck to draw her in for a kiss, but she had other ideas. Instead, she brushed her lips over the Band-Aid on his eyebrow, light as a butterfly's wings, yet he felt that tenderness all the way to his bones.

She kissed the center of his forehead. The bridge of his nose. His eyelids, taking special care with the swollen one before gliding down his right cheek to the cut on his lip. She kissed it gently. Once, twice, while desire and anticipation coiled tighter inside him, his body already hard and ready for her. He took over and pulled her mouth to his, ignoring the sting of the cut.

He was starving for this. For her to trust him enough to lower the protective wall she'd put between them and let him in completely. He was going to worship her, show her how good it would be between them. Wanted to imprint himself on her on an elemental level so that she would never want to pull away after this.

His hand cradled her jaw as he consciously gentled the kiss, teasing her tongue with his. He wanted her to be as desperate as him. Never wanted her to forget tonight.

She made a soft sound of yearning that ripped through

him and pressed closer, her rounded breasts flush against his chest. Mindful that Carly was just down the hall, he stood, taking Autumn with him.

She locked her legs around his waist, her arms wrapped around the back of his neck as he carried her to his room. He gave her more slow, decadent kisses along the way that had him hard as a pole and her squirming in his grasp.

He pushed the door shut with one hand, locked it, then turned and swiftly crossed the plush carpet to lower her onto his bed. He'd imagined her here so many damned times.

She moaned softly into his mouth when he came down on top of her, bracing most of his weight on his elbows as he covered her face in more kisses. Trailed them down the side of her neck while his hands found the hem of her top and pulled it over her head, leaving her in a black bra sheer enough that her pink nipples were visible through the lace.

He stroked them with his thumb. Delved his tongue into her mouth while he pinched them gently, drinking in her plaintive cry.

One hand slid beneath her to undo the catch. The scrap of fabric slid easily off her arms, leaving her breasts bared to his ravenous gaze. They were fuller, softer than he remembered.

He cradled them, dipped his head to suck one, then the other, rubbing his tongue across the sensitive tip. This was so much better than last time. More intimate.

Autumn's hands plunged into his hair and held him there, arching up to his mouth like an offering. By the time he got her pants off, they were both breathing fast.

He eased off her and sat back on his haunches, looking down the length of her gorgeous body to the scrap of lace between her thighs. Helped her strip his shirt off, the swift burn across his ribs barely registering under the heat roaring through him.

"Oh," she breathed, sitting up to gingerly stroke her fingers across the deep bruise that was turning from black to purple and green. "Oh, Gav."

"I'm fine," he assured her, and lifted her chin to capture her lips once more. He didn't want her worrying about him right now. He wanted her so far gone she couldn't even speak, much less think, focused only on the orgasm he was about to deliver.

He pressed her down onto her back, sat up to glide his palms down the length of her shapely legs, over her thighs and calves. Then he slid them back up, slowly, pausing to tease the center of her panties with his thumbs.

She sucked in a breath and parted her thighs more, watching him with glowing green eyes. He tugged her panties off, slid his arms under her thighs and parted them to make enough room for himself between them.

The sight of her slick, pink folds made his mouth water, her clit peeking out at the top. He lowered his head, tightened his grip around her thighs, and dipped down to run his tongue along her.

This is how it should have been the first time. But the wait made it all the more intense. More meaningful.

She gripped handfuls of his hair, a tight sound of need coming from her throat. He did it again. And again, a little firmer, pausing at the top to swirl around the sensitive bud.

"God, Gavin," she groaned, pulling him closer.

He went willingly, delving deeper, stroking and sucking her tender flesh, then sliding a finger into her core to make it even better. She whimpered and threw her head back on the pillow, breathing fast.

He slid a second finger inside her. Caressed the edge of her clit with the flat of his tongue. Felt the ripple that sped through her taut muscles.

He'd dreamed of her like this so many times. Fantasized about his tongue between her legs while he made her mindless, made her beg for him. But it went way deeper than just the physical now. He wouldn't settle for anything less than all of her, body and soul.

He focused on her every reaction, the ache in his cock almost unbearable as he pushed her higher. When her thighs and belly tensed, her fingers clenching in his hair, he stopped to quickly strip off the rest of his clothes. He pulled out the condom he'd put in his pocket, came up on his knees to tear it open.

Autumn sat up to run her palms over his chest and down his belly, the feel of her hands on his bare skin forcing the remaining blood out of his head to pool in his groin. Her soft, slender fingers slid lower, finally wrapped around his cock and stroked up to the tip.

He hissed in a breath as pleasure licked up his spine, grasped her hand to still it, and they rolled the condom down him together. Feeling her hands on him was incredible.

"Lie down." His voice was guttural.

She twined around him as he came down on top of her, kissing her slow and deep as he positioned his throbbing cock at her entrance. He settled his thumb along the edge of her clit, stroked gently as he slid the head in.

The heated friction was so fucking good. His chest heaved with the effort of holding back when all he wanted to do was bury himself to the hilt.

He broke the kiss, braced on one forearm to cradle the side of her face in his hand as he slowly eased forward, stroking that sweet spot inside her. The sound she made set his blood on fire.

She clung to him, moving with his slow, shallow thrusts

while he drank in every nuance of her pleasure-drenched expression. Reveled in the way she writhed beneath him.

She was close. So close while he felt like he was slowly dying, tendrils of ecstasy wrapping along his spinal column.

Steeling himself, he pushed deep in a smooth, controlled thrust that seated him to the hilt in her slick heat. His heart pounded, his pulse thudding in his ears over the sound of his strained breathing. He smothered her fractured cry with another sensual kiss, flicked his tongue along hers before lifting his head, the pleasure eating him alive.

"Tell me you love me," he demanded, watching her face. He needed to hear the words from her. Now. Nothing held back.

Her eyes opened slowly, hazy and heavy-lidded as she gazed up at him while he was buried deep inside her.

He caressed her clit again, driving the point home. He was in charge, wouldn't let her come until she gave him what he wanted. What he needed. "Say it."

"Yes, yes, I love you, I always have," she gasped out, her voice tight, breathless.

He growled low in his throat, drew his hips back slightly and thrust again, this time faster, his heart about to burst with triumph and tenderness. Seeing that level of enjoyment on her face while he was buried deep, knowing he was responsible for it and about to give her an incredible orgasm, was the biggest rush he'd ever known.

"Tell me you're mine."

Autumn nodded helplessly, her eyes squeezing shut, fingers biting deep into his back. "I'm yours. Gavin—"

He rocked his hips forward again, every slick, exquisite inch of friction along his cock sending streamers of fire licking up his spine. Again. And again. A steady, endless rhythm while the last of her control disintegrated.

Her core rippled around him. He captured her lips with his just in time to drink in her shattered cry as she started coming, the slick pulses milking his cock.

A low growl of mingled pride and ecstasy locked in his throat. He rode her just like that until he couldn't take it anymore and the orgasm ripped through him, more intense than he'd ever known.

There was nothing but this moment. Only him and Autumn, the two of them connected as deeply and intimately as humanly possible, clinging to each other while release crashed through them.

When the sensation finally began to fade into little pulses he groaned and slowly lowered his full weight onto her, his body sinking into her soft, warm embrace. She sighed and stroked a lazy hand through his hair, down his nape to his damp back, gliding up and down. Soothing. Calming.

She was the center of his universe. Always had been.

"I love you," she murmured into the stillness of the room.

He slid his arms underneath her torso to hug her tight. Hearing her say those words in the quiet aftermath when she was clear-headed was even sweeter than when he'd been inside her. "Love you too."

Her touch gentled even more when her fingers paused on his bruised ribs. "You okay?"

The bruise was throbbing with its own heartbeat, but he had zero regrets. "Are you kidding? I'm fantastic. Don't even feel it now."

"Liar." She kissed his shoulder, made a contented sound and was silent for a long moment before speaking again. "What do you want to do about Carly? We have to tell her."

"We'll tell her tomorrow. Then my family. Then your parents."

"You sure you want to tell everyone this soon?"

He didn't even hesitate. "Positive."

"They're gonna be shocked."

"They'll deal. And Tris already knows."

Her hand stilled in the middle of his back. "He does?"

"I told him when we were out looking for Carly."

"Oh. How did he react?"

"He was surprised, and I'm pretty sure if we hadn't been in the middle of the search, he would have done a Decker and taken a strip off me for having a one night stand with you back then."

"Well, he's always been my other favorite twin."

The unhurt side of his mouth lifted at her sass. "You know he's always loved you like a sister. And that he adores Carly. I think he's ecstatic to know she's his blood."

"He can take over being her funcle now."

He chuckled softly. "Yeah." He sobered, a moment of self-doubt hitting hard.

As if sensing his tension, she tipped her head back to look up at him. "What's wrong?"

"I'm kinda late to the parenting party. I have no idea what I'm doing."

She snorted. "Hate to break it to you, but none of us really know what we're doing with the whole parenting thing. We just do our best as we go."

"You say that because you're a natural. You're an incredible mom, have been since day one."

"I've had my moments over the years, believe me."

"You've been Carly's rock and biggest supporter, providing her constant love, guidance and stability her entire life. She doesn't know how lucky she is to have you as a mom." Autumn had always had her shit together, had provided a stable, loving, and supportive home for Carly all by herself while juggling a job and managing her household.

Sure, her parents had helped out when she needed, but Autumn had borne the day to day things alone for the past dozen years.

"Aww, that's lovely of you to say so. But for the record, I already know you'll be an amazing father. You've loved her since she was a baby. Today you risked your life to save her. That should tell you everything you need to know about what kind of parent you'll be."

Okay, there was that. If love was enough, and with Autumn there to guide him, maybe he wouldn't fuck up too badly.

"And besides, she's about to be a teenager. I'm gonna need all the backup I can get," Autumn said dryly.

"God help me," he moaned. "Suddenly a dad to a teenage girl. It's like a bad comedy." He thought about himself going through puberty and the teenage years, all the attitude he'd thrown all over the place. Poor Marley.

"No, you'll be fine. I have faith in you." She cuddled up again, her cheek nestled over his heart. God, he loved holding her like this and knowing she was his. "We still have so much to talk about."

"We'll handle it all starting tomorrow, so don't worry about anything else. The rest of tonight's just for us."

She hummed softly, and her lips curved into a smile as he leaned in for another kiss. "I love the sound of that. I didn't dream all this, right? This is really happening?"

"You need more proof?" He stroked the pads of his fingers down her spine, making her shiver.

A naughty gleam twinkled in her eyes. "I might."

"Sweetness, I'm more than happy to oblige."

He rolled her onto her back and blanketed her with his weight. But as incredible as it felt, he couldn't fully relax. Because Autumn was right. They had a lot to figure out in a short time since she and Carly were still leaving in only a few days. "Can you change your flight back and stay another week or two?"

She stroked her fingers down the side of his face. "Wish we could, but Carly has to present her report at school, and then there's her grad ceremony that Friday."

Yeah. Damn. "I'll ask for some time off tomorrow. I want to be there for that."

"Carly would be thrilled. We both would."

He came up on his elbows, ignoring the flash of pain in his ribs, and stared down into her eyes. "Stay here with me."

Her lips twitched. "I already am. All my stuff's in your closet and bathroom."

"No, I mean come live here with me."

He could feel her surprise and rushed on before she could voice any protests. "Don't say it's too fast, because it's not. We've known each other our whole lives, and we love each other."

"All right. I won't say it."

"You told me once that your boss would let you work remotely. Carly's moving to a new school this summer, and she told me most of her friends are all scattering to different districts, so she'll have to make new ones anyway. The high school here is great, and there are tons of sports teams and clubs for her to join if she wants. We'll get our own place, find a little house with an ocean view. Carly could finally get a cat."

Autumn snickered and wrapped her arms around his back, the way her curves cushioned his weight pure perfection. Soothing him on a level he hadn't known existed until now. "I'll think about it. But mostly because of the ocean view and the cat."

His lips twitched. They still had a lot of things to work

out, and everything was moving at warp speed. Even so, this didn't feel rushed. So fuck it. He was putting it all out there right now, making it clear. "I'm marrying you."

Her eyebrows rose. "Are you asking, or telling?"

He dropped a tender kiss on her upturned lips, his heart overflowing with love for this woman. "Just giving you fair warning that I plan to make you mine forever."

TWENTY-SEVEN

Carly stopped scrolling through the animal videos on her laptop when a message from a friend on their group chat popped up.

No way, you were in the riots yesterday? Are you okay?

She'd talked to her closest friend back home last night, told her all about it. Apparently the word was out, but she didn't want to talk about it anymore.

I'm fine, back in Crimson Point now. You finished your project yet?

Her friend started typing a response. *No. Been procrastinating. You?*

Getting there. Going to try to finish today.

Good idea. You sure you're okay?

Yes. Going offline now to get some work done.

Carly didn't much feel like working on her project today, but she was almost done, wanted that stress off her plate, and was sick of dwelling on what had happened yesterday. She could use the distraction. Might as well just get it done so she could try and enjoy her last few days here.

She closed the chat and video windows, grimaced when

the scrapes and bruises on her knees and elbows stung as she shifted on the bed. Her eyes weren't bugging her anymore, and she'd stopped coughing soon after Gavin had brought her to the conference center. Yesterday felt like a bad dream she just wanted to forget.

Her mom had sent half a dozen or so screenshots of information for her to use in the report so she wouldn't have to waste time searching the genealogy website. Carly used it to fill in everything possible, then stared at her completed family tree, feeling down.

One side of it was completely bare except for her dad's name next to her mom's directly above hers at the bottom of the trunk. It sucked that she didn't know anything about him or his side. She'd been hoping this project would give her answers.

It used to embarrass her when someone asked about him and she couldn't answer. Everybody else knew their dad. She'd learned to shrug it off. But it would always bother her.

A soft knock came at her door, and her mom poked her head in. "Hi, babe. You working?"

"Yeah. Just trying to finish up my project." All that was left was to write up the last bit of her report. Shouldn't take more than an hour or so if she stayed focused.

"Ah. Hey, Gavin's here. Can you come out? There's something we want to talk to you about."

Carly's insides tightened. She hadn't heard Gavvy come in, and while she loved him, she didn't want to talk about yesterday. She wished she could just put it behind her and never bring it up again. "Um, okay."

"We'll be in the living room."

Carly saved her work, shut her laptop and blew out a breath. Whatever they wanted to tell her, at least she would get to see

Gavvy again. When she thought of the way he'd rescued her yesterday, the way he'd put his vest on her and carried her all the way to the conference center through that terrifying crowd…

She sucked back a hot rush of tears, shook her head. No. She was fine. Everything was fine now.

She brushed her teeth and hair before leaving her room. Her mom and Gavin were sitting beside each other on the living room sofa when she came in. Gavvy smiled at her. "Hey, squirt. How you feeling?"

She stopped short, smothering a gasp. "Better than you." His eyebrow had a bandage on it. His eye was all swollen and bruised, and his lip had a cut on it. And he was sitting stiffly, as if he were hurting somewhere else too. "Are you okay?" She'd been so scared yesterday, she hadn't even noticed he'd been hurt.

"Yeah, I'm fine, just a little banged up."

He didn't look fine. She went to the loveseat, curled up at the far end and tucked her feet under her. Neither of them said anything as they stared at her in a way that made the pit of her stomach buzz. "Am I in trouble?"

Gavin grinned. "No, course not. It's just… Your mom and I have something really important to tell you."

Carly waited, trying to figure out the vibe going on here. Their expressions were relaxed enough, but their body language seemed tense. They were both acting weird.

"Okay," she said slowly. Something was wrong. She could feel it.

Gavin looked at her mom, who rubbed her palms over her thighs of her jeans. She only did that when she was nervous. "Well, honey, you know the DNA test you did for your project?"

Carly nodded, still worried.

"And you know the results came in the morning we flew here."

She nodded again. "But it didn't show anything about my dad's side."

Her mom and Gavin both went dead still.

"Well, that's not entirely true," her mom finally said, knotting her fingers together on her lap. "The website can show matches within the company's database to anyone you're genetically linked to. And while there weren't any Batesons listed in the results, there was one perfect match."

There was? "Who?"

"Marley."

Carly frowned, not understanding. "Auntie Marley?" She wasn't her real aunt though. Just in a sort of adopted way.

"Yeah." Her mom tucked her hair behind her ear, holding her gaze. "And if Marley is your biological aunt, then it means that…" She trailed off, her gaze sliding to Gavin, who was watching Carly.

Carly's heart started to pound as her brain connected the dots. No way. What her mom was saying seemed impossible, but it would explain the weird tension coming from them. She gaped at Gavin in shock. "*You're* my dad?"

A big grin broke over his face. "Pretty awesome, right?"

The shock of it clouded her brain. Gavin? And her whole life, neither of them had known? She flushed at the thought of Gavvy and her mom together that way. Ugh, no, she didn't want to think about that. Gross.

And while it felt so weird to suddenly find out that he was her dad…

It was also exactly what she'd secretly wished for her entire life.

"Yeah," she said with a grin, and as she studied his face, for the first time she saw some similarities between them.

Their eyes were almost the same color, and the shape of their mouths were similar. Maybe their noses too. Joy leapt inside her.

"Oh, wow, this is so crazy." She giggled, clapped a hand over her mouth, but it couldn't be contained.

"What's so funny?" he asked.

She shook her head, tried to stop. Gavvy was her *dad*.

He looked at her mom. "Well, safe to say she's not traumatized."

Carly laughed harder, but then a different swell of emotion hit her, and all of a sudden the laughter turned to tears. All her life she'd wanted a dad. To find out it was Gavvy after all this time was too much.

"Oh, sweetie, no," her mom said in an anguished voice and got up to go to her.

Carly shook her head and waved her away, instead standing up and reaching for Gavvy. Instantly, he drew her onto his lap and wrapped his arms around her. "Hey. It's okay, squirt. It's gonna be okay."

She couldn't answer. Was embarrassed to be blubbering in front of him but couldn't stop. She didn't even know why she was crying. She was happy. Maybe the happiest she'd ever been.

"N-not s-sad," she gasped out, hugging him tight.

His arms stayed firmly around her. "That's good to hear."

She melted into him, sucking in shaky breaths as she tried to pull herself together. She'd loved him her whole life, and now he was really hers.

Her mom sat next to them, stroking her shuddering back. Carly finally got hold of herself and calmed down enough to sit up and wipe her face. She stared at Gavin, gave him a watery smile and sucked in a jerky breath. "I'm s-still gonna c-call you G-Gavvy. 'kay?" She couldn't call him Dad yet. Maybe ever. He'd been Gavvy forever.

He grinned, and he was so handsome and brave and strong her heart skipped a beat. Her *dad*. She was so lucky. "Absolutely. Because I'm still gonna call you squirt."

She wiped her face again, took a hiccupping breath and looked between him and her mom. "So…are we g-gonna be a f-family now?" She wanted that desperately. He and her mom weren't together as a couple, but a lot of her friends had divorced parents who didn't live together, and they were still a family.

Her mom's eyes got all teary, and Gavvy wrapped an arm around her. Carly's heart jumped. Were they together now?

"That's the other thing I wanted to tell you," Gavvy said. "When you guys came out here, I was waiting to tell your mom something important. I missed you both like crazy while I was away, and when I finally got out of the military a few months ago, I knew exactly what I wanted. Both of you, forever, because I love you both more than anything in the world."

Hope flared, hot and painful, and more tears clogged her throat. Gavvy and her mom were together, and he loved them both. "So we are gonna be a family?"

"We already are one, squirt."

Carly grinned and flung her arms around his neck, hugging him tight.

Her mom wrapped her arms around them both. "Are you happy, baby?"

She nodded and kept her face tucked into Gavvy's neck, afraid to answer in case she started to cry again. This was so unreal. If she was dreaming, she didn't want to wake up. And she couldn't *wait* to tell her friends back home about this. They were gonna lose their minds.

Wait. She leaned back to look at them both. "Does everybody else know? Auntie Marls, Uncle Tris and Uncle Deck? And Nana and Papa too?"

"Just us and Uncle Tris," her mom said. "Nobody else yet."

"I told him yesterday when we went out to look for you," Gavvy said. "Your mom and I wanted to tell you as soon as we had a chance to talk about everything. But of course, we have to tell the others now too."

Carly nodded, her excitement growing. "They'll be so happy, especially Auntie Marls. Is Uncle Tris happy?"

Gavvy smiled. "I think you're right. And, yes, he's very happy."

Carly smiled back. Uncle Tris, Auntie Marls and Uncle Deck were her *real* aunt and uncles. Man, she was lucky. And Nana and Papa had always adored Gavvy. They were going to be so excited when they found out. "When are you going to tell them?"

"Later today. That okay with you?"

She nodded. "Can you guys do it though? I want to finish my homework so I can spend the rest of the time with you." She didn't want to be there when they told everyone. It was too awkward.

He and her mom laughed softly. "Yeah, we'll handle it," Gavvy said.

"And you'll tell me what they said?" She was dying to know.

"Yes," her mom promised. Carly kind of wanted to ask if they could video it, but held back. Probably wasn't appropriate.

"So…what's going to happen now? Are we going to live together, or…? And are you going to get married?"

"We're working through all that right now," Gavvy said.

"But yes, that's the plan." He slanted a meaningful look at her mom.

"Are we going to move here?" Carly asked her.

Her mom blinked. "Would you like to?"

She thought about it a moment. Leaving home and her friends would be sad. Leaving her grandparents would be even harder. "I would miss Nana and Papa the most, but…" Here she would have Gavvy every day. As well as Uncle Tris and Auntie Marls and Uncle Deck in the same town. "Yes."

"Okay, then, we'll figure it out," her mom said with a happy smile. She looked happier than Carly had seen her in a long time.

"Do you have any more questions for either of us?" Gavvy asked, wiping her damp cheek with the side of his hand.

She shook her head. "Not right now." She was curious about their relationship before she'd been born but didn't want to know that stuff yet. Maybe someday. "What about the riots? Are they over now?"

"Yes, everything was contained yesterday. All the bad people have been arrested."

"Including the man who grabbed me?"

Gavvy's eyes darkened. "He's in jail. And he won't be getting out for a long time."

"Good." Everyone who had hurt people or set fires or destroyed things deserved to go to jail for what they'd done. "What about that man who rescued me and put on my gas mask."

"No, he's not in any trouble."

"Who was he?"

"We're not sure, squirt. But your uncle Tris is going to try to find that out today."

"Okay. Gavvy?" She cocked her head. He was so handsome and strong, even with all the bruises.

"Yeah, squirt?"

She loved it when he called her that. "I love you too."

He exhaled roughly and hugged her tight. She gave him a squeeze, then leaned back to grin up at him, feeling like she might burst with happiness.

"What?" One side of his mouth lifted in the exact same way hers did sometimes.

"I'm so getting an A on my project."

TWENTY-EIGHT

The two-hour drive to Portland from Crimson Point passed mostly in silence while Cassie drove the company SUV and Tristan rode shotgun, answering messages, texting back and forth with HQ. He'd volunteered to accompany her on this mission to find their mystery good Samaritan because Carly was his niece, and they'd been asked to pass on any information to the police they could get about the man who had used Carly as a shield.

And…maybe also partly because he was more than a little bit curious about CPS's only female personal security agent.

She was easy to work with, always professional, but didn't mix much with the rest of them outside of work and seemed to prefer keeping to herself. But then being the only female on the personal protection team couldn't be easy.

"You hungry?" she asked when they were a couple of miles from their exit.

"I could eat if you want to stop somewhere. If not, I'm good." He'd learned from day one that she preferred to be in the driver's seat, and he was pretty sure that went beyond actual driving.

He didn't mind being a passenger with her. She was a controlled, experienced driver, always paid attention to what was happening around them, was never reckless or arrogant behind the wheel.

A little smile tugged at the corner of her mouth, her lips shiny and pink. He liked that she didn't wear much makeup, just a little lip gloss and subtle touches on her eyes that enhanced their unique silver color. She had seriously gorgeous eyes, and her short cap of black hair made them stand out even more. "Little secret about me, I'm always hungry."

She must have a crazy fast metabolism, because she was slim and trim. Tall too, around five-eleven. "Okay, then let's stop."

She took the next exit. "Coffee shop okay?"

"Sure."

They used the drive-through. She ordered herself the biggest vanilla latte they had, a chocolate croissant, and an apple turnover. He got a black coffee and a double chocolate muffin.

"Want a bite?" she asked, holding out the turnover as she turned back onto the street.

"I'm good."

She eyed his muffin. "You gonna share some of that?"

He hesitated. Knew it was fucking weird that as an adult he still wanted to hoard his food like a dragon guarding its treasure. He'd put it in his right hand without even realizing it, instinctively holding it out of her reach.

But those times he'd gone hungry as a kid when his mom had started to decline, the constant uncertainty about when he'd get his next meal, had left an indelible mark. He and Gavin had wound up over at Autumn's place to eat countless times. If not for her and her parents, they would have gone hungry a whole lot more.

He broke off a little piece of his muffin and put it in Cassie's upturned palm, fighting the discomfort.

She spared a glance at it, gave him a sardonic look. "So generous. Thank you."

He didn't answer, just tightened his hold on what was left and took a sip of his scalding hot coffee that melted off a layer of tastebuds, resisting the urge to wolf the rest of the muffin down so she couldn't ask for more.

See, he could control it.

"You're from Kentucky, right? All you guys."

"Yeah. You?" He hadn't heard from Gavin yet this morning and hoped that was good news. Yesterday's news had come as a shock, but Autumn was awesome. So was Carly. And in spite of Gavin's hangups about being a parent, Tristan would love to see his twin settled with them as a family unit.

"Nevada." She didn't elaborate, and they lapsed back into silence as they ate.

A few minutes later, they got their first look at downtown Portland since yesterday's chaos. The skyline was no longer full of smoke, but the damage to the city center was evident the moment they exited off the freeway.

"What a mess," Cassie muttered.

Cleanup was well underway, with heavy equipment and crews assisting in the effort. Security in and out of the city center was still tight. They were stopped at two different checkpoints to verify their identities and purpose for entering the city.

Using GPS, they found the construction site they were looking for easily enough. "We didn't even need an address. All we needed to do was head for the cranes," she said.

"True enough." The same company logo that was on their person of interest's vest emblazoned signage along the fences and modular buildings at the entrance to the site.

Cassie slipped on sunglasses as she parked the SUV beside the main gate, and they walked through it, pausing inside to look at the image of the man they were looking for. Ivy hadn't been able to get a shot of him head-on, but it showed his profile just as he pulled off the gas mask. Straight nose. Short-trimmed dark beard, collar-length hair.

"There's something familiar about him," Cassie said, surprising him.

"You recognize him?"

"I think so, but I'm not sure from where." They continued farther into the site.

A man exited one of the modular buildings up ahead on the right, tugging on work gloves on his way across the site. His hard hat covered his hair, but the profile and dark beard were right. "That's him," Tristan said.

"Yeah, and I've definitely seen him somewhere. It's driving me nuts."

Rather than call out or try to intercept him, Tristan instead loped up the wooden steps of the first building and opened the door. A fortyish guy with a big paunch sat hunched over a keyboard, a mug in one hand.

He looked up at them, paused. "Can I help you both?"

"Yes." He and Cassie pulled out their IDs. "We're with Crimson Point Security, following up on an incident relating to the riots yesterday. We need a word with one of your employees."

The man frowned. "Who?"

"He just walked out of here a minute ago."

"TJ?" He seemed surprised.

"What's that stand for?"

He blinked. "I'm not sure. He's a good worker, but he's not full time. Only works shifts here and there when we need extra guys."

"What's his last name?"

"Barros." He gave them a skeptical look. "You sure you got the right guy? He's low key, never any trouble. Doesn't seem the type to get involved in that kinda thing. Not like some of the other homeless guys we take on here."

Barros was homeless? That wouldn't make finding out about him easy.

"We're sure," Tristan said. Interesting that the foreman didn't seem to think Barros would be linked to the riots. Zero chance he had just been caught up in the mess. The guy had come prepared, wearing a gas mask. "Would you mind calling him over for us? It's about an investigation we're working on."

The police were overwhelmed with the sheer number of individuals charged over the weekend. Any intel he and Cassie could get about the suspect who had grabbed Carly would help their case against him.

He glanced from Tristan to Cassie and back again. "Yeah, all right." He got up, rounded the desk and strode for the door with Tristan and Cassie right behind him.

Time to find out who their good Samaritan really was.

TWENTY-NINE

"Hey, Barros!"

TJ stopped just before he reached the elevator and looked over his shoulder. Standing at the base of the stairs, his foreman waved him back. "Some folks here to see you."

He hesitated, his gaze moving to the two people standing behind him. A tall guy around TJ's age and a woman, both dressed in business attire.

What did they want with him? He didn't recognize either of them from this distance. Didn't feel like talking to them—or anyone else for that matter. He just wanted to get back to work and put in his hours, resume and maintain his low profile after the craziness of yesterday.

The foreman gave an insistent wave. TJ inwardly sighed and turned around, sizing up his visitors as he approached. When he got closer, a jolt of recognition hit.

It was the guy from yesterday. The one who had come for the little girl. TJ had surrendered her to him because it was clear from her reaction that she knew and trusted him.

Keeping his expression closed, he stopped near the base

of the stairs and eyed them. Big guy, confident posture, auburn hair, green eyes. The woman was slender with a cap of short black hair, sunglasses hiding her eyes.

"Help you with something?" A lot more polite than the *what the fuck do you want* he was thinking.

"You already did," the guy said, and something was off. Yesterday, his face had been bleeding and today he didn't have a mark on him. "You're TJ?"

He dipped his chin, suspicion taking hold. Why were they sniffing around? They weren't cops. He didn't think they were Feds either. "Who are you?"

"We're with Crimson Point Security," the woman said. "We wanted to talk to you about yesterday."

He'd heard of CPS. Good rep within the industry, big list of rich clients. They'd probably been providing VIP security at the conference. "What about it?" He hadn't done anything wrong.

"You saved a little girl yesterday," the guy said.

He didn't answer.

"You rescued her from a man using her as a shield against the cops," the woman pressed, and the way they studied him made his spine tingle. It was like they were trying to place him.

"Was just in the right place at the right time."

"You saved her life," the man said.

"No. I just got her behind cover."

"And then put your mask on her, exposing yourself to the gas to protect her. I wanted to thank you personally for everything you did." He held out a hand.

TJ stared at it a second, then shook with him, still suspicious. They'd come all the way here to find him just to say thank you?

A tiny buzz of worry lit up the back of his brain. He was an expert at not standing out. At being unseen. A nobody.

Ordinarily he wouldn't be concerned about anyone exposing his secrets. But they were with a respected security firm with lots of contacts and resources. If they dug long and deep enough…

The woman adjusted her sunglasses. "Were you involved in the protest?"

He shook his head. Her tone and body language weren't hostile, and neither were the man's. "I was in the area. Not involved." He'd only caved and gone down there in the end because he'd been concerned that Dan would be tempted to do something stupid.

And he'd been right. But he'd gone too late. He hadn't been able to keep Dan from being arrested, but at least he'd been able to get the little girl clear.

The man folded his arms across his chest, his expression calm. "The guy you rescued the girl from. You knew him. Who was he?"

TJ shrugged. "An acquaintance."

A nod. "Daniel Rutherford, currently under arrest and awaiting a preliminary hearing on charges of rioting, arson, assault, assaulting police officers, and resisting arrest. Where do you know him from?"

"Around. We've worked some shifts together." He seriously doubted Dan would have hurt the girl even while caught up in mob mentality, at least not intentionally. But when TJ had seen him grab her like that, he'd had no choice except to intervene.

"Anything else?"

He shook his head, kept his expression impassive. Hopefully, he'd answered enough that they wouldn't keep sniffing around and let it drop so he could go back to anonymity. "I need to get back to work." Time was money. He didn't get paid for standing around shooting the shit, especially while his foreman was watching him.

"Yeah, of course. Thanks for your time."

TJ nodded and walked away, that tingling sensation still crawling up and down his spine. Not a warning of danger exactly. He hadn't got the sense that either of them posed a threat to him directly, and the man's thanks had seemed genuine.

It was more a feeling about the woman. Something his subconscious didn't like that he couldn't put his finger on. A feeling that this might not be over.

TJ had learned long ago never to ignore a signal like that. Because out on the streets, a warning like that could be the difference between life and death.

THIRTY

"Tris is here," Warwick announced to the others, looking out the front window of his and Marley's house.

Gavin stood with Autumn and hurried past everyone in the kitchen and living room, then out the front door to meet him outside.

Tris stopped partway up the front walkway and looked between them. "Everything good?"

Gavin slid an arm around Autumn's waist and pulled her into his side. "Yeah, everything's perfect."

Tris grinned and continued up the walkway. "Damned glad to hear that. I'm happy for you guys."

"Thanks," Autumn said with a soft smile. "We haven't told the others yet. We were waiting for you to get here first."

"Oh, now this is gonna be fun. Can't wait to see their reactions." He stopped at the doorstep to hug Autumn. "You good?"

She hugged him back hard, her beautiful smile filling Gavin with warmth. "So good."

"Awesome. And if Gav does anything stupid or messes

up, you just let me know, and I'll straighten him out. You tell Carly yet?"

"Yes, and she's ecstatic. You're now her favorite uncle, by the way. Funcle Tris, official."

"Well, yeah," Tris said as if it was so obvious it didn't need mentioning.

"Only because I upgraded to a way better title," Gavin said. Dad. Though it would take a while for Carly to adjust enough to her new reality to start calling him that. Whatever she was comfortable with, he wouldn't push.

"You keep telling yourself that." Tris went to move past them, but Gavin put out a hand to stop him.

"You find out anything about our good Samaritan?"

"A little. His name's TJ Barros, and he only works occasional shifts at the construction site. That's how he knows the suspect who took Carly. Word is they're both homeless."

"Was he a protester?"

"He says no, that he just happened to be in the right place at the right time."

"Wearing a gas mask."

Tris shrugged. "I know. Could've had it on him because he expected the cops to deploy the gas."

"Yeah, and a homeless guy just happens to have one of those as part of his worldly possessions?"

"Dunno. His foreman said he doesn't think Barros is the type to get involved in the protests."

Gavin filed that away, more curious than ever. There had to be more to the puzzle. Not many people would put themselves at risk to do what Barros had done for Carly yesterday. "Nothing else on him?"

"Not so far. We sent his name and a picture of him to HQ to forward to the cops. I asked Ivy to do some digging."

"Great." Ivy could work outside the usual parameters and

use some magic tricks that weren't strictly legal. If anything on this dude existed, she would find it. "And?"

Tris gave him a meaningful look. "She didn't find anything."

He frowned. "Nothing?"

"Nope. It's like the guy doesn't exist."

How was that even possible? Barros being homeless might be a stumbling block, but there should still be plenty of information on him somewhere. Birth records, driver's license, tax returns, health, dental, and census records. Something.

"She's gonna keep looking." Tris glanced back and forth between him and Autumn expectantly. "So, when we doing this?"

Gavin looked down at her. She shrugged. "Guess now's as good a time as any?"

"Hell, yeah," Tris said, rubbing his hands together.

Decker, Teagan, Marley, and Warrick greeted Tristan when he walked in, then everyone fell silent when Gavin and Autumn stopped together in the entrance to the kitchen to face them all.

"We need to tell you guys something important," Gavin said.

"Just a sec. Lemme grab a drink first," Tris said, hurrying to the fridge. He pulled out a beer, twisted off the cap, and sauntered back to plunk himself down on a high stool beside Decker, eyes glinting with anticipation.

Marley shot him a frown then looked at Autumn and Gavin. "What? Is something wrong?"

"No." Gavin wrapped an arm around Autumn, suppressed a grin at the way four of their five faces went blank with surprise. He glanced down at Autumn. "You wanna tell them?"

"Noooo. You go ahead."

All right. He drew a deep breath. "There's really no easy way to tell you this, so I'm just gonna say it."

The silence in the kitchen was almost deafening. Warwick's beer was paused halfway to his mouth, his gaze flicking back and forth between them. Decker was dead still in his seat, looked like he was hardly breathing.

"Autumn and I are together," Gavin announced.

"I fucking *knew* it," Teagan breathed, her words almost drowned out by Marley's smothered yelp of excitement.

"But there's more," Gavin said, enjoying the comically rapt expressions on his siblings' and their partners' faces as they fell instantly silent again. "We just found out, but… Carly's mine."

Marley's mouth fell open. Warwick's eyes widened. A Cheshire cat grin spread across Teagan's face. Decker's eyebrows pulled into a deep scowl. Tris took a pull of his beer, the gleam in his eyes making it clear he was enjoying the shit outta this.

"You're…no," Marley said to them with a perplexed frown.

Gavin nodded. "Yep."

"It's true," Autumn said, pressing closer to him.

He tightened his grip on her, wanting to comfort her and make her feel more at ease. There was no need for her to be embarrassed about what had happened, and there was zero chance his family would reject either her or Carly. It was gonna be fine.

"Carly did a DNA test about two months ago for her family genealogy project. I got the results the other morning before we left for the airport." Autumn drew a steadying breath. "There was nothing about the…uh, the other guy whatsoever, but Marley was listed as a direct match, and that's how I found out."

The room exploded in noise as all of them except Tristan started talking at once.

"You're kidding!"

"Are you serious?"

"I can't believe it— Wait." Marley stopped suddenly, looked over at Tristan in suspicion and gave him an accusatory glare. "You knew. You tight-lipped little shit, how long have you known and not said anything?"

He looked up at the ceiling as if doing a mental calculation, then made a show of checking his watch. "Bout twenty-three hours, give or take. That about right, Gav?"

"More or less."

"What?" Marley demanded, shooting an accusing look at them both.

"I'm his twin," Tris said as if that explained everything.

Leaving Marley to continue the interrogation, Gavin's gaze slid along the line of people until he reached the far end and locked eyes with Decker. No surprise, his eldest brother's accusing stare was slowly boring a hole in the middle of Gavin's face. And Deck didn't have to say a damned thing, because Gavin knew exactly what he was thinking.

Yeah, he'd slept with Autumn when he was eighteen, and, yes, technically it was a one-night stand. "It was one time, the night before I shipped out for bootcamp. And yes, we used protection. But here we are."

Decker's gaze shifted to Autumn, his expression softening slightly. He'd always been fond of her in his own aloof way.

"I didn't know until I saw the DNA results, I swear," she told him.

"It's not that," Gavin said. "He's mad because he thinks I took advantage of you before I left town."

Marley stopped interrogating Tris long enough to shoot Decker a stern look and lean over to smack him on the shoulder. "Oh, my God, stop it, *Dad*." She jumped up, rushed at them with her arms open, a gigantic smile on her face. "I can't believe this. You guys! It's unreal." She hugged Gavin, then Autumn, hopping up and down in excitement. "I already loved that kid so much, but now I'm officially her auntie! And I already loved you, too, which you knew," she said to Autumn, still hugging her. She whipped her head around to beam at Warrick, who was still seated on his stool at the island. "Oh, my God, can you believe this?"

"No, aye," he said, looking a bit shellshocked. "Champion news, well done."

"That makes you her uncle. Ooh, you can be her funcle—"

"Nope, that spot's already taken," Tris said, then shot a glance at Decker, whose scowl was almost gone now. "Obviously, since I'm about a thousand times more fun than him."

Teagan and Warwick came over to hug them. Then Decker was there, his hard features morphing into a smile that made Gavin blink. "Welcome to the family officially," he said to Autumn, and hugged her.

And damn if Gavin's throat didn't get tight all of a sudden.

Deck's gaze shot to his with a stern look. "You're making it official, right?"

He opened his mouth to answer, but the doorbell pealed. Everyone stopped and looked at Marley. "I dunno who that is, I'm not expecting anyone," she said, hurrying to the front door. "Oh!" she cried when she saw whoever was on the other side, and threw out her arms to hug them.

The door opened wider, and Autumn gasped when she saw her parents standing there. "Mom, Dad! What are you guys doing here?" She rushed for the door to greet them.

"We were worried sick about you and Carly, that's what," her mom said, hugging her as she looked over Autumn's shoulder at him and the others.

"How did you even find me here?"

"She used the find my phone thing," her dad said, taking his turn for a hug. "I told her it wouldn't work this far away, but I was wrong."

"Yes, and I'm not sorry," her mom said, hitching the strap of her purse higher on her shoulder as she came inside. She gave Gavin a warm smile. "Gavvy, sweetheart, how are you? Oh, your poor face."

He returned her hug. "I'm fine. Better than fine." He met Autumn's gaze, almost chuckled at the warning look she gave him with widened eyes and a tiny shake of her head. They'd told everyone else, no sense in stopping now.

Autumn's parents came in, hugged Marley, Deck and Tris, and were introduced to Teagan and Warwick. "Where's my baby?" Autumn's mother said, looking around.

"Finishing up her capstone project at Gavin and Tris's place," Autumn said. "She's fine," she added quickly when her mother looked aghast. "She's secured in there all snug as a bug and trying to finish before dinner so we can all go out to celebrate…" She stopped, realizing what she'd almost said.

"Celebrate what?" her mother prompted.

Autumn paused and turned to the others. "Would you guys mind giving us a couple minutes?"

"Yup, absolutely," Marley answered, grabbing Warwick by the hand to haul him off his stool. "We have to go into town anyway."

"Us too. We'll go with you," Teagan said, dragging Decker after them.

"Good. And you're coming too," Marley told Tris, who was still sitting there enjoying the show.

"Nah, I'm good, you guys go ahead."

"Tristan." Marley gave him The Look. The one that warned he had exactly two seconds to get off his ass and do as he was told or there would be consequences.

Chuckling, he got up. "Yeah, okay." He shot Autumn and Gavin a wink. "See you guys at dinner, I guess."

Everyone filed out the front door. Marley paused to give them a grin and a thumbs up before shutting it behind her.

"Well, what on earth was that all about?" Autumn's mother said in the sudden quiet.

Autumn pulled in a breath. "Mom, Dad, come sit down." She ushered them into the living room and seated them on the sofa, then took the loveseat and waved Gavin over. He sat beside her, letting her take the lead. "We have something to tell you."

"What?" her mother said worriedly. "What's wrong?"

Gavin curled an arm around her shoulders, enjoyed the way her parent's eyes shot to the hand curved around her upper arm before they bounced back to his face.

Autumn broke the news about them, then Carly. Her mother cried out, her hands flying to her cheeks as she and her husband stared at Autumn, aghast. "You're sure?" she asked finally.

"Yes, Mom, I'm positive."

Time for him to jump in. "Mr. and Mrs. Bateson, for what it's worth, I—"

"Gavin Abrams, you took advantage of our daughter?" Autumn's mom yanked off her decorative scarf and tried to hit him with the end of it. Missed because it was so light if fluttered past his shoulder like a falling leaf.

"I took advantage of him, truth be known," Autumn said, deflating her mother's outrage and earning some slow blinks. "It was all me."

"Well, it wasn't *all* you," Gavin said.

Mr. Bateson cleared his throat. "This is a…big surprise, but not an unwelcome one." He turned to his wife. "How many times did we say we wished he was our son?"

"Well, yes, of course, you know we've always loved you like a son," her mother rushed out, but there was still some lingering outrage in her eyes. "Which is why we didn't say anything about you climbing up the tree into her bedroom all those years—"

"Mrs. Bateson, I love your daughter. And Carly. I'd been waiting to tell Autumn that in person when they came out here, hoping she would feel the same way. The news about Carly was a huge surprise to us all, but it doesn't really change anything because I already wanted them both forever." He looked into Autumn's eyes. Saw the deep, lifelong love he felt for her mirrored back at him. "I wanted to ask her to marry me before I even found out."

"Oh…" Autumn's mom blinked fast and put a hand to her chest as if that was the most romantic thing she'd ever heard in her whole life. "Oh, Autumn."

"I know, Mom, I'm so lucky. Because I've loved him forever."

"Well, that's all I needed to hear." Autumn's dad grinned slightly and extended a hand toward him across the coffee table. "Son, let me be the first to congratulate you both, and officially welcome you to the family."

EPILOGUE

Gavin suppressed a groan of pure contentment when he woke to the feel of Autumn curled up against him, warm and naked, the curve of her ass nestled snugly against his rapidly tightening groin. "Mornin'."

"Mmm, mornin'." She sighed and stretched in a catlike motion, stroking her soft, silken skin against his aroused flesh.

Soft, dawn light came through the partially open window above the headboard as they lay cuddled up in their king-size bed in the main bedroom of their small, two-story house on a hill north of town overlooking the sea. Birdsong filtered in from the backyard, along with the faint hush of the restless waves at the base of the cliff.

They'd lucked out on finding out about the listing while Autumn and Carly were packing up everything back in Kentucky. A brand new, upgraded heritage house that had been completely renovated by a local company run by a veteran named Beckett Hollister. It had been a case of love at first sight, so they'd jumped on it.

Three weeks later the deal had closed. Ten days ago, they had moved in. And six days after that...

A deep rumble vibrated in his chest as Autumn turned in his arms and began nuzzling the side of his neck. His fingers sifted through her hair while she began a trail of kisses over his bare chest, pausing to flick her tongue over his nipples before moving south.

He rolled onto his back when her hands moved up his thighs, his whole body tightening in anticipation as her fingers curled around the length of his erect cock and squeezed tight.

She rubbed her cheek against it. Darted her tongue out to glide a wet path around the underside of the head. He inhaled, fingers contracting in her hair as her lips parted and slid down to envelop him, her tongue doing naughty, wicked things to the ultrasensitive spot.

He drifted in a haze of pleasure, letting her enjoy sucking and teasing him, pushing him closer to the edge of his limit.

As good as it was, it got even better when she shoved the covers back to expose her head. With her blond hair all tousled around her face, she looked up at him with hungry green eyes and gave him a long, slow pull with her sexy mouth.

His muscles locked, pleasure rocketing up his spine. Just before he reached the point of no return she sat up and threw a thigh across his to straddle him. She shook her hair back and rose on her knees, one hand wrapped around him to hold him in position, the other stroking her rosy clit with her slender fingers.

He couldn't speak, could barely breathe as she held his gaze and slowly, torturously sank down on him, taking him inch by inch into her slick heat. Christ. His hands tightened on her hips, fingers squeezing her soft flesh as she closed her eyes and rode him, moaning softly.

Slowly. Smoothly. Erotic as fuck while her fingers played between her legs and her tight pink nipples peaked out between locks of her hair, the strands turned into liquid flame by the rosy sunlight coming through the window above them.

He reached up to play with one of her nipples, gently squeezing and twisting the tip between his fingers, his dark titanium wedding band catching the light. Their wedding had been a simple one on the beach beneath the lighthouse, with his family, her parents, and the CPS crew there to celebrate. Carly had been the flower girl and maid of honor. Tris had been his best man.

Autumn's expression tightened above him. She planted her free hand on his chest to give her leverage, and rocked a little faster.

Gavin stared up at her and let incredible sensations flood through him, drinking in the sight of her riding him like a fucking goddess as she took her pleasure from his cock, the slick sound of each glide making him insane.

Her features tightened more, her breathing coming shorter and faster as she neared the peak. He knew exactly when she got there. The tiny hitch in her breathing, the way her lips parted a split second before the gorgeous, throaty moan spilled out.

He felt her core contract around him, the ripples flowing up and down his swollen, bursting cock. He grabbed hold of her hips, pulled her down hard as he thrust up into her again and again.

His throttled shout mixed with her cry of release. It washed through him in wave after decadent wave, left him sinking into the bedding as Autumn's weight came down to blanket him in satiny warmth.

He groaned and wrapped his arms around her, holding her tight.

"Goddammit, I love you," he murmured when he could remember how to speak again. She'd been on the pill for a few months now, eliminating the need for condoms.

She laughed softly against his chest. "I know."

Smiling, he ran his fingers through her hair. He didn't know how he'd gone all those years without her. He'd been fucking starving for her and hadn't realized it.

"Now I'm all sticky," she muttered.

"I'll help clean you up in the shower," he promised. With the shower head adjusted to the perfect setting and aimed right at the exact spot that made her quiver and beg. He'd never spent so much time in the shower in his life as he had these past few weeks with her.

A faint scratching at the door caught their attention. "Did you fill her food and water bowls before bed last night?" he asked.

"Yes, and I gave her extra so she'd let us sleep in," Autumn said without lifting her head. "There's no way she emptied it yet."

A plaintive meow and more scratching said otherwise.

"Such a diva," Autumn muttered.

He kissed the top of her head. "You stay. I'll go give her a refill." He rolled her to her side and got up, pausing a moment to stare down at his wife's naked curves displayed against the white cotton sheets. She looked like a naughty fallen angel, all sated and tousled in their bed. His angel.

"Pervert," she accused, and snatched the comforter over her.

Chuckling, he grabbed a pair of sweats from the dresser, tugged them on and went to open the bedroom door. Big yellow eyes stared up at him from within a mass of long black fur that needed to be brushed at least a couple times a week to keep from getting matted or giving her hairballs. Not his job, however.

Carly had been thrilled when they'd told her she could adopt a cat and dragged them to a local shelter that same afternoon. There they'd met Bella, who was connected to the CPS crew. After listening to Bella's spiel about which cats had the hardest time being adopted, Carly had insisted on this black five-year-old female that was currently gazing up at Gavin with a pathetic expression as if she was on the brink of starvation.

"Hello, Meowy Pawpins." He felt stupid saying it, but unfortunately that was the name Carly had chosen.

The spoiled creature meowed and wound back and forth through his ankles, trying to manipulate him into going down and filling up her dish. He shook his head. He'd never had a cat, didn't consider himself a cat person, but she was pretty neat as far as felines went, and she made Carly ridiculously happy.

If only she'd just let them sleep in on the weekends. "Come on."

She stayed right underfoot, doing her best to trip and kill him on the way down the stairs to the kitchen. When he rounded the corner, he saw her food and water dishes were still full and glared at her.

"Are you serious right now? You dragged me out of bed for nothing?" He could be asleep right now with Autumn draped over him like a naked blanket. But no, he was standing here in the kitchen watching the cat eat her breakfast while she purred, all because she'd wanted company while she ate.

He waited until she paused to sit back on her haunches and lick her lips, then scooped her up and carried her up the stairs. "You're gonna stay with your girl for a while now." He had another hour's sleep curled up with Autumn, and then a long, intimate shower afterward that he was very much looking forward to.

Carly's door was partly open from Meowy Pawpins' earlier exit. She was curled up on her side facing the door, her sweet little profile bathed in soft morning light, a perfect blend of his and Autumn's features. He still couldn't believe neither he nor Autumn hadn't ever put it together before.

He set the cat down on the bed next to Carly's face. Carly opened her eyes, smiled sleepily and reached out a hand to stroke the cat's back. "Hi, Pawpins," she murmured sleepily.

The cat arched her back and held up her tail for Carly to stroke, purring and making little biscuits on Carly's quilt. Gavin stroked his fingers over Carly's hair. "Morning, squirt."

"Morning, Dad."

He stilled, his chest squeezing tight. It was the first time she'd called him that, and he didn't care that the only reason she might have done it just now was because she was still half asleep.

He pressed his lips together for a moment, swallowed. "Go back to sleep," he whispered, bending to kiss the top of her head. "It's still early."

"'kay," she murmured and closed her eyes, one hand tucking Pawpins closer to her.

Gavin left them and eased the door closed until it just rested against the jamb in case Pawpins wanted back out. In the hall, he closed his eyes and pulled in a deep, steadying breath, his heart suddenly too big for his ribcage.

Autumn was asleep when he went back into their room a minute later, sprawled on her stomach. Her eyes blinked open when he slid in beside her. Automatically, she edged closer to snuggle into him, draping one thigh across his as she nestled her cheek in the curve of his shoulder.

"Everything good?" she murmured drowsily.

"Yeah, perfect," he whispered, gathering her close.

More perfect than he would ever have dared let himself dream up until a few months ago.

It was incredible to think that that day so many years before when she had shared her lunch with him and asked if he wanted to be friends had changed the trajectory of both their lives without either of them realizing it.

But that was Autumn. It had always been Autumn.

And now she and Carly were his to love and cherish forever.

—The End—

TJ AND BRISTOL'S story is next in Guarding Bristol

Dear readaer,

Thank you for reading ***Guarding Autumn***. If you'd like to stay in touch with me and be the first to learn about new releases you can:

- Join my newsletter at: http://kayleacross.com/v2/newsletter/
- Find me on Facebook: https://www.facebook.com/KayleaCrossAuthor/
- Follow me on Instagram: https://www.instagram.com/kaylea_cross_author/

Also, please consider leaving a review at your favorite online book retailer. It helps other readers discover new books.

Happy reading,
Kaylea

Excerpt from

Guarding Bristol
Crimson Point Security Series
By Kaylea Cross
Copyright © 2024 Kaylea Cross

Chapter One

B ristol finished wiping the gel off her pregnant patient's rounded belly with a flourish and a smile. "*Voilà.* You'll no doubt be happy to know this means you can finally empty your bladder. Not here, though," she added.

The woman laughed in the middle of sitting up, then put a hand on her stomach and grimaced. "That's cruel, making me laugh when I'm literally about to burst. Do you know how hard it is to hold it in right now? I've got half a gallon of water in my bladder, which is currently a quarter of the size it normally is. Well, you saw it," she said, waving one hand at the ultrasound screen and accepting Bristol's hand with the other to help get her upright on the edge of the table.

"You're right. That was mean. I'm a terrible person."

"I'll try to find it in my heart to forgive you." She slanted Bristol a look. "By the way, was that what I thought it was?"

"Was what what you thought it was?"

"You know. That…shadow down there." She gestured to the area between her legs.

"What shadow?" Bristol asked, all innocence. The patient had specifically told her she didn't want to know the baby's sex.

"It was! I knew it!"

Bristol shook her head and held up a hand. "Whoa, I didn't say anything."

"You didn't have to, I can read your face."

"You can read my face?"

"Yep. You have a very readable face."

Shoot. She really did. She sucked at poker and was a terrible liar. "I can neither confirm nor deny that there was a shadow…down there." She adjusted her glasses, kept her face straight.

"It's okay, I was pretty sure on my own." The woman patted her belly. "This is my fourth, so I've had some practice reading ultrasounds. Now help me off this thing and point me to the bathroom before I embarrass myself and pee on the floor."

Bristol got her up, pointed her to the bathroom, then wiped down the table and equipment before exiting the ultrasound room and making her way to the lockers inside the staffroom with a spring in her step. It had been a good day. She loved her job, but sometimes it was hard. Today she hadn't needed to pass on a single piece of bad or worrying news to the radiologist for confirmation.

"There she is," Travis said, looking up at her as he laced up a shoe. He was an incredibly popular Physician Assistant here at the hospital, as well as a PJ with the Air National Guard. "All done for the day?"

"Yep." Since his hands were busy she bent to pick up his discarded boots and set them in the bottom of his locker for him. "Guess you're just starting?"

"Thanks. You know what they say, no rest for the wicked."

"Please, you're the furthest thing from wicked." There was something in the water here in Crimson Point. Most of them were either former military or law enforcement. All the men were ridiculously hot. And most of them were also taken.

He stood, shrugging into his lab coat, his arm muscles straining the sleeves. His wife Kerrigan was a lucky lady. "Got any plans for tonight?"

"Cassie's coming over soon. We're having wine and lady tapas."

"Lady what?"

"You know, picky plates." She mimicked picking something off a plate and popping it in her mouth, then chewed, rolling her eyes in ecstasy.

Travis laughed. "Well, you enjoy."

"I sure will. Later."

"Later," he said, heading for the door to start his shift.

Outside the hospital, Bristol paused to raise her arms over her head and stretch, closed her eyes and pulled in a deep breath of the warm, August evening. Even up here on the top of the hill overlooking Crimson Point the air held the faint salty tang of the ocean.

The drive home was gorgeous as always. The sun hung low on the horizon, spilling its deep golden rays across the sea that stretched out as far as the eye could see as she headed south to her quiet little neighborhood nestled on a rise facing the water. The three-story townhouse was the first place she'd ever owned, and she loved every square inch of it.

Everleigh, a physio at the hospital, was pruning the hydrangeas bordering the walkway when Bristol got out of her car. "Hey, neighbor."

"Hi. Got big plans tonight?" Everleigh called out. She looked like an angel sent to earth with the deep golden sunlight shining on her silvery-blond hair.

Bristol stopped to pick up a few cut branches and toss

them in the pile on the tarp. "Lady tapas with Cassie. You wanna come over?"

"Love to, but I'm taking Grady on a date when he gets off. They're on exercise this coming weekend, so we're getting quality time in before he leaves."

Grady was also a PJ in Travis's unit, and an L&D nurse at the hospital. Seriously, Crimson Point was a hotbed of gorgeous military men. "Awesome, enjoy."

"Oh, I will," Everleigh replied with a sly wink that made Bristol grin.

Cool, citrus-scented air greeted her when she opened her front door and walked in. She rushed upstairs to change, then hurried back down to the kitchen to put together dinner. Crackers with hunks and slices of various cheeses she'd bought from a shop in town, fresh berries and other fruit, toasted nuts, sliced veggies, ranch dip, hummus, rotisserie chicken, a few roasted pepper slices, marinated artichokes. All the good stuff, and the best part was, she hadn't had to make any of it.

"Knock-knock," a familiar voice called from the front entry.

"Come on in. I'm in the kitchen putting the finishing touches on this masterpiece."

Cassie appeared around the corner a few moments later, tall and slender in snug cropped jeans and a form-fitting top that hugged her trim figure to perfection. Her short cap of black hair was wispy around her face, the dark color a sharp contrast to her pale skin and startling, silvery eyes. "Hi, honey. How was your day?"

"Great, you? Oooh, yeah, you brought the good stuff." Bristol took the bottle of red from her and fished in the drawer for the corkscrew to open it.

Cassie examined the board she'd built. "Lady tapas? Nice."

"Right? I love not cooking." She handed over two wineglasses. "Make yourself comfy. I'll be right there."

Cassie took the glasses to the couch and stretched out. "Oh, yeah. Been looking forward to this all week."

"Same." It was so nice to have Cass around. It hadn't been easy to convince her to make the move out here from Vegas, but Bristol knew her stepsister was way happier here, and now they got to hang out whenever they felt like it.

She finished arranging the board and carried it to the coffee table, accepting a glass of wine as she settled into a corner of the couch. "Cheers, babe."

"Cheers." Cassie clinked glasses with her and grinned. "Look at us, hanging out all on our own like we actually like each other."

"I know, right? We've come a long way."

"I'll say. You hated my guts when we first met," Cassie said with a smirk. "Stone cold Elsa freeze treatment."

Yeah, because her dad had decided the best way to introduce them was to bring Cassie over to dinner one night and announce over roast chicken that they were going to be sisters when he eloped with Cassie's mom in a few weeks. Bristol had been singularly unimpressed. "I know. Sorry I was such a moody bitch."

Cassie snorted a laugh in the middle of taking a sip of wine, wound up choking. Bristol leaned forward to pound on her back.

"It always cracks me up when you swear," Cassie wheezed when she finished coughing a minute later. "You're so damn adorable, you look like sugar wouldn't melt in your mouth."

"Whatever, I swear," she argued with a frown.

"Hardly ever. And I don't think I've ever heard you say the word 'fuck.'"

Bristol brushed at a crumb on her pants. "Be grateful. Because that would mean I've gone nuclear."

Cassie's eyes danced with silent laughter. "I think I'd pay good money to see that."

"You say that only because you haven't witnessed it first-hand." She gestured to the mostly demolished food left on the board. "Want more? I've got lots more."

Cassie groaned. "No, I couldn't. Maybe another glass of wine for dessert though."

"It's fruit. It counts." Bristol topped up Cassie's glass and took the mostly empty board to the kitchen. "So, tell me about work. What's the latest at CPS, the best security company in the entire Pacific Northwest that you love working for and will be eternally thankful I made you apply to earlier this year?" Being a cop in Vegas had burned Cassie out. Private security work—and the pay—suited her way better.

"Yeah, all right, I'll give you that one." Cassie took another sip. "Got a gig coming up this week, not sure what yet. And after that there's a security detail for a celebrity coming into town. Good friends with Ryder, apparently."

"Who?"

"Dunno, I don't have the details yet." Cassie took her wine across the living room to examine the framed photos lined up on the shelves.

"Is this upcoming gig a solo thing, or will you be working with a partner?"

"Partner."

Bristol paused to look up at her. Cassie's back was to her, and that plus the nonchalant tone was a giveaway. "With who? Tristan?"

"Maybe." Cass swirled her wine, kept her back to her.

Bristol chuckled softly. "Man, you are so twitterpated."

Cassie looked over her shoulder at her. "Twitterpated? Who the hell uses that word?"

"Me. And I'm right," she added smugly.

Cassie huffed and went back to looking at the photos. "You're not always right."

"Mostly. What's he like?"

"He's…fine," she said with a shrug.

"Girl, that goes without saying. As in, fiiiine." She'd seen him and his twin Gavin around town. And like most men around here, they were definitely both *fine*. "But I meant his personality. I'm seriously curious about what kind of guy would have you all tied up in knots."

"He doesn't have me tied up in anything, he—wait." She grabbed a framed photo from the shelf, stared at it a second before looking over at her. "Who's this?" She marched over, holding it out for Bristol to see.

The one of Eric and four guys in their utilities on a deployment overseas. "Some guys in my brother's unit in Afghanistan." Seeing him didn't hurt as much anymore. Time had softened it to an ache instead of jagged grief.

"When was it taken?"

"I dunno, a year or two before we pulled out of Afghanistan. Why?"

"This guy." Cassie tapped the guy on the far left. "Who is he?"

"Buddy of Eric's. You recognize him or something?"

"Remember the good Samaritan I told you about from the Portland riots?"

"The one who rescued Gavin's daughter from the bad guy?"

"Yes. I swear this is him. God, I knew there was something familiar about him."

Bristol looked at the photo again. "You sure?"

"Almost positive. We don't have much information on him. Even Ivy couldn't dig up anything."

Ivy, the legendary female badass living right here in Crimson Point. Rumored to be some kind of former government assassin or something. "Huh."

"Do you know his name?"

"Tomás." Eric had been pretty tight with him while they were deployed. Would be such a weird coincidence that he had wound up here, just a few hours away from her.

"That fits, he told us his name is TJ. I swear this is him, minus the beard and longer hair."

A disturbing thought occurred to her, erasing the warm contentment she'd been basking in. "Didn't you say he's homeless?"

"Yep. On the streets in Portland, working odd jobs when he can get them."

"Oh no…" Bristol took the photo from her, staring at Tomás's smiling face.

He looked so young, so cocky and full of life. To think that he'd earned a Ranger tab, survived the war and come home only to wind up hitting rock bottom just like Eric had…

Her stomach tightened in distress. It hurt to think about, dredged up all sorts of painful memories she tried not to think about.

"He seems to be doing okay, all things considered," Cassie added softly. "I mean, relatively speaking."

His situation filled her with sadness and anger. What if it was Tomás? She couldn't stand the thought that he was on the streets. Discarded. Alone, like Eric had been. "Do you think you could find him again?"

Cassie's gaze shot to hers. Then she shook her head. "Oh no. No, come on, don't do this to yourself. He's not Eric, you—"

"I can at least find out if it's him, can't I?"

"And then what?" Cassie folded her arms, looking every inch the protective sister Bristol hadn't had until their lives had intertwined six years ago. "Save him from himself?"

She lifted a shoulder, feeling suddenly defensive as dark, ghostly memories swirled in her head.

Of walking the darkened streets and alleys in search of her brother, the awful fear and uncertainty that she was too late. The endless, painful weeks that followed once she had.

"Maybe." She'd helped pull him from the abyss, if only for a short while before tragedy had taken him from her forever.

Tomás deserved at least a chance to turn his life around.

"If it's him, then he was Eric's friend, and I can't turn away." Eric would want her to do what she could for him. "Maybe he just needs to know someone still gives a crap about him."

Cassie sighed and rubbed her forehead. "Shit, now I wish I hadn't said anything."

"I don't." Bristol would never have known about his situation otherwise. "Just help me find him, that's it. It might not even be him."

Cassie eyed her a long moment, exasperation clear on her face. "If I say no, you'll go try to find him on your own, won't you."

Bristol didn't deny it. "I need to see if it's him. For Eric."

"For Eric, or for you?"

Okay, point taken. "For both of us."

Ultimately she hadn't been able to save her brother. But maybe she could help save Tomás.

End Excerpt

ABOUT THE AUTHOR

NY Times and USA Today Bestselling author Kaylea Cross writes edge-of-your-seat military romantic suspense. Her work has won many awards, including the Daphne du Maurier Award of Excellence, and has been nominated multiple times for the National Readers' Choice Awards. A Registered Massage Therapist by trade, Kaylea is also an avid gardener, artist, Civil War buff, Special Ops aficionado, belly dance enthusiast and former nationally carded softball pitcher. She lives in Vancouver, BC with her husband and family.

You can visit Kaylea at www.kayleacross.com. If you would like to be notified of future releases, please join her newsletter.

Direct link: http://kayleacross.com/v2/newsletter/

COMPLETE BOOKLIST

ROMANTIC SUSPENSE

Crimson Point Security Series
GUARDING TEAGAN (Decker and Teagan)
GUARDING BELLA (Creed and Bella)
GUARDING AUTUMN (Gavin and Autumn)
GUARDING BRISTOL (TJ and Bristol)

Crimson Point Protectors Series
FALLING HARD (Travis and Kerrigan)
CORNERED (Brandon and Jaia)
SUDDEN IMPACT (Asher and Mia)
UNSANCTIONED (Callum and Nadia)
PROTECTIVE IMPULSE (Donovan and Anaya)
FINAL SHOT (Grady and Everleigh)
FATAL FALLOUT (Walker and Ivy)
LETHAL REPRISAL (Warwick and Marley)

Crimson Point Series
FRACTURED HONOR (Beckett and Sierra)
BURIED LIES (Noah and Poppy)
SHATTERED VOWS (Jase and Molly)
ROCKY GROUND (Aidan and Tiana)
BROKEN BONDS (ensemble)
DEADLY VALOR (Ryder and Danae)

DANGEROUS SURVIVOR (Boyd and Ember)

*** Kill Devil Hills Series***

UNDERCURRENT (Bowie and Aspen)

SUBMERGED (Jared and Harper)

ADRIFT (Chase and Becca)

Rifle Creek Series

LETHAL EDGE (Tate and Nina)

LETHAL TEMPTATION (Mason and Avery)

LETHAL PROTECTOR (Braxton and Tala)

Vengeance Series

STEALING VENGEANCE (Tyler and Megan)

COVERT VENGEANCE (Jesse and Amber)

EXPLOSIVE VENGEANCE (Heath and Chloe)

TOXIC VENGEANCE (Zack and Eden)

BEAUTIFUL VENGEANCE (Marcus and Kiyomi)

TAKING VENGEANCE (ensemble)

DEA FAST Series

FALLING FAST (Jamie and Charlie)

FAST KILL (Logan and Taylor)

STAND FAST (Zaid and Jaliya)

STRIKE FAST (Reid and Tess)

FAST FURY (Kai and Abby)

FAST JUSTICE (Malcolm and Rowan)

FAST VENGEANCE (Brock and Victoria)

Colebrook Siblings Trilogy

BRODY'S VOW (Brody and Trinity)
WYATT'S STAND (Wyatt and Austen)
EASTON'S CLAIM (Easton and Piper)

Hostage Rescue Team Series
MARKED (Jake and Rachel)
TARGETED (Tucker and Celida)
HUNTED (Bauer and Zoe)
DISAVOWED (DeLuca and Briar)
AVENGED (Schroder and Taya)
EXPOSED (Ethan and Marisol)
SEIZED (Sawyer and Carmela)
WANTED (Bauer and Zoe)
BETRAYED (Bautista and Georgia)
RECLAIMED (Adam and Summer)
SHATTERED (Schroder and Taya)
GUARDED (DeLuca and Briar)

Titanium Security Series
IGNITED (Hunter and Khalia)
SINGED (Gage and Claire)
BURNED (Sean and Zahra)
EXTINGUISHED (Blake and Jordyn)
REKINDLED (Alex and Grace)
BLINDSIDED: A TITANIUM CHRISTMAST NOVELLA (ensemble)

Bagram Special Ops Series
DEADLY DESCENT (Cam and Devon)

TACTICAL STRIKE (Ryan and Candace)
LETHAL PURSUIT (Jackson and Maya)
DANGER CLOSE (Wade and Erin)
COLLATERAL DAMAGE (Liam and Honor)
NEVER SURRENDER (A MACKENZIE FAMILY NOVELLA) (ensemble)

Suspense Series
OUT OF HER LEAGUE (Rayne and Christa)
COVER OF DARKNESS (Dec and Bryn)
NO TURNING BACK (Ben and Samarra)
RELENTLESS (Rhys and Neveah)
ABSOLUTION (Luke and Emily)
SILENT NIGHT, DEADLY NIGHT (ensemble)

PARANORMAL ROMANCE
Empowered Series
DARKEST CARESS (Daegan and Olivia)

HISTORICAL ROMANCE
THE VACANT CHAIR (Justin and Brianna)

EROTIC ROMANCE (writing as *Callie Croix*)
DEACON'S TOUCH
DILLON'S CLAIM
NO HOLDS BARRED
TOUCH ME
LET ME IN
COVERT SEDUCTION

Printed in Great Britain
by Amazon